# A RAGE OF SOULS

*Also by Chris Nickson from Severn House*

### The Simon Westow Mysteries

THE HANGING PSALM
THE HOCUS GIRL
TO THE DARK
THE BLOOD COVENANT
THE DEAD WILL RISE
THE SCREAM OF SINS
THEM WITHOUT PAIN

### The Cathy Marsden Thrillers

NO PRECIOUS TRUTH

### The Inspector Tom Harper Mysteries

GODS OF GOLD
TWO BRONZE PENNIES
SKIN LIKE SILVER
THE IRON WATER
ON COPPER STREET
THE TIN GOD
THE LEADEN HEART
THE MOLTEN CITY
BRASS LIVES
A DARK STEEL DEATH
RUSTED SOULS

### The Richard Nottingham Mysteries

COLD CRUEL WINTER
THE CONSTANT LOVERS
COME THE FEAR
AT THE DYING OF THE YEAR
FAIR AND TENDER LADIES
FREE FROM ALL DANGER

# A RAGE OF SOULS

## Chris Nickson

SEVERN
HOUSE

First world edition published in Great Britain and the USA in 2025
by Severn House, an imprint of Canongate Books Ltd,
14 High Street, Edinburgh EH1 1TE.

severnhouse.com

Copyright © Chris Nickson, 2025

Cover and jacket design by Piers Tilbury

All rights reserved including the right of reproduction in whole or in part in any form. The right of Chris Nickson to be identified as the author of this work has been asserted in accordance with the Copyright, Designs & Patents Act 1988.

*British Library Cataloguing-in-Publication Data*
A CIP catalogue record for this title is available from the British Library

ISBN-13: 978-1-4483-1629-8 (cased)
ISBN-13: 978-1-4483-1616-8 (paper)
ISBN-13: 978-1-4483-1683-0 (e-book)

This is a work of fiction. Names, characters, places and incidents are either the product of the author's imagination or are used fictitiously. Except where actual historical events and characters are being described for the storyline of this novel, all situations in this publication are fictitious and any resemblance to actual persons, living or dead, business establishments, events or locales is purely coincidental.

No part of this book may be used or reproduced in any manner for the purpose of training artificial intelligence technologies or systems. This work is reserved from text and data mining (Article 4(3) Directive (EU) 2019/790).

*All Severn House titles are printed on acid-free paper.*

Typeset by Palimpsest Book Production Ltd.,
Falkirk, Stirlingshire, Scotland.
Printed and bound in Great Britain by
TJ Books, Padstow, Cornwall.

The manufacturer's authorised representative in the EU for product safety is Authorised Rep Compliance Ltd, 71 Lower Baggot Street, Dublin D02 P593 Ireland (arccompliance.com)

# Praise for the Simon Westow Mysteries

'Brimming with Nickson's trademark period details, memorable characters . . . but also filled with frightening twists, bloody violence, suspense, and danger'
*Booklist* on *Them Without Pain*

'Well-drawn characters, plentiful historical details, and a real feeling for Leeds in all its gritty glory'
*Kirkus Reviews* on *Them Without Pain*

'A riveting read'
*Booklist* on *The Scream of Sins*

'This gritty and surprise-filled mystery will enthrall both newcomers and series fans'
*Publishers Weekly* Starred Review of *The Dead Will Rise*

'Nickson's richly authentic descriptions of life in . . . Britain combine with a grisly plot and characters who jump off the page'
*Booklist* on *The Dead Will Rise*

## About the author

**Chris Nickson** is the author of eleven Tom Harper Mysteries, seven highly acclaimed novels in the Richard Nottingham series, eight Simon Westow books and the Cathy Marsden thriller series set during World War II. Born and raised in Leeds, he moved back there more than a decade ago.

www.chrisnickson.co.uk

*To Candace Robb, such a good, true friend*

*Leeds, February 1826*

The scream sliced through the sky. Loud, clear, a cry of pure terror that crashed into her thoughts. Everyone near Seaton's old mill turned to look. Carts halted, their drivers searching for the sound. Men and women walking together clutched each other's arms.

All of them stopped except the couple Jane was following. Heads down, they kept moving steadily along, as if they hadn't heard a thing.

A second scream, stronger, more awful than the first. Two men ran along the road, carrying a girl on a wooden hurdle. She was a small creature, no more than nine, clothes drenched in blood. Her dress was torn, showing a leg where the flesh hung ragged, ripped through to pale bone. Her fists were clenched, thrashing against the wood to try and stop the pain.

'Be quiet,' one of the men ordered in a harsh voice. 'Surgeon will take care of it.' They all knew what that meant: the leg would go. People shuddered and stepped back as the girl wailed no, no, no, no, the fear raw in her voice.

Only a few seconds and the sound began to fade. Like an exhalation, life began again. Most would have forgotten it all long before they arrived home. But the one who really needed to lose the memory never would. A single moment and her life was changed. An accident under the loom, some failure of the machine. For her, the cause didn't matter.

Jane realised she'd been digging her nails hard into her palms. Pain arrived so suddenly; it could touch anyone. She knew; seeing the girl had brought back the torment of losing her own little finger. Hers had been a deliberate act of violence, but in some small way she understood. She was still for a moment, trying to push everything she'd just seen out of her mind. She knew it would return later. As soon as she closed her eyes that night.

# ONE

'My wife enjoyed playing cards,' James Barton explained, and his expression turned rueful. 'Unfortunately, she was never as skilled as she liked to believe. She acquired some debts. A number of them.' He lowered his eyes, embarrassed by the admission. 'She told me, and I offered to pay them, but she said she wished to cover the losses herself. Selling the gold bracelet was her idea. She'd inherited it from her mother, but she never cared for it.' He gazed at nothing for a moment. 'Now I think, I don't recall ever seeing her wear it. It all had to be done quietly, of course. No hint of a scandal.'

Of course not, Simon thought. Everything quiet and discreet. 'Would the sale have brought in enough to cover what she owed?'

'Yes. The debts weren't outrageous, and it was an expensive piece. What you have to understand is how difficult it was for her to admit the problem in the first place.' A small sigh. 'Especially to me.'

Simon Westow rubbed his chin, feeling the rasp of bristles; he needed a shave. 'How did you come to meet this man Fox?'

'I didn't. He met me.' Bitterness and regret curled behind his words. 'I'd never even heard his name before I received his letter. I have no idea how he discovered I was looking to sell the bracelet, but he said his name was Frederick Fox and he knew people who were in the market for items like that.'

'Weren't you suspicious at all?'

'Of course I was.' Barton gave a grim smile. He had thin lips and deep-set eyes, his thick hair turning grey. 'Anyone would be. I didn't know him from Adam. But my wife needed to do something quickly to keep the debt quiet. I invited Fox here to examine the bracelet. It didn't seem as if that could do any harm.'

The first step to gaining someone's trust: getting inside their house. 'What did you think when you met him?'

'I realise it must sound stupid now, Mr Westow, but he impressed me. I liked him.'

Barton was hardly the first to be taken in by someone charming and plausible. He wouldn't be the last; the ruse was probably as old as time. Fox claimed to be the youngest son of a landowner, one who'd never inherit, explained he existed on a small quarterly allowance from his family.

'He dressed reasonably enough and gave me the names of people he said he knew,' Barton continued. 'Titled, connected to court. All of them with money. As soon as he saw the bracelet, he told me he was sure there was one man who'd snap it up as a gift for his mistress. He was convincing.'

'His type always are,' Simon said. 'That's part of their game. What else did he tell you about himself?'

Rage and frustration reddened the man's face. 'Not enough, and I didn't ask questions. He said he was from North Yorkshire, somewhere around Richmond, but he was never exact.' Barton sighed. 'The truth is that he took me in, and I was foolish enough to allow him to do it.'

'Was it just the bracelet you intended to sell?'

'Yes.' A single, terse word. 'Two days after we first met, Fox came to see me again, saying the man he'd mentioned was definitely interested in buying the bracelet.' He snorted. 'Believe it or not, I felt grateful to him. My wife could settle her debt.' A long pause as he tried to let his anger subside – at Fox, at himself for being gulled that way. He was a businessman who'd made his money building factories for manufacturers, a smart, canny person in a thriving market. 'The buyer wanted to see it, and he asked permission to take it. He promised to return later that day with the bracelet or the money.' He looked into Simon's face. 'One thing about Mr Fox, Mr Westow. He's gently persuasive. I believed him. I liked him and I *wanted* to believe him. I trusted him. When he left, that was the last I saw of him or the bracelet. I never heard from him that day and I sent him a note the next morning.'

'He'd never lived at the address he gave you,' Simon suggested. It was a story he'd heard often enough before.

Barton nodded sadly. 'They'd never heard of him. I asked and nobody seemed to know who he was, so I contacted you. Now, with all that, do you think you can retrieve the bracelet?'

Simon Westow was a thief-taker. Work like this was his trade.

'If he's still in Leeds, there's a good chance I can. If he's gone . . .' Then it would be close to impossible. 'I explained my terms to you.'

'I agree. Worth every penny if you succeed.'

Fox hadn't vanished from the town. It had taken less than two days to discover where he was living with his wife, putting on an honest, respectable appearance. He'd been brash, hadn't even bothered to change his name. Another three days and Simon had woven a web around the man, planting word of a fence who might be willing to buy his bracelet. Lies to snare the liar. Easy enough to do; Fox needed to be rid of the jewellery that could hang him. Far more, he wanted the money so the couple could move on. A man who was eager to believe. In some ways, not a penny's worth of difference between him and Barton.

Simon's wife Rosie would be the fence.

The meeting at St John's Church was set. That was where the trap would be sprung. Everything as smooth and straightforward as he could have hoped.

# TWO

Looking up, Jane couldn't spot the couple and began to hurry, alert, watching. She wasn't worried; she knew exactly where they were going.

Soon enough, she spotted them on Briggate. Mr and Mrs Fox were promenading like honest citizens, laughing and smiling, taking their time as they paused to glance into shop windows, pointing to the things they might buy with the money they anticipated having in their purses very soon. On the far side of the Head Row, they passed Davy Cassidy, the blind fiddler, not even catching the sweetness of his music, then strolled through the entrance to St John's churchyard.

Jane never worried they might notice her. With a shawl clutched over her hair, dressed in faded, dark colours, she was just another drab in the crowd, faceless and invisible to everyone. Following like this was her skill, her art. As the couple strolled along the path towards the church, she was a shadow behind them, bearing away to the side, over the grass.

It was a day of late winter sun, bright but with little warmth. Sally was there, kneeling by a gravestone and brushing away dirt and moss like a dutiful granddaughter. Jane caught a glimpse of the carved names: James Wood, John Wood and his wife Magdalene. The Foxes passed her by without a glance. Simon stood back in the shadow of the Bluecoat school at the far edge of the yard, dressed in the well-worn coat he used for work and a low crown hat.

The couple entered the church porch. Rosie was waiting. She was carefully overdressed in a plum-coloured gown, wearing cheap, glittering bangles and baubles. On Jane's sign, Simon and Sally drew closer, cutting off any escape.

'My wife,' Fox said with a gesture to the woman beside him. He had a confident, melodious voice.

Rosie nodded at the woman. This was business; no need for more than that. 'Did you bring it?'

'As we agreed,' Fox replied. 'Provided you have the money, of course.' The man produced a packet from his greatcoat, unwrapping it as Rosie watched, the greed gleaming in her eyes.

He held up a heavy gold bracelet set with rich red and blue stones.

'It's worth every penny,' the man said.

'I daresay it is,' Rosie told him. In an instant her face changed, turning predatory and unforgiving. 'A pity I won't be giving you anything.' Her hand darted out and snatched the bracelet from him.

He took a small step back. 'What—'

The church door creaked open and James Barton stepped from the gloom. 'Did you truly believe I'd let it all go so easily?' He shook his head as Rosie handed him the piece of jewellery. 'You can't have been that stupid.'

'Is this the bracelet?' she asked.

'It is.'

'You've been caught by thief-takers,' Simon told the couple. They turned quickly to see him standing with Sally and Jane beside him, knives drawn. He turned to Barton. 'Do you want to prosecute?'

For a few seconds there was a heavy silence. The man stared at the couple. His gaze gave nothing away. 'What will happen to them if I do?'

'They'll hang,' Simon told him. No question about the sentence; the bracelet was easily worth fifty pounds.

'Just him,' Barton decided finally. 'He's the one who swindled me. I've never seen her before.'

# THREE

*Leeds, April 1826*

Simon looked up from the *Leeds Intelligencer*. The house was quiet, their twin sons Richard and Amos off at their lessons at the grammar school.

'Do you remember Frederick Fox?' he asked.

Rosie was stirring a pot on the range. 'Of course I do. What's happened? Have they finally hanged him?'

'He's been pardoned.'

'What?' She let the spoon clatter against the pan. 'Why?'

He folded the newspaper and placed it on the table. 'It doesn't give the reason. All done at the last minute, apparently. He was standing on the scaffold in York when the message arrived.'

'That's probably an exaggeration. You know they always try to make it sound dramatic.' Rosie pressed her lips together. 'Still, I wonder what happened. Maybe he knows someone important.'

'Perhaps he does. He did tell Barton he came from a good family; I suppose it could have been true and someone had a quiet word. I'll have to ask the constable.' He stood, leaning heavily on his walking stick, one where a twist of the handle let him pull out a blade as thin as a rapier.

Almost a year before, Simon had been stabbed in the thigh while trying to catch a thief. If it hadn't been for Dr Hey's delicate skill, he'd have lost the leg, possibly even his life. In the end luck had held himself close; he'd escaped with no more than a vicious scar and a bad limp for the rest of his days. It had left him cautious, aware how life could end in the space of a heartbeat. It had taken months to ease him back to full health; longer still to rediscover his will. He'd been forced to understand that there was so much he could never manage again. No running, no fighting. For a long time he'd felt defeated, overwhelmed and lost. Gradually, with help from Rosie and

Amos and Richard, he'd come to terms with what he could do, to accept the limits. There were still plenty of days when fury roared inside. But as the weeks passed, he'd worked his way back into being a thief-taker, the only trade he'd known.

Simon had always been good at his job. He was successful. People in Leeds knew him; he'd earned his reputation. But he understood full well that he could no longer manage the old ways. He'd spent hours talking about it with Rosie, sitting with Jane and Sally, the two young women who worked with him. If he was going to return to the business, he'd need their assistance more than ever.

Simon would remain the public face. That was how it had to be. People expected a thief-taker to be a man. He would be the one they hired, who came to agreements. They could do business with him; and a man could do things that were impossible for women: talk to those in power or go to the inns and beershops and sit with criminals. Simon knew people; they'd learned to trust him.

But for everything else, he'd have to rely on Rosie and Jane and Sally. His wife was no novice to the business; they'd worked together before their sons were born and she had the time and desire to do more. With the boys now growing towards manhood and flourishing at the grammar school, she had time to take on a full share of the load again.

Jane had been with him for a long time. She'd grown up on the streets, thrown out by her mother when she was eight years old. She'd quickly learned how to survive, turning into a ruthless fighter who had an uncanny ability to follow without being noticed. More recently she'd drifted away into another, quieter life in the curious little house she shared with old Mrs Shields. Sometimes a fortnight or more would pass without him seeing her, yet she was ready when he needed help.

It had been Jane who'd discovered Sally, another feral girl, a younger, deadlier version of herself, small enough to slip unnoticed in and out of crowds. She was sharp and observant, the most dangerous person with a knife he'd ever seen, an odd mix of fury and compassion. Now her home was in the attic of Simon's house on Swinegate; she'd become a part of the family, almost a sister to the boys. Yet two, sometimes three nights a week, she'd slip out of the house to help the young ones who had nowhere to live. Money, food, someone who'd listen. It wasn't an obligation she felt, he decided, more a vocation.

The four of them made a curious, ragged crew. But a very effective one, Simon thought as he hobbled up Briggate. They'd done well together. He passed the place where the Moot Hall had stood for centuries in the middle of the street, until it was pulled down the year before. Now the cobbles on the road looked so sad and worn that it was hard to remember it had been any other way. He grimaced. Each step took effort; these days, every journey required thought. He'd dressed in his good clothes: the carefully brushed dark wool coat with the swallow tails, the trousers cut loosely to make movement easier. A top hat today. But always the work boots with the hobnails on the soles.

George Mudie was busy in his printing shop; as soon as Simon opened the door he was assaulted by the heavy tang of ink. Mudie had edited a newspaper once, before he fell out with the owner. Now this business kept him alive. But his curiosity for gossip and news had never flagged.

'Let me guess, Simon,' he said as he stretched out his back and wiped his hands on a rag that was close to black. 'Fox.'

He grinned. 'That obvious?'

'You're not the only one who reads the papers.' He poured himself a small glass of brandy and sipped. 'Besides, who wouldn't have a few questions about a thing like that?'

'What do you make of it?'

The man shrugged. 'Influential relations, perhaps. A good lawyer who has someone's ear. But that costs money.'

'I doubt Fox and his wife could afford it.'

Mudie sighed. 'Then who knows? Good fortune, perhaps. Someone has to have it, because God knows it's certainly never visited me. If this Fox has any sense at all, he'll never show himself in Leeds again.'

Constable Porter shook his head. He looked strained, tired. 'Nobody's told me the reason and I haven't asked. All I know is what was in the newspaper. I've been too busy to ask any questions. Have you heard about the troops from Chapeltown barracks and the feud with the drinkers at the Old King's Head? They're at it every night.'

'People are taking bets on who'll come out on top.'

'None of the bastards if I have my way.' His voice became grim. 'If it carries on, we'll end up with one or two dead. Fox is old business, Westow. It stopped being my concern when we shipped him off to the assizes.'

# FOUR

*Leeds, June 13, 1826*

The knock on the door disturbed a doze. Simon had developed the habit since his wounding, closing his eyes and slipping into a light sleep for a few minutes. The time of day didn't seem to matter; just a few moments of rest. He pulled the watch from his waistcoat pocket. Not even nine in the morning. For the love of God, he was becoming an old man.

A man in dark, sober livery was standing on the step, a serious look on his face. Someone's servant, Simon thought. He made a hasty bow and handed him a folded note.

'Mr Barton said to bring you this, sir.'

'Thank you.' He fumbled in his pocket, found a halfpenny and pressed it into his hand. With a smile and a thank you, the man drifted away.

At the kitchen table, Simon broke the seal.

> Mr Westow,
>
> No doubt you saw the news that Fox was granted a reprieve from death. When that happened, I imagined he and his wife would go somewhere nobody knew them and find a new life.
>
> However, since last week, I believe I've seen him following me three times. At first, I decided it had to be my imagination. With the second instance, I was a little less sure. The third happened yesterday morning, and I'd swear an oath it was Fox. Always at a distance, with no attempt to speak to me or threaten me.
>
> I'm not a man easily given to fright, but this worries me, more for my wife than myself. I will gladly pay you to discover what's happening and to keep us safe.
>
> Your servant,
> James Barton

He read it through once again and began to plan.

'It's what you've always done best,' Simon said. 'Following people.'

Jane sat by the empty hearth in the cottage behind the wall in Green Dragon Yard. Summer and the air was warm. With no need of a fire, she'd swept the grate clean then blackleaded it until it gleamed. Mrs Shields, the only person she really cared about, was busy in the kitchen.

'How long will it take?' she asked. She remembered Barton, the dark glint of revenge in his eyes when he said he wanted to prosecute Fox.

'That's up to him. As long as he's willing to pay for it. It'll have to be you and Sally. Fox barely saw the two of you. He knows Rosie, and I . . .' He tapped his leg. 'You've seen him.'

She had, and still remembered his face when he learned he'd been trapped. Jane sighed, staring down at the book beside her chair. *Woodstock*, the new novel by Walter Scott. She'd borrowed it from the lending library the day before and the tale had been gripping her ever since. She was reluctant to do anything before she'd finished it. But she'd agreed to help when Simon needed it.

'What if Fox tries for revenge?'

'You know the answer to that,' he said. She'd killed often enough in the past; she would again if it was needed. 'I don't know what's in his mind. Fox didn't seem violent. It should be easy enough, and Barton has money.'

Jane nodded. She'd given her promise, but she preferred her quiet days and nights with Mrs Shields. They suited her spirit these days.

She gazed out of the window, making up her mind. The sun was shining, as fine a June day as anyone could wish to see.

The night before, the screaming girl had visited her dreams yet again, as she had so often in the past months. Crying, terrified. Enough to wake her, make her clutch hard at the sheet and weep small tears of her own.

As she sat in bed, letting the beating of her heart slow, that day felt like something from a different life. If the girl had survived the infections after her leg was amputated, she'd still wonder how to live now she was unable to bring a wage home to the family.

Maybe the dream had been an omen of some kind, she thought.

'Tell me where he lives,' she said. 'I'll follow until two o'clock. Sally can take over then.'

The joy of *Woodstock* would have to wait. Jane laced up her stout work boots, gathered her shawl, kissed Mrs Shields farewell and followed Simon out of the cottage.

She saw no sign of anyone following Barton as he strode here and there around Leeds during the morning. Calling on friends, dipping in and out of offices on business. A man with a very full day.

They passed Dodson, the beggar who'd lost his leg fighting against Napoleon; she smiled at him and dropped a few coins in his mug.

Barton never looked back. He had no idea she was there. Curious behaviour, Jane thought, if he really believed Fox was following him; she'd expect him to be constantly peering over his shoulder. At the corner of Boar Lane and Briggate she paused long enough to give Kate the Pie-Seller three pennies for two of her pies. All the time Jane was watching people move.

Nothing suspicious at all. Certainly no sign of Fox.

Barton arrived home for his dinner not long after noon. He lived in one of the old mansions tucked back from North Street, houses built for rich wool merchants a century before. Jane kept her distance, hidden away in the shadow of a wall, never stirring until she felt someone close.

'Have you had any problems?' Sally asked as the church clock struck two.

'Nothing at all.' Jane handed her one of the pies. 'No sign of Fox.'

'How do you think he managed a pardon?' the girl asked. 'He didn't seem like anyone special, did he? Simon asked the constable, but he didn't seem to know.'

Jane didn't care. It had happened, and the man had plenty of reason to return to Leeds for revenge.

'It's probably all to do with money. Everything is.' She stretched. 'I'll come back at six.'

\* \* \*

She sat outside the cottage, quietly reading her book and relishing the warmth of the afternoon sun. Even through the fine layer of haze and smoke that always hung over the town, the heat was comforting.

When the bell at the parish church pealed half past five, Jane set the book aside and brought a knife from her pocket, spending five minutes honing its sharpness. She knew this blade. It had saved her life and served her well. Readiness could mark the distance between life and death. Her attention had slipped once, and she'd paid for it with her little finger. Simon had let down his guard for a single moment and now he walked with the consequences.

As she approached Barton's house, she paused to study Sally. When they met, the girl had been a child of anger. It was fury that had kept her alive on the streets. But living with Simon and Rosie and their boys, she'd found a family who cared for her, and much of that hardness had blunted, tempered with compassion. She was growing, taller every month it seemed, and starting to fill out. How old was she? Thirteen, Jane decided. That, or perhaps a year older.

Still a strange one, a child of two families, one with the Westows and the other with the homeless children who relied on each other. God help her if she was ever forced to choose between them, Jane thought.

'Barton left about an hour after you,' Sally said. 'The servant brought a gig from the coach house. He and a woman went off in it. I decided to stay in case Fox came sniffing.'

'Any sign of him?' Her gaze slid around, but there was little to see. The house was quiet, nobody visible through the windows.

She shook her head. 'Nothing at all.'

'I'll stay for a few hours and come back again in the morning.'

When she turned her head again, Sally had vanished.

Toward eight, the light began to change, growing paler and thinner as dusk edged closer. Jane waited, but Barton and his wife didn't return. Time seemed to slow, the minutes dragging by. Then, from the corner of her eye, she spotted a movement. A dress. A woman leaving a hiding place and slipping away. Before she was gone, Jane caught a brief flash of a face she'd last seen months earlier: Mrs Fox.

How? She'd never sensed another soul there.

Jane took out her knife and twisted the gold ring on her finger for luck. Her heart began to beat faster. Then she tucked the shawl over her hair and followed.

# FIVE

'Are you certain it was her?' Simon asked, and Jane saw him frown. Barton had only mentioned the man, not his wife.

'It was. I remember her,' Jane replied. 'It was Mrs Fox.'

Upstairs, Richard and Amos moved around noisily, a brief swell of raised voices that quickly died away again. She looked at the window. It was becoming darker outside; she'd come to tell them all what had happened.

'I never felt anyone close when I was watching the house,' Sally said.

'I didn't either. If I hadn't seen her . . .' That had worried and nagged at her all the way here. It had shaken her. She should have sensed *something*, an indication, a small tingling that something was wrong. Instead, there had been emptiness. Jane looked around the faces at the kitchen table. 'She might be good at this.'

'Where did she go after she left Barton's house?' Rosie asked.

'I followed her to Middle Fold.' It lay on the far side of Mabgate, a ragged street petering out towards the back of Burmantofts Hall. 'She never realised I was there. I'm positive of that, but I kept my distance. I couldn't see which house she went into, but there aren't too many of them.'

Simon nodded. It was well over a year since he'd been around there, but he could picture it clearly in his mind. Still plenty of green all around, but buildings were encroaching – there were already a few new ones on Skinner Lane, only a stone's throw from the Sheepscar mill pond.

'The question is, what do the Foxes intend to do to the Bartons?' He paused for a second. 'Is there anywhere to stay out of sight near where they're living?'

'A few places.'

'I'd like you and Sally to start there in the morning.' Simon told them. 'Follow them when they leave.'

'What if they go in different directions?' Sally asked.

'Split up. One of them will probably watch Barton.'

Frederick Fox had felt the noose around his neck before he'd been given back his life. He was bigger, stronger than his wife. He had to be brimming over with hatred. What else but revenge could have brought him back to Leeds?

The coffee cart outside the Bull and Mouth always opened before first light. A coach arrived, the sweating horses pulling under the high arch and into the yard as Simon took a sip from the mug and gazed at the people who'd gathered. Familiar voices, and many of the same faces he'd seen for years, always a good place to catch the early gossip. But nobody had any worthwhile gems today.

He'd heard Sally slip away from the house in darkness. Off to Middle Fold.

There was little he could do until the Foxes acted. Nothing but wait. That had always been the most frustrating part of this business, even more so these days. He liked to be out, beating at the bushes and stirring things up to see what followed. That was much harder to do now. He needed to rely on others and it could never be the same.

'You're miles away, Westow. Not woken up yet?'

He turned at the sound of Constable Porter's voice, the inspector a few feet behind.

'Don't often see you here.'

Porter looked at the tin cup with disgust. 'I don't know how you can stand the taste of that muck.'

'Sometimes I hear useful things.'

'Anything on Fox?'

Simon felt a ripple of panic up his spine. 'Why? Should there be?'

'I saw Mr Barton yesterday. He told me all about it.'

'Fox and his wife are living in Middle Fold.' He gave the man the rest, the precious little he knew.

'What do you think? Are they likely to try anything?'

'We only started yesterday. It's too early to tell.'

'There's something about this . . .' Porter took off his hat and scratched his scalp. 'It bothers me. Why have they come back?'

'I doubt they're here to apologise.'

That brought a flicker of a smile. 'Are those two lasses doing the following?'

'Yes.'

'I hope they're as good as you've always claimed.'

'They are.'

'Right. I need to go to the barracks and try to calm this problem with the soldiers and the town once and for all. Damned thing seems like it doesn't want to end.'

Sally and Jane squatted deep in the shadows, two faint outlines in dark cotton dresses, shawls covering their hair. They'd arrived early, moving quietly through the streets well before dawn peered over the horizon. A hundred yards away, carts trundled slowly along the road to the turnpike. A single passenger coach rushed past in a welter of noise, the driver cracking his whip above the horses.

Jane felt the other girl's nudge and glanced up. The Foxes were leaving the house together. She kept her eyes on them, not moving at all until they were a good forty yards ahead. Then she stood. Only a few people around; they'd be easy to follow.

'Which one do you want?' Sally asked softly.

'Her.' The man seemed like the real danger, and Sally was the quick, furious fighter; she'd be on him before he could act. It was the woman who intrigued her. Able to hide without giving away any sense of herself. She seemed like someone with experience, likely to be wary and alert.

At North Street the couple exchanged a few words then parted company. Jane watched Sally slide away, keeping the man in sight.

Mrs Fox walked into town with quick, deliberate strides. Jane followed and thought about *Woodstock*; she'd read more of the book last night. The glitter of Charles the king arriving from abroad, and the monarchy restored. All the colours and the pageant of it. It must have felt as if London was coming alive after sleeping for so long.

The woman walked down Briggate, stopping often to look at the displays in windows. A little beyond the place where the

Moot Hall had once stood, she disappeared into a shop. A dressmaker, Jane saw as she passed. An expensive one to have her premises here.

That was curious; the Foxes didn't look as if they possessed real money. Their clothes were neat enough but unremarkable. They were living in a very ordinary house, hardly a fashionable, expensive address. Yet somehow Frederick Fox had secured himself a pardon from death, then come back to the place he'd been arrested. Try as she might, Jane couldn't fit any of those pieces together.

Ten full minutes passed before the woman came out again, nothing in her arms. She looked up and down the street, as if she couldn't decide which direction to take. Finally, she retraced her steps. Jane stayed behind her, well back and on the other side of the street. Rosie probably knew the dressmaker; she could discover what Mrs Fox had wanted in there.

The woman returned to Middle Fold. A single errand. Never glanced over her shoulder to judge whether someone was behind her. Something felt wrong. She couldn't understand the purpose of the trip, and Jane worried: could the woman have seen her? She didn't think so but . . . Mrs Fox was tricky.

The morning passed slowly, another hour until the front door of the house opened and the woman came out again. She'd changed into simpler clothes, a plain cotton dress, and a thin cotton shawl wrapped around her shoulders. She was carrying a basket, eyes moving all around before she began to walk.

From the hidden spot, Jane watched her go. She allowed the woman a long start, then very cautiously she began to follow.

Jane stayed well behind her all the way down Mabgate, past the clamour and hot metal stink of Hope Foundry to Lady Bridge and across Timble Beck, towards a tangle of small streets where the houses were so new they weren't yet black with soot. For a moment Jane wondered if Mrs Fox might try to vanish in there, but she kept to the main road.

At the parish church, she turned up Kirkgate, still walking purposefully. Between a pair of ancient houses she took the ginnel that led into Grey's Court.

Jane stopped. She couldn't follow the woman there without being seen, and the court had three entrances. She found a place by the passage through to Fleece Yard to settle and watch. It was a chance to think, to see if she could understand exactly what was happening.

Had the earlier trip out, when Mrs Fox wore her good clothes, been a test, to judge whether anyone was behind her?

But why? What was she doing? Had Grey's Court, with its different exits, been a way to throw off any possible pursuit or was she visiting there? Jane glanced at the entrance again. She wasn't going to find the answers now.

# SIX

Simon watched Rosie frown as she listened closely to Jane. None of this made sense. Perhaps they simply didn't know enough yet, but he couldn't find a path into it. They were staring at mysteries. At shadows.

'Do you think she knew you were there?' he asked.

'I can't tell.' Jane's answer came slowly, thoughtfully. 'At Barton's house yesterday, I never sensed her.'

Did that mean anything? He couldn't be sure. The woman might be anywhere in Leeds by now.

'You did everything you could,' he assured her.

'What do we do now?' Rosie asked after Jane had gone.

'Something I should probably have done right at the beginning,' he said, pushing himself up. 'I'm going to try to find out about the Foxes. See if that pardon came from any type of connection.'

'What about me? Where do you want me to go?' There was eagerness in her voice. She enjoyed working again.

'You could talk to that dressmaker.'

'It sounds like Mrs Carson's shop.' Her face brightened into a smile. 'I know her. She loves to gossip.'

This was a time when he could have used Barnabas Wade's knowledge. A disbarred lawyer, he'd spent years scraping a living by selling worthless stocks to travellers as they passed through Leeds on their coach journeys. Each season he seemed to grow poorer. Finally, one morning last winter, his landlord had found him dead in his cheap room when he came to collect the rent.

Wade had known about money: who had it, who'd lost it. About families and ancestors. He'd have had information about the Foxes, unless their story was all lies. But with Wade gone, who else was there to ask?

'I can't help you, Simon,' George Mudie said. He rubbed his

hands on his leather apron. 'I asked a few questions after he was given that pardon.'

'You never said.'

He shrugged. 'I was curious. Didn't find any reason for it. Nobody I talked to knew about him. There's supposed to be a wealthy family called Fox up towards Richmond, but I've no idea if he's related.'

'He told Barton he came from around there.'

'Perhaps it's true, then. You'll need to ask someone from that area.'

Plenty of people had wondered about the pardon, Simon discovered as he moved around Leeds, but nobody had answers.

Porter sat behind his desk at the courthouse, papers piled around him. The windows were open, all the noises of the street drifting in.

'I can write to the constable in Richmond,' he offered. 'I'm curious myself, especially if he's back in Leeds. You say he hasn't threatened Barton?'

'Not yet. Hasn't even approached him.'

He frowned. 'Fox is a free man. He received his pardon; he has every right to be here as long as he doesn't break any laws. You said you have your girls on him?'

'One of them. The other's following his wife.'

The constable nodded. 'I'll see if they know anything up there, but don't expect too much. Fox probably isn't even his real name.'

Simon snorted. 'I doubt it is. Still, it would be useful to know.' He paused. 'If anyone up around Richmond can describe him—'

'I'll ask.'

After she left Simon's house on Swinegate, Jane started for home. The day sat still and heavy on Leeds. She had time to sit with Mrs Shields, maybe learn a little more from her about the plants growing in the small garden outside the cottage.

But her feet didn't take her back to Green Dragon Yard. The pull of curiosity was too strong. She ambled along Vicar Lane, down Templar Street and Crown Street, between the houses to Prince Street, then across the small footbridge over to Mabgate and the few yards to Middle Fold. What game was Mrs Fox playing?

The woman obviously knew Leeds; going to Grey's Court, with its many ways in and out to watch, made that obvious. There had to be some reason for whatever she'd done; Jane wanted to discover what it was.

She was still there, deep in the shadows, when the woman returned almost two hours later, walking, a basket heavy with groceries in the crook of her arm.

Quietly, Jane moved away, certain that Mrs Fox was done for the day. She'd had all the time she needed for her tasks.

On the way home she spent a few minutes with Dodson, the one-legged old soldier who begged around town. He was a good, quiet man, someone who saw and remembered things. But there was little he could do to help her on this. She tipped a few coins in his cup and kept walking to Green Dragon Yard.

'Fox walked around for almost an hour after he left his wife this morning,' Sally said. She drank, then tore off a piece of bread. 'He was trying to see if anyone was behind him.'

'He never realised you were there?' Simon asked.

'No.' Not pride; a simple matter of fact. Jane had taught her the art of following and she'd learned well.

'Did he end up at Barton's house?'

'Close enough to watch it.'

'What about Barton? Any sign of him?'

'The servant brought the little gig and he drove off. Not long after that, his wife went out with the maid. They were gone for the rest of the morning and came back about half an hour before he did. Then they stayed at home for the rest of the day.'

'How about Fox? Did he stay there or leave?' Rosie wanted to know. She was leaning forward, listening intently, forearms resting on the kitchen table.

'He stayed where he was the whole time.'

'When did he leave?'

'The church clock had just struck four. After it was obvious he was going to Middle Fold, I came back here.'

'He never strayed on to Barton's property?' Simon wondered. That could be a trespassing charge.

'No.' She stood and stretched, and he heard her footsteps on the stairs, clattering up to her room in the attic. How could she be so silent sometimes and so loud at others?

'What are these people doing, Simon?' Rosie said. 'I talked to the dressmaker. She remembered Mrs Fox. The woman never said much, just came in, examined some fabrics and patterns but never bought anything. Wasting her time, Mrs Carson said.'

'I don't know.' He stared at her, wondering what they were planning. 'I have no idea at all.'

Jane was dragged back to the world by the knock on the door. She'd been so caught up in *Woodstock* as Scott's words carried her along with the Cavaliers and Roundheads that she had to blink a few times to be certain where she was as Mrs Shields looked up from her own novel and smiled at her.

'A good book can do that, child.' Another knock. 'You'd better see who wants you.'

Sally was standing in the deep twilight, wearing the same old dress she put on every day, with a thin shawl spread across her shoulders and a face filled with anguish.

'Can you come and help me? It's the children.'

She led the way through town, past the drinkers and the travellers gathered around the inns and the beershops, down Wellington Road and beyond Bean Ing to the patch of empty ground between Park Mills and Airedale Mills. All about them, buildings were rising day by day, growing walls of brick and stone for new factories. The place had changed in such a short time, Jane realised. No more than four years since she'd buried her money out here to keep it safe, in a tin under a tree; now a machine or a loom covered that ground.

A fire had been lit, sending sparks into the night. The children had used old wood, scraps gathered from the sites where people were building, anything they'd been able to scavenge that might burn. It gave warmth and comfort, welcome even on a June night. More than that, it offered safety.

There were twenty or thirty of them, the youngest no more than three, looking lost and terrified, rising to somewhere around Sally's age.

On the way down, the girl had been silent, shaking her head as Jane asked questions. Now she beckoned a boy forward.

'Wilfred, this is Jane. Tell her what's been happening.'

He was ten, possibly eleven, all elbows and knees, wearing a torn, grubby shirt under a coat made for someone much older and bigger, with ragged trousers torn at both knees. His toes stuck out from the broken front of his buckled shoes. Just a stick of a lad with grazes and cuts across his knuckles and cheeks and sadness at the back of his eyes.

'Men have been coming,' he began, wondering how much to say. He glanced at Sally; she nodded. 'It started a few nights ago. They have knives. One of them carries a pistol. They force us to give them any money we have and they take our food. They . . .' His voice tailed off and she saw his face redden in the firelight. 'They catch some of the girls.'

'I've seen them,' Sally said. 'There are four of them. Too many to fight them all on my own.'

She'd grown wiser, Jane decided. Now she was thinking and planning. Not too long before, she'd have charged in.

'How long has this been happening?'

'The past three nights.'

Wilfred looked from one of their faces to the other. She could see the hope in his eyes, that they could save the children.

'Did you try to stop them?' Jane asked him.

'I wanted to.' He hung his head, ashamed of not being able to protect the others. 'Before I could do anything, they hit me and laughed at me.'

'You tried,' Sally told him. 'You tried hard.'

Jane had known camps like this. They'd helped her stay alive during the years she lived on the streets. Out here, life was so brittle, so easily ended. She'd seen too many mornings when someone had disappeared or died, beyond help.

'What do you want me to do?' she asked.

'We stop them when they come,' Sally told her. 'After that, we find them.'

'What do you want to do then? Kill them?' she asked, relieved when the girl shook her head.

'Not unless we have to. But we need to make sure they don't come back.'

How could they do that? She looked around the faces. Probably most of the children here wouldn't see another year on this earth. She'd been different; she'd had the will to survive. The desire to live that pushed her through each night and into the next day, and the ruthlessness that required. So had Sally. They were survivors. Now the girl used much of the money she earned with Simon to try and keep all these alive. It was a losing battle, and she knew it, but she had to keep fighting it. She was always so certain about it. About so much. At her age, Jane had been unsure about the world. Each time she made a mistake, she'd cut herself. To punish herself and make sure she remembered. She still carried the faint scars on her arms. All that lay far behind her now.

Jane understood why the men came. They believed it was sport, amusement after a night of drinking. Easy game. Something a little different that let them swagger around and made them feel big and important. She'd seen plenty like that. Strutting and preening, and underneath it all, little men.

There was no chance that she'd refuse to help. 'Are they likely to return tonight?'

'Yes,' Sally replied, no doubt in her voice. 'They'll keep coming until someone fights back and beats them. We're going do that.'

There was never any real silence at night in a camp. Always an undercurrent of voices in the darkness. The crackle of the fire as someone fed it with more branches. Finally people settled, but even then she could hear the sniffles and coughs and the cries of bad dreams.

Jane was comfortable, sitting quietly, wrapped in the blackness. Sally stayed on the other side of the group. The girl had decided that would be best; a greater chance of keeping everyone safe.

She let her thoughts roam, shifting from *Woodstock* to the Foxes. Whatever plan for revenge they had, it was impossible to follow. She searched until she recalled a word from a book she'd read: labyrinth. Twisted and tangled. Everything would have to come clear in time. Until then, her job was to wait and watch. To be ready.

The noise sliced through her thoughts. In an instant, she was on her feet, knife in hand. A shout from thirty yards away in the darkness, the heavy sound of men running. From the corner of her eye, she picked out a silhouette in the firelight. Sally. Crouching, prowling as she edged forward. Jane stood her ground. Let them come.

Four of them. Even at a distance, she could smell the brandy on their breath and catch the glint of a knife. Jane tightened the grip on her blade and kept still as they drew closer. And closer.

They were yelling, here to torment and scare. None of them anticipated a fight.

It didn't last more than twenty seconds.

She stood facing a pair of men. They stopped as soon as they saw the weapon. One tried a wild swipe at her. Too slow; he only found air. His friend lunged for her and discovered she'd cut his arm.

They both turned and fled as their courage failed them.

After another moment, only one of the four remained, shifting nervously from foot to foot as he faced Sally. Dodging back, never daring to strike. Jane ran at him, yelling as the children cheered. As soon as he saw her, he scurried away.

'You stay with them,' she said to Sally. 'I'll follow him.'

It was easy to do. He was loud enough to rouse the dead as he dashed through town. She didn't even need to be careful, but moved along behind him with her skirts flying. Fear was pushing him along.

He never looked back, running all the way to North Street, so easy to follow. No chance to see his face, but she watched as he used a key, then the click of a lock as he let himself into the Barton house.

# SEVEN

'A son?' Sally asked.

'It has to be,' Jane told her. The girl had arrived at the cottage early, eager to hear everything that had happened as they walked down to the house on Swinegate. But the news took her aback.

'We need to tell Simon.'

Jane had spent a long, wakeful time weighing that once she settled in bed. The thoughts had crowded sleep away. They might well have terrified the young man; his simple sport had suddenly proved too dangerous. If he and his friends had learned their lesson . . . perhaps they could let it lie.

But if he hadn't? What if he returned with more men and did real damage? She'd always carry that guilt in her heart.

'We need to be there again tonight,' Jane said.

Sally gave her a curious look and nodded. She'd have gone anyway. Two of them would offer the children some fleeting sense of safety.

'What about Simon?'

'I think we should wait and see what happens.' If the men were going to return, it would be in the next two nights. She felt certain of that. If young Barton was with them, then they'd tell Simon. 'For now, I think we ought to stay quiet.'

'I need the two of you on the Foxes again. I don't understand what they're doing, but sooner or later they have to make a move of some kind on Barton.' He paused and looked around the kitchen at Rosie, Sally, Jane. 'Why else would they come back to Leeds?'

'How long do you want us to follow them?' Sally asked.

'As long as it takes. Barton's paying us.' For a second, he imagined a glance between the young women as he mentioned the name. Simon turned to his wife. 'I'd like you to call on

Mrs Barton. All of this began because she liked to gamble and was in debt. Find out if she still does it.'

Rosie smiled. 'It'll give me a chance to wear my best gown.' Her eyes flashed. 'I don't often have the opportunity to impress.'

The house was quiet, Amos and Richard already off at school. No more tutor's voice in the background all day. The silence had seemed strange at first, an emptiness that had gradually become normal. Space for him to think, but so far he hadn't made head nor tail of all this.

'I'll come with you,' he decided suddenly. 'I need to speak to her husband.'

It took time. He couldn't stride along Briggate the way he once had. A slower pace these days.

'I'm sorry. At this rate we might get there tomorrow.'

'It doesn't matter, Simon.' She made a small curtsey to Mrs Williams on the other side of the street. 'There's no rush.'

No sign of Sally or Jane near the house. No sense of the Foxes anywhere close. Simon knocked on the door. When it opened, he gave the servant their names.

Inside, everything was old-fashioned. Sumptuous and grand when it was built, but that had been a century before. Now it seemed dark, with heavy panelling and too many shadowed corners. Small, mullioned windows that didn't let in enough light. Even on a warm June day, the room carried a chill.

No fire burning in the parlour, where the Bartons rose to greet them. A few polite greetings, then down to business.

'What have you learned, Mr Westow?'

'You were right, the Foxes are definitely here,' Simon told him. 'Both of them.' He glanced at Rosie. She said something to Mrs Barton before the women disappeared.

'At least it wasn't my imagination.' Relief, but the man's face stayed clouded. 'What do you think? Has he come back to take his revenge?'

'I can't see why else they'd be here.' The man was paying to know the truth.

'I've started carrying a knife and a loaded pistol.'

Those were fine if he knew how to use them, but he'd wager good money that Barton had never learned.

'We're following both of them. If they attempt anything, we'll stop them.'

Barton gave a long, studied look. 'Tell me, Mr Westow, can you make them leave?'

'No. They haven't broken any laws.'

He nodded his acknowledgement. 'Perhaps not, but that's not the question I asked, Mr Westow.'

It wasn't one he wanted to answer. Instead, he said, 'Do you know why Fox was pardoned?'

'No, I don't. Why, do you?'

'I've been trying to find out. They're up to something, but we don't know what that is yet.'

Barton's voice hardened. 'Revenge. You just said so yourself.'

'But what kind?' Simon asked. 'If Fox wanted to kill you, he's had plenty of opportunity to do it and vanish before anyone knew. I think he must have other plans.'

'What kind of plans?' He was brusque, tense. 'He's keeping them damned well hidden.'

'As soon as we discover that, we can stop him.' Simon paused, hearing heavy footsteps on the staircase in the hall.

'My son.' Barton shook his head in dismay. 'Not an early riser. I used to hope he'd learn the business so he could take over in time, but he's only interested in the money it makes and how much pleasure it can buy him. Do you have children?'

'Two boys. They're at the grammar school.'

'Then I wish you better fortune with them than we've had. Andrew has brains, his teachers told us that. He just doesn't seem to believe he needs to work. Out at night, roistering around and drinking his life and my fortune away. Every time we talk, it becomes an argument. It's been worse since the winter.' Barton sighed. 'My apologies, it's not your trouble. Just one more thing weighing on me. Where were we?'

'Trying to learn what the Foxes are doing. Both of them are involved.'

'Strange,' he said once Simon finished telling him what they'd learned. 'Now tell me, are we in danger?'

'If you mean are you likely to be attacked, then no, I don't believe so.' He kept a calm, reassuring tone to his voice. He'd considered the possibilities; he believed what he said. Fox hadn't come to murder. If he'd really wanted that, he'd have done it much sooner, then vanished. He seemed to have something else in mind, something Simon couldn't puzzle out yet. But there was always the chance of violence. 'Still, you should both be careful. We're watching them, but we can't do it every hour of the day.'

'Of course.'

'Do you want us to continue?'

'Yes.' No hesitation at all. 'Find out what they're doing and stop them.'

When he'd sent his note, he'd wanted Simon to keep him and his family safe. This was a little different.

Mrs Fox was the first to leave the house on Middle Fold.

'Do you want to stay with her, or change?' Sally asked.

'I'll keep following her,' Jane replied. She watched the woman move along the road, in no hurry, and wondered what was on her mind for today.

'Good. I prefer him,' Sally said. 'He's simple.'

'I hope he stays that way.' She drifted away, keeping a good distance between her and the woman as she turned on to Mabgate. Not too many people out on the street, just the dirt and the roaring and hammering of the foundry along with the other workshops that had sprung up around it.

Over Lady Bridge, but not on to Kirkgate this time. The woman followed Vicar Lane to Leadenhall, where the butchers had moved their shops after the Moot Hall and Middle Row had been demolished, a street where the stink of blood ran high.

Plenty of folk around, easy for her to keep close but out of sight.

Mrs Fox had never learned how to shop. She didn't understand the value of things. Jane was close enough to watch as she paid too much for a poor cut of meat, never trying to bargain on the price. Round to the Central Market on Duncan Street, browsing the stalls. Jane climbed the stairs to the balcony. It was a perfect place to observe; nobody ever looked up.

The woman had no idea she was being followed; Jane was utterly certain of that.

An easy amble back to the house. Sally had gone. She settled back to wait, wondering if the woman would emerge again. But it was a fruitless day of sitting, studying a door that never opened.

'What did Mrs Barton tell you?' Simon asked as they strolled home. Briggate teemed with people going in and out of the shops, gazing at the goods on display in the windows, pushing their way along the pavements. Carts and carriages rattled over the cobbles; a coach driver shouted angrily at vehicles blocking his way. A ragged man with a cart and shovel scooped dung from the cobbles. He saw Simon, nodded, and paused to light his pipe. Elias, always reeking so badly from his work that his wife could barely tolerate him. But he made enough to keep them in a fair house and put food on the table. And occasionally a snippet of information.

'She says she's stopped gambling.' Rosie paused and thought for a moment. 'For now, at least. The hunger for it is still there, though; I could see it in her eyes. But the episode with Fox and the bracelet has chastened her.'

'For their sake, let's hope so it stays that way. No other vices?'

'Come on, Simon. Would you blurt out your secrets to a complete stranger?' she asked with a gentle smile. But he knew his wife too well; after so many years together, he could read the hesitations and doubts in her voice.

'Go on.' They passed Turk's Head Yard and he glanced at a smith hammering metal on an anvil at the back of the court.

'She wouldn't look at me as she answered. I think she has something she's keeping quiet.'

Simon pushed his lips together. People. Why couldn't they be straightforward? But if they were, how much work would he have?

'Any idea what it might be?'

She took her time answering. 'If I had to guess, I'd say a lover. That's the obvious thing. She didn't say anything to indicate, but . . . it's just a feeling I have.' After a moment she added, 'Maybe she just wishes she had one. I don't know.'

He knew to trust her instincts; all too often she was right. One more thing to consider, he thought. Or maybe it had no bearing at all.

'Did you see the son?'

Rosie shook her head. 'Heard him, that's all. His name's Andrew. She didn't have much good to say about him. She talked about their daughters instead. Both in good marriages to men with plenty of land.'

'They sound like a family that values connections,' he said thoughtfully. 'It could explain why Barton was so ready to believe what Fox told him. An old family from North Yorkshire that's distantly related to the people who've owned Temple Newsam for centuries? He might feel flattered by that.'

'The Ingrams own it.' She rolled the name round her tongue. 'Wasn't there a whisper that they had a daughter who was the mistress of the Prince Regent?'

'I have no idea.' He paid no attention to that kind of gossip. He'd never been out to Temple Newsam; there had never been a reason. All he knew was that it was a grand house with sprawling grounds a little to the north-east of the town.

'If there really was a family connection like that, it could explain a pardon, especially with that affair,' she continued. 'The prince is King George now.'

'I could hire a cart and go out there,' he said. 'Someone at the house should be able to tell me.'

She glanced down at his leg. 'Could you manage the journey?'

'Sally grew up in the country. We know she can ride. Maybe she knows how to drive a cart.' He chuckled. 'I could be the passenger and be carried in luxury. What do you think?'

Rosie frowned. 'It could be useful to know. But if Sally's busy, who's going to follow Fox?'

He smiled. 'Jane. Why don't you go after his wife? She only ever had a very brief look at you.'

'Yes,' she agreed with a smile. He knew she was glad to be part of the hunt again.

Sally had placed the children in two camps. The younger, weaker ones stayed farther back, towards the riverbank, gathered around their own fire. The older boys and girls moved forward. She'd had them collect stones ready to throw, to fight back if the men returned.

'I hope they won't need to,' she said. But the worry floated through her voice. Hardly surprising, Jane thought; a few rocks would never stop determined men. A few of the children carried knives, but how many would be willing to kill?

It was late, long after dark, no more than a sliver of moon showing between the clouds. Still too early for a group of young men spending their evening drinking in the inns and dram shops.

'Simon said you're going with him tomorrow.' They'd met at the house at the tail end of the afternoon and she'd seen the excitement on the girl's face when he told her about the dog cart. That was just a name, he'd explained; it was pulled by a horse. 'Have you driven one before?'

'My father showed me.' She stayed silent for a long time, thoughts drifting back towards a time she'd chosen to keep walled away. 'I've never heard of Temple Newsam. What is it?'

'It's a big house,' Jane told her. 'Very big, with a lot of land.' When she'd asked, Mrs Shields had told her about the place.

'I went there for a ball one summer when I was a girl.' The old woman's eyes had sparkled; in her mind she was hearing the music again. 'There were so many people, even more than at the assemblies here. They held it in the great hall, and people wandered out into the grounds and down to the lake. Torches were burning to make a path. I don't believe I've ever seen anything so magical in my life. Have you ever heard of Mary, the one they called the Queen of the Scots?'

Jane nodded; she'd seen the name in a book she'd read.

'Her husband was Lord Darnley. He was born at Temple Newsam. That's what my governess taught me. Their son was the James who succeeded Queen Bess in England.'

She'd been rapt, falling back through time as the old woman spoke. But none of the history would interest Sally. She only believed in the things she could see and touch.

Around the fires, quiet murmurs of conversation scattered through the night as the hours passed. They were only a small distance from Leeds; Jane sensed the town quietening and going to sleep.

'They won't come,' she said finally.

'Not tonight,' Sally agreed. She spoke to the boy who seemed to be the leader. Almost a young man, his cheeks covered in spots. Giving him instructions before they left, just in case.

Sally and Jane walked together through the empty streets to Swinegate. Maybe the men had learned their lesson, Jane thought as she covered the final yards to Green Dragon Yard. But that felt unlikely. They were young, they'd been humiliated; they'd return, craving their revenge. She kept the knife tight in her fist as she walked, alert and wary, all her senses sharp.

Sally told him she'd driven a cart before. Simon spotted the lie as soon as they settled on the seat and she took up the reins. For five minutes she was tentative, warily nudging the horse along until she had the feel of the vehicle and could keep the animal under close control.

He'd dressed very carefully, wearing his finest clothes, out at first light at the coffee cart to listen for any useful gossip, but hearing nothing. Then on to George Mudie's printing shop for a little history about the family at Temple Newsam.

'Easy for someone to claim he's related to the gentry.'

'I hope I'll be able to find out if there's any proof,' Simon said.

'Chances are that you won't. The aristocracy all have so many by-blows and mistresses that they must spend half their lives in bed. It's the murkiest world you can imagine. Lucky devils.' He gave a harsh laugh. 'You'll probably need to scrub yourself clean afterwards.'

It would be worth the short trip to try and discover a little truth, Simon thought as they trotted along the road. Knowing more about Fox and any connections he might have could help them anticipate his moves.

Or it might make no difference at all. Then there was the man's wife to consider. What game was she playing? He couldn't begin to penetrate that yet.

Sally was grinning. Once she understood what she was doing, she relished every second of this. Driving sensibly, not too fast, taking no chances.

'Better than riding a horse?' he asked.

She pursed her lips and stared at the road before shaking her head. 'No. I like it, but it's different. We had a waggon and I drove that a few times. It's like this. But up on a horse you . . .' She struggled for the words. 'Up there you feel free.'

Simon had tolerated being in a saddle, never more than that. With the damage to his leg, he could never ride again. But Sally had started life in the country; riding was natural to her. Driving the cart was the best he could offer her for now. She was enjoying this. He gritted his teeth. Each bump and jolt shot through his leg like a blow. He was going to ache later.

It was strange to be standing next to Rosie, waiting deep in the morning shadows for the Foxes to leave their house. She was a very different presence from Sally. Larger – not as hidden. She stood quietly, with a thoughtful gaze, but Jane could feel her eagerness.

Jane knew that Simon's wife was good at this work; she'd seen it enough times over the years. Someone to be trusted. But Mrs Fox had her skills, too. Not a woman to take lightly.

'Do they have any servants?' Rosie whispered.

'I've never seen any,' Jane replied. 'Which of them do you want to take?'

'Her.' Never a moment's hesitation.

The silence returned. Then a flurry of movement as the couple emerged. They parted at the end of Middle Fold. The man was hurrying along; Jane had to move quickly to keep him in sight. A hurried glance over her shoulder to see Rosie start to walk, pulling a shawl over her hair, her face set hard.

Fox kept to his brisk pace. She had to hurry to keep up – never a good way to stay inconspicuous. Jane twisted the gold ring on her finger for luck. But nobody looked twice as she glided between people on Lady Lane, then Briggate, up Commercial Street and Lands Lane, all the way to the Head Row. A curious route, but Fox never slowed. He didn't appear to know she was tucked in twenty yards behind him. A safe distance on a busy morning when the pavements were full.

The day was warm again, the air still and weighted with humidity. Men sweated in their heavy woollen suits. Women waved small fans as they walked, trying to cool their faces. All around her, Leeds was a cauldron of noise. Voices, rumbling cartwheels, the relentless sounds of hammers from small workshops down in the yards.

She knew every inch of this town. Leeds had always been

the background to her life, easy to ignore as she kept her attention on Fox. He crossed the Head Row, following the streets behind St John's Church and its alms houses, finally finding a place out of sight that offered a good view of Barton's house.

It was simple to settle in a hollow between the tree roots where she could keep her eyes on him. Nobody had built on this ground yet. Soon enough that would change. People arrived in Leeds every day, all of them desperate for somewhere to live, lured by the blind promise of a fortune.

As she sat, Jane thought about the man watching the house. Why had he taken such a twisting way here? She'd swear he had no idea she was following him. Perhaps it was some cautious habit. She couldn't look inside his head; there had to be a reason she didn't understand. After a while, her mind strayed to the men who'd tormented the homeless children. The house where one of them lived stood in front of her. She hoped he'd learned, and that was an end to it for him. She'd have no need to mention it to Simon. But deep inside, she had her doubts. A gnawing in her belly said it wasn't over yet.

Then the screaming girl from the factory came back to her, a waking dream that made her cringe. The sound raced through her skull, as real as if she was hearing it all over again. She had to close her eyes and shake her head to force it away.

Jane was grateful when the parish church struck the hour and cut off her thoughts. The front door opened and Barton came out, striding briskly away. She was ready when Fox left. He paused by a tree and slipped something into a hole in the trunk.

Very odd. Making sure he couldn't see her, she pulled it out. A slip of paper with one thing on it: the number three scribbled in pencil. What did it mean? A time? A meeting? Who was meant to see it?

For a moment, she wondered if she should wait and see who collected it. No. Her job was to follow Fox and keep Barton safe.

# EIGHT

Sally pulled on the reins and the horse stopped. He watched as she stared open-mouthed at the house in the distance, unable to find words for it. It had risen in front of them as they topped the hill. A U-shaped building with red brick that seemed to glow in the sunlight, stately and magnificent, overlooking acres and acres of carefully landscaped grounds. A view to steal the breath away.

'Do you know what it's like inside?' she asked finally.

'No.' Simon had never seen how people with titles and the real riches lived. He stared; like her, he was drinking it all in. This was beyond his imagination. How could anyone find the words to describe it? An advertisement of wealth and power that hit him in a way he couldn't have anticipated. Not envy, but . . . awe. 'We'd better move,' he said after a long while.

'Will they let us in?' she asked doubtfully, looking down at her dress and heavy boots.

He smiled. 'We'll be talking to the servants. The people who own this probably aren't here.'

She kept the horse at a sedate pace, glancing at the roll of the hills. A shepherd was counting a flock of sheep, calling out as he moved among them: 'Yan, tan, tethera, methera, pip,' and more and he walked among the animals. Simon saw the girl smile.

'What's he doing?'

'That was how we count in the country. I don't think I've heard it since I came to Leeds.' She blinked. 'It made me remember. Look over there.'

She pointed off into the distant sky, picking out the red kites, the kestrels and buzzards over the woods. Something to change the subject. But her eyes always returned to the house.

'There are letters at the top of it,' she said in astonishment. 'What do they say?'

George Mudie had told him. He hadn't understood, but now

the words in white-painted stone seemed to make a curious kind of sense.

'"All glory and praise be given to God the father the son and the holy ghost on high peace on earth goodwill towards men honour and true allegiance to our gracious king loving affection among his subjects health and plenty be within this house,"' he recited.

Those things would certainly be plentiful inside those walls, he thought.

'All those words?' She sounded doubtful.

'Yes. It's their motto.' Sally turned her head quizzically. 'Words they're supposed to live by,' he explained.

A gardener directed them to the proper entrance. The rear of the house, where no carriages or gentry were likely to spot them. When he stepped down, his leg was stiff, a sharp, angry pain with each step.

A few questions and a footman wearing a dark apron over his livery was leading him with quiet grace towards the butler's pantry.

'Talk to the maids and kitchen girls,' he told Sally. She nodded as she looked around, completely overwhelmed by the scale of things. She'd soon discover the truth as she met girls her age who spent their days sweating near the ovens and endlessly cleaning the house. Drudges.

Mr Dawson, the butler, was a man defined by his dignity, one who'd worked his way up to his position. Soberly dressed in a dark jacket and trousers, black shoes polished to a high gloss, his shirt and stock immaculate and white, he stood and listened to Simon, eyes slowly narrowing. For a long minute he remained silent.

'You need to talk to Mr Holroyd,' he decided. 'He's the estate clerk, been here for years. If anyone here would know about any family called Fox, it would probably be him.'

He rang a bell and another footman quickly appeared, escorting him along the passages and up a back stair that kept them out of sight of the grand rooms.

The office was neat, with tall bundles of papers carefully stacked and tied. The man behind the desk looked to be well into his sixties, with thin white hair, a pale, genial face and kindly blue eyes behind a pair of thick spectacles. The light from the window fell on the desk where he was working. Out beyond, the ground rolled away for miles.

'Over my time here I've had dealings with many families related in some way to the Marchioness,' he replied with a wan smile when Simon had finished. He didn't need to consult any old books; very likely the entire history of Temple Newsam rested in his head. He'd know the grounds, the buildings, the people, better than the owners. It had probably been his life since he was a boy. 'Others who claimed to be, too. I can assure you that none of them was named Fox from anywhere near Richmond.' He spoke with an odd, stilted formality. 'I'm sorry, you appear to have had a wasted journey.'

'Believe me, it's been worthwhile to learn that,' Simon told him. 'At least I know there's no connection.' He stood. 'Thank you.'

'It's nothing.' He dismissed it with a small wave. 'A boy will show you the way out.'

The silence of the house came as a surprise. So many servants moving around, working, but never talking. No chattering or gossip to help pass the time. It was like being inside a tomb. Everything was communicated with gestures and looks. Sometimes a hurried whisper, as if they daren't risk disturbing the owners.

Sally was waiting by the cart, wearing an expression he couldn't read.

'What did you make of it?' Simon asked. He walked in small circles, trying to ease his leg before the trip back.

'It's beautiful,' she replied. 'But none of it seems real, does it? A house like this . . . look at the grounds . . .' She frowned with frustration. 'I can't put it the way I think. It's *like* the country, but it's not the *real* country. There are sheep, but where's all the dirt?'

'Money,' he replied. He climbed back on to the seat and shifted around, trying to find a comfortable spot. 'This is what it buys you. An illusion. The look without the problems.'

She nodded, grimacing. 'Yes, and all those people working away to make your life easier.' Sally twitched the reins and the cart rolled on. 'A girl showed me some of it.' The wonder grew in her voice. 'Did you know there's a passage under that courtyard at the front where they carry dishes from the kitchen for the feasts, and hidden stairs so guests don't have to see the servants.'

He chuckled. 'I can easily believe it. I was on a staircase like that. Out of sight.'

'There's a ghost in the house, too. The girl said she knew someone who'd seen it, it's a blue lady.'

He was quiet as she recited the story, wondering if he'd ever heard her speak so much. Everything from ghosts to kitchens, the passages with stone floors that stretched away, and the uniforms the servants had to wear; she'd learned so much in a short time.

'Half of them seem to spend their time in the cellars,' Sally finished and shook her head. 'They even eat there. I don't understand how anyone can do that, with no light and air around them.'

Not that there was much good air in Leeds, Simon thought as they turned towards town. Out here it was fresh, clean enough to taste. A different world. For a few minutes he'd stepped into it, just long enough to learn what he needed. That was enough. It wasn't somewhere he could live, not with the deference it demanded.

'Could you be content there?' he asked.

Sally set her mouth in a straight line. 'I don't think so. Maybe if I hadn't known anything else.'

He smiled. Not knowing anything else. Perhaps that was the key to it. Expecting nothing more from life.

She guided the horse back down the drive, halting at the top of the rise for a final look back. Just like her, Simon would carry this with him for the rest of his life. His eyes caught her face, noticing the way her eyes shone to be out in the country. Sooner or later they'd lose her, he thought. The pull would be too great. Once she was old enough, she'd probably marry a farmer. Maybe create a home for some of those stray children. Growing food and raising animals. It was in her blood.

The day slithered away from her. Fox trailed Barton around Leeds, always keeping a good distance: too far to threaten, still close enough to worry.

After the church clock struck two, Fox began pulling out his watch. Finally he left Barton, moving away in a loping walk. Which to follow? It was an easy choice; Fox was the danger. Jane stayed behind him all the way to a warehouse where the river met the start of the Leeds and Liverpool Canal.

Jane stayed out of sight, a hidden, crouching figure in a shawl. If anyone looked, their eyes would pass over her.

As the bell in the distance tolled three o'clock, another man appeared and she understood the morning's note; it was to arrange the meeting. The man who appeared was younger, moving in gawky strides. Well-dressed in a dark coat and a dark waistcoat, pale, tightly fitted trousers and a top hat with a high crown.

Fox was talking, anger and frustration leaving his face stormy. He gestured and waved, as if they were arguing; Jane was too far away to pick out any words. The other man stood, head bowed and face stern, pushing a few words into the gaps. Finally, after five minutes, they seemed to reach an agreement of some sort and the younger man left, looking around him before he disappeared.

He never spotted her, but she'd know him when she saw his face again. Fox began to move away, back into the heart of town and she stayed behind him as he returned to Middle Fold.

Who was the other man? Why the secrecy of the note and meeting out of the way? Yet more questions about the Foxes. Too many. Maybe Rosie had managed to find a few answers about the wife.

They met at the house on Swinegate.

'She went to buy food, then home and never came out again,' Rosie said, with a sour smile.

'We learned that Fox has no connection to the Ingrams,' Simon said, hobbling around the kitchen, trying to smother the pain coursing through him. 'But with that meeting he's obviously planning something. How old was this other man?'

'Young. Probably not much more than twenty,' Jane answered. 'The way he moved, it was like he hadn't quite grown into his body yet.' She thought a moment longer. 'He was trying to look confident, but Fox seemed to take charge.'

'He shouldn't be difficult to find.' Simon leaned against the door jamb. 'It seems there's nothing more we can do today.' He nodded at her. 'I'd like you and Sally back on the Foxes tomorrow. Whatever they're planning must be ready to take shape by now.'

'Are they going to come?' Sally asked. They stood, silhouetted by the small fire, two outlines in the dark.

'Yes.' All the way here, Jane had felt it. Through the long twilight, she'd sat outside the cottage behind Green Dragon Yard and run a whetstone over her knife while Mrs Shields read. Finally, when night fell, she'd put a thin shawl around her shoulders.

'Are you sure you know what you're doing?' the old woman asked in an anxious voice.

Jane nodded. 'Sally's going to need me.'

Catherine Shields's gaze lingered, then finally she nodded. 'Please be careful, child. I don't want to lose you.'

'I will.' A smile, a squeeze of the old woman's hand and a kiss on her head. 'I promise.' She meant the words. She'd return, whole and sound.

Sally had gathered a small group of children around her as she told her tales about Temple Newsam. The dark underground passage where candles had to be hung on the walls and the story of the ghost called the Blue Lady.

Jane listened as she stared out into the darkness. The stories helped to pass the time as the fire crackled. But they were nothing more than words to fill the waiting, before whatever was gathering. Once the quiet returned, it seemed fuller, stronger than before. Sally wandered around the group, pausing for a kind word here, some encouragement there. Last night had been a lull, a chance to breathe. They all realised something was coming. The real wave would crash over them tonight.

As she sat by Jane, Sally said, 'When we were out at that house today, I could taste the clearness in the air. I realised how much I've missed that. Everything's so dirty here. All the smells and the muck. Don't you ever notice it?'

How could she? This was what she knew. It was home. She shook her head. She'd seen the way the girl's eyes sparkled whenever she talked about the countryside. That was the real core of her. Leeds was just a thin layer over the top, a place of constant battles.

'Is everyone ready?' It was all Jane could think to say. She twisted the gold ring on her finger; they might need the luck tonight.

'They are,' she replied. They had their stones. Some had gathered branches. She looked at them as if they were her family. In a way, they were. 'They'll fight.'

'There—' Jane stopped, catching something in the distance. 'It's them. They're coming.'

Six this time. No blundering tonight; they were moving cautiously. Too many for her and Sally to fight alone. The young ones would need to play their part.

Maybe the men believed they were keeping quiet. They kept their voices low, as if they imagined no sound would carry on the air. She knew where they were, right to the yard, ready when one let out his war cry and they started to charge.

The children were good, halting them with a barrage of stones. At the very first resistance, two of the men turned tail. Suddenly the numbers were more balanced. The four who remained tried to gather themselves in a ragged line as more stones and branches pelted them. Jane launched herself at the one on the end. He ran as soon as he saw her knife, before she had chance to strike a blow.

The battle was quickly withering. Barely even a skirmish now. It was rapidly becoming a repeat of the last time.

Only three left. Sally was fighting furiously against one, her face rigid with fury. From the corner of her eye, Jane saw her start to push him back.

Then another took a run straight at her, murder in his eyes. Someone had taught him a few basics of knife fighting. How to hold a blade. But not enough to turn him into any kind of warrior. He flinched as she feinted close to his belly, then she slid inside and cut the back of his hand. With a yelp, he dropped his weapon, stared at her in panic for a second before he dashed away.

Sally was still fighting. That left one more. The children were trying to hold him off, but he was beginning to overwhelm them. He'd already wounded one, a boy who clutched his arm and held back tears.

Time to end things.

Jane shouted. He turned towards her. She saw his face and for a second she froze. It was the same man she'd seen talking to Fox that afternoon. Crouching now, ready for her.

He slashed. Pure instinct made her parry and the jolt that ran through her arm startled her back to her senses. She began to fight. He possessed enough skill to cause her a few doubts. But all too soon she could hear him panting. No stamina, no experience of fights where the outcome was staying alive or dying. The man had scrapes and blood on his face from the stones the children had thrown. Another ten seconds and he had the brains to realise he wasn't going to win.

He raised his hands.

'No more,' she warned him. 'No coming back. Any of you.'

He agreed with a curt nod before he turned and dashed away.

Sally's opponent was limping off into the distance. It was over. They wouldn't return. One boy had a knife slash on his arm. Not deep; it would heal well. Sally bound it with a strip of cloth one of the girls handed her.

Nobody dead. No serious injuries. Nothing to attract the constable and the night watch. That was a victory.

The surge of war began to drain from her body as the two of them walked into town.

'The last one I was fighting . . .' Jane began, not sure how to continue.

'What about him?'

'I've seen him before.'

Sally stared at her. 'So have I. When did it happen?'

'He met Fox this afternoon. When—'

'He's Barton's son.'

# NINE

Jane passed Richard and Amos as they ran along Swinegate, scampering away on a Saturday morning. A nod, a quick 'Good morning, miss,' and they were gone again. Growing so fast, she thought, already taller than her. When she began working for Simon, they were only small boys.

But the house remained exactly the same. They sat round the table in the kitchen, and she and Sally explained what they'd seen yesterday.

Simon stared at the floor as he listened. First light had seen him haunting the coffee cart, craving some useful news and hearing nothing. Now the surprises had come into his own home and he had no idea what to make of them.

'We need to tell the Bartons,' Rosie said.

'Yes.' They'd made it clear they didn't have much regard for their son. This news that he'd been talking to Fox and attacking homeless children would destroy whatever was left. If he was conspiring against his parents . . . 'The sooner the better.'

He stood, leaning heavily on his stick. Every step hurt today; the journey in the cart had taken its toll; finding a comfortable position for sleep had been close to impossible. One more thing the injury had stolen from him.

'You'd better come with me.' To Jane and Sally: 'Stay with the Foxes. Are you sure this problem with the young men and the children is really over?'

A fleeting look between the pair. 'Yes,' Sally answered firmly.

The groups of children were a familiar sight in town. Easy targets for any man with a temper or wanting to prove himself after a night fired by drink. He knew how much Sally cared for them. Of course she'd be their defender, too.

\* \* \*

'Mr Westow . . . Mrs . . .' Barton looked confused as the servant showed them into the room. 'This is a surprise. Have you discovered something?'

'We have,' Simon told him. He began with Temple Newsam, seeing anger flash across the man's face at falling for a lie. That was the easy part. Barton's expression grew darker as he learned about his son. First the children, then the meeting with Fox.

'There's no doubt?'

'None.'

The man reached across and took his wife's hand and called for a servant.

'Tell Andrew I want him down here in five minutes.'

'He was—'

'Five minutes.' Barton didn't raise his voice. No need; the tone was steel. He turned to Simon. 'I'd like you to put it all to him, the way you did to me. I want to watch his face.'

Andrew Barton wore a sullen expression as he came in, struggling into a jacket. No stock, hair uncombed and wild. Grazes on his cheek.

'I came in late last night,' he began. 'I was still asleep—' He stopped as he noticed Simon and Rosie.

'This is Mr and Mrs Westow,' Barton said. 'They settled the business with Fox.'

Simon saw the young man staring at him, uncertainty and desperation behind his gaze. He was taller than his father, shifting from foot to foot, not yet completely at home in his body.

'What does that have to do with me?'

'I believe you know Mr Fox,' his father said.

'No.' The young man stepped back as if he'd been hit. 'Of course I don't.'

'You met him yesterday afternoon, down by the canal,' Simon said. 'He left a message for you with the time.'

He shook his head. 'He's lying to you.' He turned to his parents. 'I never did that.'

'What happened to your face?' Mrs Barton asked. 'It wasn't like that yesterday.'

He rubbed his hand across his cheek. 'Some roughhousing last night. That's all.'

'You and some of your friends attacked some children.'
'I—' He turned to Simon. 'Why are you lying to them?'
'It's the truth.'
'What are you doing with Fox?' Barton asked.
'Nothing, I told you. I never saw him.'
'Andrew, I've known when you've been lying since you learned to talk.' His mother's voice overflowed with sadness. 'It's time for the truth.'

Frantic, Andrew looked around, hoping for . . . Simon didn't know. Then he turned on his heel and ran from the room. All they could hear was the rush of his shoes on the stairs.

'I'm sorry,' Rosie said into the silence.

'No need.' Barton shook his head. 'I'm grateful you told us. It's better to know what we harbour in our own house. We'll have it out of him later. I'll send you a note.'

He sounded weary at heart, Simon thought. The last few minutes had aged him, brought a new kind of pain into his life.

'We still don't know what the son was plotting with Fox,' Rosie said as they strolled along Briggate. She kept turning her head to look at the enticing displays of fabrics and baubles in the shop windows. They'd dressed well for the meeting, Simon fashionable in his tight swallowtail coat and his best trousers. Rosie wore her favourite plum-coloured gown with a small hat and an Indian cotton shawl covering her shoulders. Clothes intended to impress.

'No,' he agreed. 'But we've set things in motion. That's a start.'

Last night, the air had crackled around them with anticipation as they waited with the children. This morning felt lighter, Jane thought. The air was warm, sticky and close as they stood hidden in Middle Fold. But the tension had drained away.

'They're out,' Sally warned.

No rush; the couple were ambling arm-in-arm. This time they didn't part as they reached Mabgate, but turned away from town, up the road, then on to Skinner Lane, following Long Balk Lane, into Cobourg Street to the tidy gentility of Queen Square.

It was only a few years old, standing off Woodhouse Lane

above the city to look down on the grime. Another desirable Leeds address for people with means. The Foxes knocked on a door and vanished inside.

'Did you see which house they went into?' Jane asked.

'Yes.' Sally was staring at the building. Thoughtfully, she said, 'I followed someone to this square once before.'

'The same house?'

'I don't know. They disappeared before I was close enough to see.'

Leeds might be loud and bustling, but it was still small. They took advantage of the coolness of a tree, climbing into the low branches and out of sight, shaded by the leaves. Resting with her back against the trunk, Jane smiled to herself. Mrs Shields would chide her if she could see; young ladies didn't climb trees. But young ladies wore delicate shoes and slippers, not sturdy boots with hobnails in the soles. They didn't carry knives and know how to use them. They hadn't come of age on the streets. They didn't work for thief-takers and relish any comfort as they waited outside in all weathers.

Almost an hour passed before the Foxes came out again, strolling back down Woodhouse Lane and into town. It was harder to follow out here; too few people around. But as soon as they were fully into Leeds, they'd be swallowed by the crowds. They needed to be ready.

Sally slipped ahead, hurrying across the fields and sites marked out for new homes, down to wait by Wormald Place, while Jane lingered behind the couple. She crossed the road, shawl tucked around her hair, moving with her eyes down, but constantly flickering to see the man and his wife.

Who had they been to see? What business had they done? She'd never seen either of them greet people or stop to talk, so it was unlikely to have been a social call.

They needed to know much more. But this was a thread for Simon to tug.

Sally slid in beside her just before they reached the Head Row. Not far away, Davy Cassidy was playing his fiddle. The quick notes of a jig lifted into the air and for a fleeting moment Jane wished she could stop and hold the music close. But the Foxes kept walking and so did she.

Once the couple reached the main road, they parted.

Jane stayed with the woman. Down Albion Street, past the elegant new buildings of Commercial Street, where dressmakers' windows displayed expensive gowns few women could afford, past the subscription library and the jewellers. Mrs Fox kept a determined stride, her gaze straight ahead, not distracted by any of the items on display.

She crossed Briggate, started down Kirkgate, and Jane began to suspect she was going to Grey's Court again.

She could keep following, but that would mean stopping when they reached the court. Or she could take a risk, rush along the back ways she knew, and be there first, able to spot exactly where Mrs Fox went.

If the woman was going anywhere else, she'd lose her.

Jane dashed through the ginnels to the far side of the court and in through one of the three entrances. The flagstones were smeared with the night waste people had tossed out, a burning stink to inhale as she stood close to the water pipe, head down, waiting, hoping she'd been right.

A blink and Mrs Fox was there, eyes moving around, passing quickly over Jane. She was nothing, part of the landscape. Her gaze followed the woman as she climbed the steps, knocked on a door and entered without waiting for an answer.

Later they could find out who lived there and the connection to whatever the Foxes were doing. Now it was time to leave before the woman came out again.

Queen Square, then here. Who were the people behind the doors? What connected them to the Foxes?

'Two, please,' she said to Kate the pie-seller. Jane had first known her when she was still a girl living wild. Back then, the woman would sometimes give her a pie, often the only thing to keep her going that day. Kate was a big woman, a widow now the husband who beat her was dead. But she didn't feel free, she said. She missed him.

'Why?' Jane asked.

'I loved him.' Her voice was a mix of sorrow and surprise. Kate gave a rueful smile and shook her head. 'I know, it's daft. But it's how I am, I can't help it. I was used to him.'

Now she'd finally shed her grieving, smiling as she saw Jane.

'Here you are, not long out of the oven, still warm as you please.' She squinted. 'You look . . . What is it? Are you puzzled by something?'

'I am.' The woman was right. Trying to understand this was like making out shapes in muddy water. 'It's work.'

A few moments to talk before she moved through the crowds that thronged Briggate. Some had gathered around a juggler, a new face in town. He was skilful, keeping five balls in the air and a flow of patter as people darted towards him and placed coins in his hat. A coachman's horn sounded as the vehicle emerged from Bay Horse Yard and started hell for leather towards Newcastle. Close by, a singer had an audience for the new ballad, selling at a penny a sheet.

Plenty of diversions to tempt her. But she was going to Middle Fold. Sooner or later, Mrs Fox would return.

'I'll go to Grey's Court,' Simon said after Jane finished speaking. Outside, afternoon was easing into evening. He looked across the kitchen table at his wife. 'Can you go up to Queen Square?'

She gave a thoughtful nod. 'I know a couple of women who live there. One of them should be able to tell me who's in that house.'

Sally opened her mouth to speak, then closed it again, puzzled, before she said, 'I don't understand Fox. He didn't do much. After he left his wife, he walked over to Barton's house and spent a few hours watching it before he went home. There was no sign of Barton. He didn't come back for his dinner, and he'd probably gone before Fox arrived. I don't understand it. I can't see what he's trying to do.'

'He worried Barton enough for him to employ us,' Simon reminded her.

'Yes.' She nodded and pushed her lips together. 'But what has he *done*?'

'He had that meeting with Barton's son,' Jane reminded her. 'He left a note to arrange it, so they must have set that up as a way to keep in touch. That means they already knew each other.' She turned to Sally. 'Did Fox stop at that tree? You know the one?'

'I'm not sure.' She gazed at her hands. 'I didn't want to get too close and risk him seeing me.'

'It doesn't matter,' Simon said. 'Stay with them again tomorrow.' He needed to come up with something to lift the dour mood. 'You've both been doing good work on this.'

Quietly, Jane closed *Woodstock* and set it on the small table by her chair.

'Did you enjoy it, child?' Mrs Shields asked. The older woman was bright today, spirits lifted by the warmth and sun that lasted through the long evenings.

She gave an enthusiastic nod. 'I did. I felt I was right there with them.'

'That was a bad time for the country, with the Cavaliers and the Roundheads, families split in two. Dangerous. I learned a little about it when I was a girl.'

Jane thought about that. No war, no battles in the country now, but for plenty of people today held ample dangers, too. 'I learned things I never knew about history.'

'Books can always do that. What are you going to read next?'

'I don't know.' She'd make a trip to the circulating library as soon as this job allowed. It wasn't that long since she'd learned to read, not even two years. As soon as she had, words consumed her, as if she needed to make up for all those years she'd lost. She read everything: books, newspapers, magazines, even the advertisements pasted to the walls. Anything printed caught her eye. She'd taught herself to write, and Rosie had shown her numbers. She'd discovered she had an endless thirst to know more.

Finally, as darkness arrived, Jane laced up her work boots.

'Again, child?' Mrs Shields had worry in her voice.

'It's nothing to worry about tonight.' She gave a reassuring smile. 'It's just a precaution.'

Sally was there with the children, listening to their prattle as they gathered by the fire. The talk slowly died away as the children began to settle.

'I don't think they'll come back,' she said, but there was a faint edge of fear running under the words.

'They won't,' Jane said. Deep inside, she knew it. But she

was here, anyway. Just in case. She'd become a part of this. The nights had brought too many memories of her own time living this way swimming back in to her mind.

As the church clock struck one, they strolled home. Jane stayed alert, hand on her knife. She checked on Mrs Shields. The old woman was sleeping with a sweet, calm smile on her face.

Simon nodded to the faces around the coffee cart. Sunday morning, and Leeds was quiet, but men were still out and about. Some had work to go to, others simply nowhere else to be. Faces he rarely saw anywhere else sharing a few quick minutes at the start of a day. All sorts of folk: clerks, men who owned businesses, a mechanic or engineer with burly arms and scarred hands.

The busy and the lost: which was he?

The pain from the cart trip was beginning to recede. He'd slept more easily last night, but the ache lingered, and he had to concentrate on each step as he walked. No more travelling that way, he decided; even with the pleasure of seeing Temple Newsam, the cost was too great.

He felt as if the entire affair with Barton and Fox had slid away from him. When he first received the note to say the man had returned after his pardon, it had seemed straightforward. Now he wasn't sure of anything. There had been no confrontation, no threats. Then he had to consider Fox meeting with Barton's son. For the life of him he couldn't work out what the devil it meant. But it was time to find some answers.

Simon finished the coffee, handed back the ancient tin cup and started down Kirkgate. The bells from the parish church at the bottom of the street rang through his head.

Grey's Court. As he entered, he smelled the rot rising from the ground. Nobody was shouting or moving around. Simon looked up at the door Jane had described.

A knock and . . . nothing. Empty rooms had their own sound. Hollow. He tried again. No answer, no footsteps shifting around inside. He tried the doorknob. Locked. A hurried glance around. Not a soul was watching as he drew out the small pack of lock picks from his waistcoat pocket. Only a few seconds before he felt the satisfaction of a click and turned the handle, holding his breath as he gently pushed the door open.

Immediately, Simon knew.

The room was alive with flies, thousands of them buzzing in the sticky heat. The air was heavy with the bitter stink of death. There was nothing else quite like it. Simon gripped the handle of his stick, ready to draw the sword inside. But he was the only living human here.

A shape lay on a narrow bed, covered by a grubby sheet. He took a shallow breath through his mouth and drew back the cloth. Nobody he knew. A man who might have been thirty.

A thin rope had cut deep into his neck and strangled him. Simon stepped back, eyes moving around the room. A table and chair, but no plates or knife. No clothes hanging from a nail, no shoes on the floor. This wasn't a place where anyone had made a life.

Simon glanced back at the corpse. He was wearing an old coat, dirty and dusty with just a scrap of paper in the pocket, this address scribbled on it in ink. No coins, nothing that could give him a name.

He slipped the note back where he'd found it. A final inspection to be sure he'd missed nothing, then softly back to the door. Not a soul outside as the church bells finished summoning the faithful.

He didn't pause to lock the door behind him. Where now? Vanish quietly or report what he'd found?

'A body?' Inspector Fry tried to stare him down. He had the duty today, sitting at the constable's desk in the courthouse with a copy of the *Leeds Mercury* and glaring as Simon gave him the news.

'Come and see for yourself.'

'What the hell have you done, Westow?' But he was on his feet and hurrying towards the door, calling for a couple of members of the watch.

By the time they arrived at the Grey's Court, Simon's leg ached fiercely from trying to keep pace with the angry strides.

'How did you get in?'

'It wasn't locked,' he lied.

'Round here?' For a moment the man looked ready to argue. Instead, he entered, keeping the men from the watch outside.

The inspector threw back the sheet then seemed to stare at the corpse in disgust. He moved a finger over the rope, stroking it, before he turned.

'Who is he, Westow?'

'I don't know. I've never seen him before.'

'Don't lie to me.' His eyes blazed. 'You came here. You're trying to tell me that you didn't know who you were visiting?'

'That's right.' Simon kept his voice low and steady as he explained and glanced at the body. 'I have no idea who he is. But I can tell you he probably never rented this room himself or spent much time here.'

Fry raised his eyebrows in astonishment, then looked around and nodded.

'If you don't know his name, let me tell you. He's called Daniel Shackleton.' He spat it out as he looked down at the bed again. 'I wondered what happened to that bastard.'

'Doesn't mean anything to me,' Simon said.

'He used to live in Leeds. Killed a man in a fight.' He narrowed his eyes. 'It must have been . . . close to a year ago, I suppose.'

That would explain why Simon had never heard the name. It was just after he'd been knifed, when all he could think of was staying alive and not losing his leg.

'They arrested him in Wakefield,' the inspector continued. 'Sentenced to hang, and they put him in prison in York. He escaped back in March. God only knows why he decided to make his way back here.' He stared at the corpse again. 'Strangled.' The inspector snorted. 'Some justice, at least. You say Fox's wife came here?'

'One of the women who works for me followed her.'

'All the way to the door?'

'I wouldn't have known where to look otherwise.'

'Where do I find the Foxes?'

'Middle Fold.'

He reached out and touched the rope once more. 'Remember, Westow, this is murder. It's not your business any longer.'

'You're welcome to it,' Simon told him. 'Something for you

to think about, though. If he was in York prison until March, Fox was there, too.'

The inspector considered the idea and nodded again. 'That would explain the connection. But it doesn't explain this room or how he came to be murdered. We'll need to find out who paid for it.' He nodded. 'I'll find you if I need to know more.'

It was a dismissal.

'The man's name was Daniel Shackleton,' he told Rosie. She'd been sitting with the boys, watching as they finished their homework at the kitchen table. Simon sent them upstairs to put on old clothes and collect the fishing sticks he'd cut for them from hazel branches. He explained everything while they were gone.

Her mouth turned down. 'Something's wrong. None of this makes sense.'

'I know, and it comes back to the Foxes again.'

The four of them were sitting in their favourite fishing spot by the river when Sally dashed up, calling out his name. She was breathless, eyes wide. Painfully, Simon pushed himself to his feet.

'We've been watching Fox's house,' she said. 'The shutters are still closed. Nobody's come out.'

He felt a flutter of fear in his belly.

Rosie put a hand on his arm. 'Leave it to the watch, Simon.'

He hesitated for a moment before he agreed.

'I imagine the constable's men will be there very soon,' he told the girl. 'I went to Grey's Court this morning, the room Mrs Fox visited. There was a body. He'd been strangled. Someone who'd been in York prison the same time as Mr Fox.'

# TEN

Jane lifted her head. The first footsteps she'd heard along Middle Fold in over an hour. She glanced from the shadows: Inspector Fry and two more she recognised from the watch. Nothing to do but keep still as they marched to the house where the Foxes lived and hammered on the door.

No reply, nor a second time. She saw the inspector try the handle, then stand back in surprise when it turned under his hand. He drew his knife and edged inside, the others behind him.

Time for her to leave, a figure who might have been there, although nobody would be able to recall with certainty. As she turned on to Mabgate, she found Sally hurrying back after seeing Simon.

'I didn't wait to see if the Foxes were still inside,' Jane said. 'I didn't want to risk anyone spotting me.' A murder, and something wrong in Middle Fold. The hairs rose on her arm. Much safer for them to keep as far from that as possible, she decided as she walked home. Nothing good could come of it.

She worked outside the cottage, pricking out the weeds around the flowers and relishing the feel of the sun, forgetting death and problems in the scent of the honeysuckle that climbed up the wall. Mr Richardson's *Pamela* waited for her on the bench, a book from Mrs Shields's library that she'd never read. Sitting with it would be her reward for finishing the job.

Afternoon had waned into a drowsy evening by the time Simon and Rosie arrived. As they sat together, drinking one of the old woman's cordials, Simon looked at her and said, 'Inspector Fry came to see me. He says it looks as if the Foxes left their house in a hurry.'

'Was there anything to indicate why? Or where they were going?' Jane asked.

'No.' He glanced at his wife. 'We're on our way to see Barton and tell him.' He pursed his lips. 'I'd like to hear what happened when the watch turned up at the house.'

What was there to tell? Very little; she'd only seen them arrive. It barely took a sentence. He listened and said, 'I never told the constable about his son meeting Fox. Maybe it's not important now.'

'What do you want me to do tomorrow?' she asked, although she knew the answer.

'I don't think there's anything for us at the moment,' Rosie told her.

She was happy with that. She treasured her time at this cottage, just her and Mrs Shields together. Soon Simon would pay her for the job, more money to hide behind the loose stone in the wall.

Barton exhaled slowly and looked across at his wife after Simon finished speaking.

'I have no idea what to make of all that.' He shook his head, baffled. 'I don't recall ever hearing of anyone named Shackleton. How does he come into this?'

'He must have been in prison with Fox, but I can't see how it has anything to do with you. Still, it looks as if the Foxes have vanished. You shouldn't have any more problems with them.'

The man gave a tentative nod and rubbed his chin. Off in the distance, the bells rang for evening service.

'None of this makes a scrap of sense, does it?'

'No.'

'I'd still like someone following me for the next two days. It would make me feel safer. Just in case.'

'Of course.' Simon looked toward his Rosie and she nodded. That was work Sally could easily do on her own. 'There is one other thing.'

'I know. My son and Fox. I've talked to him and badgered him, but he still denies he ever met the man. I know he's lying, but he refuses to budge on it. To tell you the truth, Mr Westow, I'm at the end of my patience with him. He announced this morning that he was going out with some friends to Kirkstall Abbey for the day and we were glad of the peace and quiet.'

'I'll come back tomorrow. I need to talk to him.' He paused, uncertain how to phrase the rest. 'I'm going to have to squeeze him for the truth. After what's happened today, it's vital.'

'Do whatever you have to do,' Barton agreed. 'Find your answers. You have my full backing. I'll be interested to hear it all. In the meantime, if you hear anything more about the Foxes . . .'

'I'll make sure you know.'

The coffee cart overflowed with Monday morning gossip about the dead man. He listened as someone recounted the murder Shackleton had committed. Another had ideas about how he'd managed his escape from the jail in York. But none of them could explain how he'd come to die in a shabby room in Leeds. Nobody mentioned Fox's name.

Simon walked to the courthouse and slowly took the stairs to the constable's office. His leg was finally back to its usual, tolerable ache. Porter was at work, smoking his pipe as he read reports. He lifted his eyes from the paper.

'You cause me more damned trouble than anyone else in Leeds, Westow.'

'Have your men found anything more about Shackleton?'

The constable snorted. 'There's nothing to find. No documents or papers, as I'm sure you know. You said his door was unlocked.'

Simon smiled back at him, his gaze steady. 'That's right.'

'Very convenient. What took you there?'

Five minutes for the tale; Porter listened intently. Simon told him everything except the meeting between Fox and Barton's son.

The constable sighed. 'The Foxes have run. There's no doubt about that. They didn't buy tickets at any of the coaching offices, and they didn't hire any type of carriage or cart. It doesn't look too planned; they appear to have left much of what they owned at that house.' He looked up. 'Does that give you any ideas?'

Just one, but it seemed ridiculous. 'What if they're dead, too?'

He saw the disbelief cross Porter's face, then he began to weigh the possibilities. 'Maybe,' he said with a small nod.

'If not, they're either walking along a road or hiding somewhere in Leeds.'

'The inspector's handling it. He has an interest; he's the one who was originally hunting Shackleton. He'll probably have some questions for Barton.'

'There's no connection, as far as I can see.'

'Of course there is. The Foxes.'

Simon nodded. 'I'll tell him.'

He'd scarcely arrived at the house before Rosie ran out of the kitchen.

'Barton sent a servant. He needs to see you. Urgent, he says.'

'Did he know—'

'No, but he said Barton and his wife are frantic.'

The man paced while his wife sat and stared, hands clasped together in her lap. Through the powder on her face, Simon could see the dried tracks of her tears.

James Barton's voice was tight. He looked like an old, terrified man. 'At first, we thought Andrew must have come home late again. But when the servant went in, his bed hadn't been slept in.' His eyes turned towards his wife but his head never moved. 'A few times he's spent the night with one of his friends after a picnic. The way things have been between us, I thought he perhaps decided not to tell us. I sent a servant to ask them earlier.'

'Maybe . . .' Simon began, but the man was shaking his head.

'They said he slipped away not long after they arrived at the abbey. They thought he must have arranged to meet a girl and when he didn't return, they left him to make his own way home.'

Shackleton murdered, the Foxes vanished, and now this. Was there some pattern that he was missing? Something to tie all the threads together?

The first thing was to talk to the friends.

It took an hour to gather the three young men in Barton's dining room. As he waited, Simon was aware of the time ticking away, and Andrew was still missing. A grown man, but one full of anger. The urgency pressed down on him.

'We know he was at the abbey. We need to search out there as soon as possible,' he told Barton.

'Of course.' The man nodded, fear bright in his eyes. 'But do you think he's still—?'

'We don't know where he is, or if something's happened to him,' Simon said. 'We have to start somewhere, and that's the last place he was seen. Lend me your gig and my wife and assistants can go.'

'Yes. Anything you need,' the man agreed without hesitation.

'If you'll have it brought round, I'll tell them.'

Standing in the warm sun, he breathed deep, then let out a low whistle and closed his eyes. When he opened them again, Sally was in front of him, appearing from nowhere.

'Find Jane and Rosie and bring them here. You're going to be driving Barton's gig out to Kirkstall Abbey and see if you can find anything to do with Andrew Barton out there.'

Her eyes grew wide. 'What do you mean? A body?'

'I hope not.' It had to be a possibility; it would fit with what they knew, but he didn't want to think about that. Simon passed on what Barton had told him. 'Rosie knows the way. I'm going to trust you to drive. Just be very careful.'

She gave a quick girlish grin, turned on her heel and dashed away.

'Did Simon say anything else about Andrew's disappearance?' Rosie asked.

'No.' Sally kept her attention on the horse and the road. 'I don't think he knows. Just that his friends thought he might have gone off with someone.' She pulled lightly on a rein. 'It all happened yesterday, so he's not sure what we can find.'

Everything was too vague, Jane thought. She was squeezed against the end of the seat, gripping the metal armrest with all her strength.

'Did his friends search for him?'

No answer to that.

Jane had barely arrived home when Sally began hammering on the door. She'd returned from shopping and the circulating library, eager to start *The Last of the Mohicans* and read the strange tale about the Indians in America. For a moment she stood in the doorway of the little house in Green Dragon Yard, torn.

'Go, child,' Mrs Shields urged her. 'The book will still be here when you get back.' Her eyes shone with memories. 'Perhaps you can find this young man. And you need to see Kirkstall Abbey. My husband and I often went on outings there.' A light squeeze of the hand. 'All that history.'

Now she could see a part of it from half a mile away, the remains of a stone tower that rose up to the sky, as tall as any church steeple. Mrs Shields was right; it was magnificent. What must it have been like when it was whole? This was the kind of ruined beauty she loved.

The road ran straight through the huge arch of a window, directly into the church. Just a few yards away, cattle ignored them as they happily grazed.

Not a soul she could ask, nobody who might answer questions. What chance was there of discovering Barton out here?

'Where do we start?' Jane asked.

Rosie looked around and shook her head. 'We'll have to look for anything at all. The smallest scrap. The river's down there. Sally and I can search upstream. You go the other way.'

Jane started with the remains of the buildings. Much of it was no more than mounds of old, dark stones, lifeless, some only foundations; everything usable had been scavenged over the centuries. There were still dark places to hide things, and she looked there; far more, she wanted a few brief minutes to revel in the place, to trace her fingertips over the stones and feel the past seep into her bones. She wondered about the monks who'd once lived there, who they'd been, what they were like. She stroked a column that had broken off above her head, caressing the weathered roughness of the stone, as if it might hold some echo of voices. High up in the ruined tower, an empty window looked out at the sky.

Jane strode across the grass, trodden flat, somewhere to sit and eat and laze on a warm day; then went further, down the slope to the riverbank. It would be a fine spot to bathe. The water looked calm and safe. No corpse bobbing there. Off in the distance, she spotted Sally examining the ground as Rosie listened to a cowherd who was pointing at something.

Jane followed a well-trodden track through some trees along the riverbank. Pale, dappled sunshine fell on the leaves. She trailed her arm through the tall grasses and flowers beside the path. At some other time, this could be a perfect place.

The sound of the water grew louder with each step, until she could see it roaring over a weir. A sluice drew a strong flow off to the side, flowing down a mill race towards the building in the distance. Another building stood on the other side of a short stone bridge. She knocked and tried the door. Locked. Nobody inside.

Jane stayed close to the river, scraping through bushes and briars, crouching as she passed under the old Kirkstall bridge, carefully watching the water for any small sign of Andrew Barton's body.

'You all know that Andrew hasn't returned.' Simon addressed the three young men who stood like awkward schoolboys. He watched their faces; they were all wary and fearful. 'People are searching out at the abbey. It's important to know exactly what happened, and when.' He glanced at James Barton. 'We need everything you can remember.'

They could have been cut from a single pattern. Slim, with fashionable clothes, the same swallowtail coats and tight trousers, all with carefully brushed hair. Faces that hadn't had time to settle into their final character yet. Another ten years and a couple of them would run to fat, he thought; they already had a faint hint of it around the neck.

'I think it was about two o'clock when we arrived there,' one said, glancing at the others for confirmation. Tim Cowley, the son of a factory owner.

'Just the four of you?'

'Yes,' a second replied. He had a tentative, reedy voice. Charles Ibbotson. 'We often do things together. Andrew suggested it and assembled the party. He arranged to hire that cart. It seemed like a good idea. Yesterday was warm, so the place was busy.'

'What happened after you arrived?' Simon asked. He studied them, alert for lies and hesitations.

'We ate and drank.' The third young man had a deep, sombre

tone that matched his dark hair. He'd introduced himself as Henry Harrison. 'We had a few bottles with us. Nothing outrageous. We weren't there to get drunk. All we wanted to do was enjoy ourselves. After we finished, Andrew said he was going for a walk.' He blinked, as if a thought had just occurred to him. 'I don't think he invited any of us along, did he?'

'No,' Ibbotson agreed. 'I remember. Just announced it and wandered off. I didn't make anything of it. He's always liked to walk.'

'I went to bathe,' Cowley said. 'It was hot in the sun.' He shrugged. 'Other people were doing it.'

An ordinary afternoon for young men. Another few years and it could be Richard and Amos telling a similar tale.

'Andrew didn't come back at all?'

'No,' Cowley told him. The others seemed content to let him do much of the talking. 'We were enjoying ourselves. I don't believe we gave him much of a thought until about seven o'clock. Most of the families with children had gone by then, so it was quieter, but it hadn't started to feel like evening. We'd been talking and playing cards and picking through what was left of the food. After we finished off the wine, we decided to come back to town.'

The others nodded their agreement. They were telling the truth, Simon had no doubt. With Barton watching them, they were too scared to lie.

'No sign of Andrew?'

Harrison shook his head. 'Not since he walked off.'

'Yes.' Ibbotson spoke, his skin glowing red. 'There are sometimes girls out there. You know . . .'

'Prostitutes, you mean?'

A small moment before he nodded and looked down. 'Andrew has . . . before.' The colour on his face deepened further as he mumbled, 'We all have.'

'Did Andrew say that was why he wanted to go to Kirkstall Abbey?' Simon probed, hoping for the smallest hint or clue.

'No,' Harrison told him sharply. 'He didn't say a word, just that it was a chance to enjoy a summer's day.'

No help for him there. 'What did you do about Andrew when you were ready to leave? Did you look for him?'

'We shouted,' Ibbotson said and turned to Harrison. 'Didn't you go after him?'

'I did. I kept calling his name, but he never answered. Finally I said the devil with it and we came back.' He gave Mr Barton an apologetic look.

'Andrew had drunk more than the rest of us, but that wasn't unusual,' Ibbotson said.

Simon watched Barton draw in a breath and narrow his eyes.

'We decided he must have arranged to meet someone and he was off somewhere enjoying himself.' Cowley stared at the floorboards. 'We thought it would serve him a good turn if he came back and we were gone, so he'd have to walk back to town.'

'You never imagined something might have happened to him?'

All three shook their heads. Of course they hadn't. They were young, they were immortal, they had money. They were safe.

'Did Andrew ever talk about a man named Fox?'

Harrison pinched his lips together and glanced at Barton. 'Is he the one who—?'

'Yes,' Simon told him. 'Did he mention the name at all?'

'No.' The surprise was genuine. 'Why would he?'

A few more questions, but they had nothing more to offer. They left, subdued, and Simon was alone with Barton in the room.

'What do you think, Mr Westow?'

Simon gripped his stick and paced awkwardly, stretching his leg. It had been a straightforward, honest account. Four young men who seemed to have no real care in the world, out for an afternoon of pleasure. But it seemed one of them had made other plans. What had happened at the abbey? Was Andrew still alive?

'I don't know,' he said and saw the fading hope on the father's face. 'Truly, I don't. There's been no report of a body. He hasn't committed a crime, and he's of age, so the constable won't start looking for him.'

'But you can,' Barton said. 'I want you to find him for me.'

\* \* \*

A little further. Willow branches hung over the water and the path grew thinner and thinner, until it was barely more than a line in the dirt, winding between heavy clumps of grass. Something was close. Jane felt it like a weight on her chest, twisting the gold ring on her finger. So close. She moved on, dress brushing against the nettles, and a memory sprang from nowhere: she was four or five years old, out with her mother and father. Suddenly she cried out and saw a red rash growing on her arm where she'd rubbed against the weeds. Her mother pulled some dock leaves and stroked them across the itch and pain until it went away.

For a moment she felt stunned. She didn't *want* to remember anything good about her mother. Why did she need fond recollections of the woman who'd thrown her out on the street?

Jane stood, breathing slowly until her anger abated. She was here to do a job. A little farther on, she saw the sunlight flash on something in a small pool at the river's edge. Heart racing, she scrambled down. A piece of cloth, darkened by the water. Reaching out, she tugged at it, pulling with all her strength until the body trapped against a branch turned slowly in the water and she could see its face.

One look, then she turned and ran.

Find him. The words filled his head.

The Foxes were gone and Andrew Barton had vanished. God only knew how, but they had to be linked. Nothing else made sense.

He walked into Mudie's print shop, drawing in its heavy smell of ink. George was turning the handle of the press and watching the sheets as they emerged. His eyes shifted to Simon and he stopped work.

'You'd better sit down. You look like you have the weight of the world on your shoulders.'

'Not the world. Just one man.'

'Maybe he really had arranged to meet someone there and went off with her,' Mudie said when Simon had finished the tale. 'He'd hardly be the first, would he?'

It could be that way. But yet . . . 'He's never stayed out like that before, according to his father.'

'What does that mean? He's a young man feeling his oats. You said he and his father had been arguing.'

'Yes.'

'He could be doing it deliberately. Have you considered that?'

He'd dismissed it. But hearing it again, it seemed more plausible. The young man had been drinking; it might have seemed like a good idea to him. Andrew Barton would probably show up later with a grin across his face.

'Maybe,' he allowed.

'It could be that something has happened, too.'

'If it has, then it's bad. Rosie's out at the abbey with Jane and Sally.'

'What do you hope to find? It all happened yesterday.'

He nodded. 'I don't expect to find anything. I don't *want* to. But we have to start somewhere. That's the last place he was seen.'

'These friends of his . . . do you think they know more than they were saying?'

'No,' Simon told him. 'I'm sure of that. They told me everything.'

'What do you think? Is he still alive?'

That was the question. Somewhere inside, he wanted to believe that Andrew Barton was fine. But was that nothing more than a forlorn hope?

By the time Jane reached the abbey, her hands were scratched by thorns and there were rips in her old work dress.

Sally and Rosie were waiting by the gig, standing ready with hands on their knives in case someone was chasing her.

'What happened?' Sally kept her eyes fixed on the distance.

'There's a body in the river.' Jane gulped down air and tried to catch her breath. 'Towards town, in a little pool.'

'Andrew Barton?' Rosie's face grew pale.

'No.' She looked up, confused. 'It's Mrs Fox.'

# ELEVEN

How? Simon thought.
Why? Why there?
They'd come through the door a little after five o'clock, all three of them with dark, hooded looks on their faces.

He saw it in their eyes; they'd found something. But he waited until they were seated and ready to talk.

'No sign of Andrew,' Rosie told him. 'But there was never much hope of it, was there?' He waited. 'Jane found Mrs Fox.'

Startled, he turned to stare at her, his head suddenly overflowing with questions.

'She was in the water,' Jane told him.

Suddenly all his thoughts were upended, reeling and sliding everywhere.

'Drowned?'

She shook her head. 'Strangled with a rope.'

The same as Shackleton at Grey's Court. This whole tale kept twisting, growing bloodier, moving beyond his reach and understanding.

'Who else knows about this?' he asked when they finished telling him.

'Constable Porter,' Rosie said. 'Mr Barton, too; he asked when we returned the gig.'

By tomorrow it would be common currency all over Leeds. Where was Fox? Andrew Barton? They'd had that meeting by the canal . . .

He couldn't begin to untangle the knot in his head. Simon looked at the three women.

'Do you have any ideas?'

Silence at first. Then Sally said: 'We talked about nothing else on the way back. None of it makes sense.'

'No, it doesn't,' he agreed emptily. 'Maybe we can find out more tomorrow.'

\* \* \*

Jane's body was tense after spending so much time in the gig. The seat was hard, jolting her over every bump. Being so high off the ground left her terrified she'd fall and be crushed under the wheels. But Sally enjoyed every moment of driving: the speed, controlling the horse, the way the vehicle bounced and skipped over the road.

Idle thoughts. Distractions to take her mind from the sight of Mrs Fox as they dragged the corpse from the river. As she lay there on the bank, sodden, the marks stood out around her neck. Strangled with a rope.

She'd seen the woman alive, followed her all over Leeds. In a curious way, Jane felt she'd known her. Now Mrs Fox was no more than an empty bag of bone and flesh.

As she walked up Albion Street towards home, she heard Davy Cassidy's fiddle and followed the sound, craving some beauty to take away the death she'd seen.

Jane stood at the back of the small crowd, eyes closed, happy to let the music wash over her. As the tune ended and people started to drift away, she moved forward until she was standing by him as he rosined his bow.

'Where do you find all that beauty?'

He turned a pair of sightless eyes to her and smiled.

'I don't,' he told her in his soft voice. 'It's already there in the music. All I do is try to let people see it. Not my doing at all.'

He underestimated himself, Jane thought. She dropped a handful of coins in the cup and he smiled at her.

Simon had his arm around Rosie, her face nuzzling his neck as she slept. Slowly, gently, he shifted in the bed, careful not to wake her. His eyes stared up into the darkness, and outside in the night he heard someone running, then nothing at all.

Rest wouldn't come. Instead, he tried to put some kind of order into the last two days. Two murders, both strangled the same way. Who'd killed them? Fox seemed the obvious suspect. He'd vanished, but so had Andrew Barton. Had they gone off together? Had they been plotting the deaths on the day they met? What was the connection between Shackleton and Fox?

He'd only discover the answers to those questions when they found the missing men. But there were still other things they could discover. Who lived in the house in Queen Square that the Foxes visited? Who'd rented the room in Grey's Court? That might shed some light on things.

Or take them nowhere.

With his son still missing, Barton wanted someone to keep him safe. With two murders to consider, it was time to put Jane and Sally together. Young, sharp, quick to handle danger.

Slowly Simon drifted away as the problems gnawed at the edge of his mind.

Clouds had arrived overnight, high and pale, trapping the heat. Jane sat in the shade, close enough to watch the front of Barton's house. Sally was checking all around once again, to make sure nobody else was observing.

Jane hadn't felt anyone, but that first day she'd never sensed Mrs Fox. She still didn't understand why.

'Nobody else here, just us.' Sally scrambled back in beside her. 'What do you want to do when he comes out? Both of us follow him?'

'No.' That was too much. 'One of us can keep watch here.'

Simon had gone early to see Barton. The worries about his son had turned him into an old man overnight, the lines carved deep in his face. No news yet.

He lifted his head, eyes rimmed red and full of pain.

'Have you told the constable about Andrew and Fox?'

'Not yet.'

'Please, Mr Westow, don't. Wait. Once he comes back, I'll make him explain.'

'All right,' Simon agreed. He felt it was a mistake to say nothing, but it was Barton's family and he was paying the bills. 'When will you report he's missing?'

'Today if he doesn't come home.' There was desperation in the words.

'When you do that, Porter is going to need to know about that meeting. He might be able to make something from it. You have to tell him.' With Mrs Fox a corpse and her husband gone, he'd be furious he hadn't already been informed. But what was done was over. It couldn't change the past.

A slow nod. 'Perhaps. Can you find him?'

'I can try.' How could anyone promise more than that?

Barton might not appear at all, Jane thought, as she sat in the shadow of a branch, watching the front door of the house. He'd probably stay inside, hoping for good news. She'd seen him through the windows, shuffling through the rooms like a man lost in his own life.

A rustle of leaves and Sally settled beside her once more.

'Are we going to spend the day here?'

'Unless he goes out or something happens.'

Time passed, and the church bell tolled the hours. Sally kept shifting restlessly.

'Why don't you go and buy us something to eat?'

The girl brightened. A movement and she was gone. Stillness returned. Nothing to see in the house.

Simon stood and admired the handsome buildings of Queen Square. Well-designed, still quite new and far enough from town that the bricks had kept their fresh, bright colour. He leaned on the stick; no more than half a mile from home, but he felt the ache and effort of walking in the summer heat.

Rosie was behind one of the doors, chatting to Mrs Golden, a woman she knew. Simon studied the front of the house the Foxes had visited. Nothing to distinguish it from any of its neighbours in the square, the same shining black paint on the wood, heavy curtains pulled back in the windows.

His wife would take her time. That was fine. It gave him a chance to think. He'd promised Barton that they'd search for his son, but the chances of finding him alive grew dimmer every hour. The man had to know that, but as long as he refused to admit it to himself, then Andrew couldn't be dead. Simon understood that all too well.

Rosie came back out, beaming as she waved farewell.

'Mrs Curtis,' she said. 'That's who we want. She's a widow, moved here two years ago after her husband died. Sarah Golden said the rumour is that she's been having some hard times.'

'Selling her jewellery, do you think?' If the Foxes had heard about her misfortune, that could explain the visit.

'She doesn't know.' She glanced at the house. 'We're here, we might as well ask.'

He was happy to let her lead, presenting her visiting card and invoking the neighbour's name to get them inside. This was something Rosie did so well.

The house felt cramped, Simon thought, with far too much furniture for the space, as if the woman had never parted with anything in her life.

Elizabeth Curtis had probably once been stout, but age had shrunk her. The skin sagged into jowls around her face, her hair had become thin and white and her teeth yellow. But her eyes still had a sharp, attentive intelligence. She pursed her lips as she listened to Rosie, showing the web of lines spreading from it. A shaft of light caught the hairs protruding from her chin.

'It's hardly a secret that I don't have much money, Mrs Westow.' She waved a scrawny arm. 'I know it's cluttered, but I'm selling things piece by piece. I need money to live. I only have a single servant now, and I can barely afford to keep her and this place.' She frowned, but her gaze was defiant. 'My errant husband didn't provide well for me in his will. Plenty for his mistress, though.' She caught Simon's look of astonishment. 'It's perfectly true, I can assure you of that.'

'The couple who came here on Saturday, the Foxes,' Rosie said hurriedly. 'Was that the name they used?'

She gave a small, girlish giggle. 'It was, and they said they knew I had jewellery. The man claimed to know people among the gentry, to come from a good family near Richmond, related to the Irwins from Temple Newsam. He had a great deal of charm, I'll grant him that, but something about him rang false.' She narrowed her eyes, as if she'd remembered something. 'You're the thief-takers who caught him, aren't you?'

'We are,' Simon admitted.

'I listened to what they had to say. I have plenty of time and visitors are rare these days. The poor man sounded so sincere. I think he might have believed what he was saying.' She shook her head.

'He has no connection to the Irwins,' Simon told her.

Mrs Curtis gave a delicate laugh. 'I'm not surprised. I've been a guest at Temple Newsam . . . well, it was a long time ago and I was young then. It was obvious he'd never been there.'

'You led him on?'

She blushed. 'A little, perhaps. For some amusement.'

'What did they offer?' Rosie asked.

'They asked to see my jewellery. I showed them the best pieces, but . . .' She paused, then, 'I kept a very careful eye on them both.'

He laughed. 'You didn't trust them?'

Her eyes sparkled with life. 'Not an inch, Mr Westow. But it was an . . . interesting experience to meet someone who'd been pardoned on the gallows.'

'What was Mrs Fox like?' Rosie asked. 'I never spoke to her.'

'Didn't you?' The old woman cocked her head and thought. 'She was polite. Too polite, really. I think she knew more about jewellery than he did. She certainly admired the pieces.' Mrs Curtis pursed her lips. 'She simpered over them, and I have no time for that. As soon as I turned down his offer to take the pieces and show them to people he said he knew, they took their leave. They must have thought I was born yesterday.'

'You did the right thing.'

'As soon as I saw them, I knew there was something not quite proper about that pair. They had an air. Once I remembered the name, I decided to enjoy myself at their expense for a few minutes. Was that terrible of me?'

'I think it's wonderful,' Rosie told her, and she reached across and squeezed the woman's hand.

'They won't be back,' Simon said.

'No, but they brought me another set of visitors. I'm grateful for that.'

Rosie looked over her shoulder as they walked away.

'They never stood a chance. I hope I'm like her when I'm old.'

'She doesn't miss a trick.' He smiled, then his expression turned sour. 'I'm surprised at the Foxes. Expecting the same act to work.'

'Why not? Barton fell for it,' she said. 'It's months since the stories about the trial and the pardon were in the newspapers. People have short memories, especially for names.'

That was true; the couple had expected easy prey and found

someone too quick for them. What had happened after that? Somehow he found it hard to imagine that Mrs Fox had killed Shackleton. Strangling someone with a rope took plenty of strength; it didn't feel like a woman's crime. He'd only seen her once, the day Rosie played fence and Barton chose to prosecute Fox; that had been no more than a few moments and he'd paid little attention to her. In his hazy memory she was a small woman: could she have had the strength to choke away someone's life?

'Now we know where the Foxes were during some part of the day on Saturday.' Rosie's voice was thoughtful. 'On Sunday there was no sign of them. Something happened.'

'Frederick Fox is the only one who can tell us what it was,' Simon replied. 'All we have to do is find him. If he's still alive,' he added. 'I need to go and talk to Porter. Find out what he's learned.'

'Don't become constable,' Porter warned, gesturing at the papers that littered his desk. He sat back and lit his pipe. 'They'll try to drown you in all this stuff. Life was easier when I was part of the watch.'

'But it didn't pay as well.'

He gave a snort. 'Maybe not. Anything more on these murders?'

'I came to ask you the same question.'

He shook his head. 'Next to nothing. The room in Grey's Court was rented to' – he looked for the scrap of paper and pulled it from the floor – 'to a woman called Smith. The landlord said she paid him for a month.'

'Woman? Mrs Fox?'

'He claims he doesn't remember what she looked like.' Porter raised his eyebrows. 'Can't describe her.'

'She paid him to forget.'

'Very likely. There's nothing more to be had from him. He says he never saw Shackleton, never even heard the name. I'm willing to believe him on that. He thought the woman was living there, since she paid for it.'

'But he's not sure.'

'He claims he doesn't remember. You said your lass saw her

go into that room at Grey's Court on Saturday. That could make Mrs Fox the murderer.'

Simon looked doubtful. 'It doesn't feel right to me.'

'It's still the obvious answer, Westow. She kills him Saturday. Sunday she and her husband run off. Monday she turns up in the river at Kirkstall, murdered in exactly the same way as Shackleton. Fox probably did it and now he's vanished.'

'It's full of holes. You know that as well as I do. I saw her. That woman didn't look strong enough to strangle Shackleton. Why would Fox wait until they were out in Kirkstall to kill his wife? He could have done it in that house on Middle Fold and left the body.'

Porter's eyes flashed with anger. 'How the devil am I supposed to know what was going through his mind? We can drag the truth out of him once we find him. I've sent letters to all the towns to arrest him.'

Where did Andrew Barton fit into this tale? Was he dead, too? If he was still alive, where had he gone? Was he alone? Could he have killed Mrs Fox?

Too many questions and not a prayer of an answer yet. As he made his way down the steps his heart was beating faster. How would he find the truth in all this?

Simon stepped out of the courthouse, blinking in the light as he gazed up at the buildings along Park Row. All very proud and impressive, no doubt about that, but the grandeur was an illusion. Their stones were blackened by the factory smoke that filled the air and the lungs. It was impossible to escape in Leeds. There was dirt everywhere, horse dung covering the cobbles of the streets. Look around and it was a filthy city.

A movement caught his eye. Sally, standing on the other corner, waving her arms. He waited for a gap between vehicles and hurried across to her as fast as his damaged leg would let him. What had happened? Had someone found Andrew's body?

'What is it?' he asked as soon as he was beside her.

'Rosie told me where to find you.' She looked up into his face. 'You need to come.'

Simon's chest was suddenly tight. He could barely speak. 'Who?'

'It's Andrew Barton,' Sally said. 'He's come home.'

# TWELVE

For a second, he didn't understand. Surely the young man was dead. So many questions started to flood into his head, but she carried on before he could begin to speak.

'We were watching the house and he walked up, unlocked the door and entered.' Simon opened his mouth; she continued, 'It was definitely him. No mistake.'

'How did he look?'

'Tired. A little the worse for wear. His shoulders were low' – she demonstrated for him – 'and there was dust and dirt all over his clothes. But he didn't seem to be injured. We couldn't see him clearly, but there wasn't any blood.'

Rosie was waiting at home, a thin, colourful cotton shawl around her shoulders. Arm in arm, they hurried up Briggate to Barton's house. By the time they arrived, Simon's leg was sore and aching; a bad day for it. A glance around. Sally and Jane were out of sight.

'You heard very quickly,' Barton said. The tension that had clouded his face just an hour or two before had evaporated.

'You wanted us to watch you.'

His eyes widened. 'Ah yes. Of course.'

'Where has he been?'

'Andrew hasn't told us yet.' Barton sighed, frowning with concern. 'When he came in, he looked bone-weary, Mr Westow. I told him to go and wash, then sleep. We'll have plenty of time to talk about everything once he's awake. We're just relieved that he's alive and back with us. That's enough. You know what we'd feared. For now, he needs to rest.'

'There are—'

'I don't care,' Barton's voice snapped. 'This is my son. He's just come home. I'll ask him questions later. We're grateful to God to have him safe.' A smile. 'I'm sure you can appreciate that.'

He could. He'd have felt the same, protective towards his sons. However much Barton and his wife had hoped, inside they must have anticipated the worst news. It must have felt like a miracle to see him come through the door.

'Does he have any injuries?'

Barton shook his head. 'Nothing that I saw.'

'As soon as possible, I'd like to talk to him,' Simon told him. 'I imagine the constable would, too.'

A flicker of worry shadowed the man's eyes. 'Why? Did you mention anything to him? I never reported him missing.'

'I haven't said a word. But we have two murders and your son might be able to cast some light on them.'

'I'll ask him once he's slept, Mr Westow.'

Pressing the man wasn't going to help. Not now. He was too relieved to have his son home to think beyond that.

'We'll keep watch on you. The way you wanted.'

A nod. 'Now . . .' Barton said, glancing at the front door.

'Yes, of course.' They shook hands. 'I'm pleased he's returned.'

'What did Mrs Barton have to say?' he asked Rosie as they slowly ambled home.

'She kept breaking into tears. She'd hardened herself to hear the worst, I think.'

Safe inside their four walls again, but where had Andrew been since Sunday evening? What had he done? A healthy young man like that could easily strangle Mrs Fox.

It was a new world in every way. So different from anything Jane had known. A war was raging between Indians and colonists in the youthful America, the British and the French who'd arrived in the place. No cities, barely a town worthy of the name, nothing more than outposts quickly erected across the landscape. No manufactories with their chimneys to darken the skies.

She kept stopping to think about the words she'd read, to imagine being a part of that landscape, out there in the wilderness with Hawk-Eye, Cora and the others.

'What's wrong, child? Don't you like it?' Mrs Shields asked. They were sitting outside the cottage, relishing the evening warmth. The old woman had a heavy shawl tucked around her shoulders; she felt the chill so easily these days.

'I do,' she answered slowly. 'It's the place . . . I've never dreamed of anywhere like it. It's so . . . I don't know.'

'Nothing like Leeds.'

Jane gave a soft laugh. The town felt tame in comparison. Too civilised. 'What do you think it's like to meet people who are so different?'

'Did I ever tell you that when I was a girl, just very small, I remember seeing someone with a servant who had black skin,' the old woman said thoughtfully. 'I'd forgotten all about it. It happened a long time ago.'

She didn't understand. 'Black? What do you mean? Rubbed with soot like a sweep?'

'No. It was his proper skin colour, the way he was born. Black and smooth, like ebony.' The wonder still filled her voice. 'We all stared, we'd never seen anything like it. But the world is filled with all sorts of people. We've only experienced a tiny part of it.'

Her eyes moved back to the page, but her thoughts were full of what she'd just heard. They had to be real, the Indians in the book, not pulled from a writer's imagination. But it was all far beyond her comprehension. How was she ever going to learn about the things around her?

What must it be like to travel and see all these different people and places? With all those different languages, how could they understand each other? Yet people had done it. They'd gone all over, even to the other side of the world, down to Australia, where they sent the convicts. She'd seen sailors, and men like Dodson the old soldier who'd gone overseas to war. Jane knew she could never do that. She'd been terrified enough on the bench of the gig. She could never set foot on a ship.

The only way she could travel to those places would be in the pages of books.

Her mind drifted, thinking back over the day outside Barton's house. After Simon and Rosie, nobody visited, no one came out. The hours dragged by, each minute weighing heavy. Sally had stayed restless, slipping away several times to make sure they were still the only watchers.

Finally, as the church bell rang five, they left.

'Do you know what it all means?' Sally asked.

Jane shook her head. It was impossible to untangle the strands and make sense of everything. Too many pieces were still missing from the puzzle. The look on Simon's face as he left Barton's house made it clear he'd discovered nothing more. Maybe tomorrow they'd learn what had happened.

'I think I'm going inside,' Mrs Shields said. 'I can feel a headache coming on and I'm beginning to feel very weary.'

'Are you all right?' Jane rose to help. She stayed alert to everything; the woman was so frail.

'It's nothing but old age, child,' she said. 'There's no cure for that.'

Once the old woman was settled in bed, she sat outside and idly ran her knife over the whetstone. A lazy, comforting rhythm. Sharp and deadly. How old was Catherine Shields, Jane asked herself as she let the darkness grow around her. Was she seventy, eighty? The woman refused to tell; a lady never reveals her age, she said. She'd never spoken much about her life when she was young. From a family with plenty of money; that was obvious. Exactly who she'd been, how she'd ended up in this small place . . . that was the story the woman had never told. Jane had tried to discover it, but all she'd received were little smiles and shards from the past, like the one she'd heard tonight. Some day, maybe . . . but she knew it wouldn't happen.

She checked the edge of her knife; satisfied, she slipped it into her pocket. When the men had come after the children, she'd barely needed to land a blow. At least they wouldn't return; that was something. Sally would probably be with them now, trying to care for them all like a mother or an older sister. Or more like a shepherd, perhaps.

'Watch Barton's house again,' Simon told them. 'If anyone comes, follow them when they leave. The same with anyone from the family.'

'Won't he expect that?' Jane asked.

'Very likely,' he admitted. What else could they do? Barton was paying for their presence. They were doing what he'd ordered.

But this would be the final day, he decided. Yesterday he'd gone around the inns and beershops, asking for any news, any sightings, even faint rumours about Fox in Leeds. Nothing at all. That threat had gone.

This morning he'd go and see Barton. Simon still wanted to know what had happened to Andrew, and whether it tied into the murder of Mrs Fox. Once he had that, he'd tell the man that his family appeared safe. Simon had no other work waiting, but this . . . what had seemed straightforward at the beginning had grown too twisted. Something was wrong, and his gut told him they'd be safer keeping their distance from it.

'Nothing else on those murders?' Simon asked Porter. The windows were open in the constable's office, but no breeze stirred the warm, still air inside.

'Not a damned thing.' He cocked his head. 'Why, have you heard something?'

Simon shook his head. 'Fox?'

'No reports at all. The best I can guess is that he's changed his name and he's far away by now.'

'I'm going to tell Barton that since he's gone, there's no need for us to follow him any longer.'

Suspicion flashed in the constable's eyes. 'It's not like you to give up on some easy money, Westow. Something smell wrong about the job?'

He gave a little laugh. 'He doesn't need the protection. There's other work out there.'

'Between you and me, I doubt we'll find Fox. It's not as if anybody's grieving over the bodies.' Porter grunted and gave a shrug. 'Plenty to keep us busy without that. At least the damned feud with the soldiers seems to be over.'

The day had warmed up quickly. Simon pulled out his watch from his waistcoat pocket. Not long after nine o'clock and already he was sweating as he made his way along the drive to Barton's house.

The servant let him in, and he was grateful for the dim coolness inside. Simon stood by the parlour window, gazing out at the tidy garden, until he heard Barton enter the room. He was in shirtsleeves, a stock very clean and white around his neck.

'I hadn't expected to see you yet, Mr Westow.'

'Have you talked to your son?'

The man nodded. 'Last night, once he was awake. He bathed and we had a conversation as he ate.'

'What did he have to say?'

'He swears he knows nothing about any murders. He's never heard of anyone called Shackleton, and he was shocked when I told him about Mrs Fox being found in Kirkstall. I made him place his hand on the Bible when he told me he wasn't involved. Is that good enough for you?'

'Where was he all that time he was missing?'

Barton gave a small, wan smile. 'It was exactly what his friends thought. He'd arranged to meet some girl, and went off with her.'

Simon raised his eyebrows. 'Until yesterday morning?'

'She found out he had money and persuaded him to go drinking with her all of Monday. By the time he woke yesterday morning, he'd spent everything he had and she threw him out.'

At least that part sounded plausible. He'd hardly be the first young man to be used that way.

'Who was she?'

'Andrew said her name was Martha. He didn't know her surname.'

'Where did they go?'

'She had a room off Vicar Lane.'

He'd rather be hearing this from Andrew, to look in his eyes and see if he was telling the truth. But that wasn't likely to happen, certainly not for now. Barton was shielding his son from the world.

'How was he when he returned?'

'Full of regrets, of course.' Barton gave a small shake of his head. 'Feeling like a fool and head still thudding. I have hopes he might learn a lesson from it.'

Maybe he would, Simon thought. But there was one other thing.

'What about the meeting he had with Fox? A few days ago you told him he was lying about that. Do you believe him now?'

Barton took a long time before he answered, then the words came haltingly. 'I asked him again. He still denies it. He insists none of it happened.'

'There was a message left for him with the time.'

'Honestly, Mr Westow, I don't know. I want to believe him, but something . . .' Silence returned. 'We prayed he'd come back. I'm so happy to have him here and safe that I have to give him the benefit of the doubt. I have to forgive him for any lies he might have told.' The man's stare grew fierce. 'He's adamant about it. Maybe your girl was mistaken. No note, and no meeting.'

Forgiveness was something for the church or a family. Simon needed truth. The young man had to be lying, but one look at Barton's face and he knew not to say more about that for now.

Jane wasn't wrong. He knew that. He trusted her with his life. But Barton had taken his position. No matter what, he was going to defend his son.

'As you wish.' Simon nodded. 'I've been asking about Fox. He hasn't been seen in Leeds since Saturday. The constable thinks he fled after he murdered his wife. I believe there's no danger to your family now. With your son home, you've had a good ending. You don't need us.'

Barton considered the idea for a few moments. 'Very well,' he replied. 'I agree. Send me your account and I'll write a bank draft for you.' He stuck out a hand and Simon shook it. 'Thank you for your work.'

Back in the hazy daylight, he let out a low whistle and began to walk away. Within fifty yards, Jane and Sally were beside him.

'No need to stay,' he said. 'The job's done.'

Jane's eyes were filled with questions, but she stayed silent. He was grateful; he had no answers for her, anyway.

'What about those people who died?' Sally asked.

'That's nothing to do with us. It's work for the constable. We'll see what turns up next.'

'I didn't make a mistake,' Jane said as they sat around the kitchen table the next morning. 'It was definitely Andrew Barton I saw talking to Fox by the canal.'

'I know it was,' Simon told her. For a moment the room was filled with noise as Richard and Amos burst in to say their goodbyes before rushing to school. A few seconds later the front door slammed behind them and calm returned. 'I never doubted you. But he still denies it, his father is willing to accept the lie, and Fox isn't here to tell us one way or the other.'

'What do we do now?' Sally asked.

'Nothing,' Rosie said quietly. 'We did everything Barton paid us to do.'

'But—' the girl began.

Simon shook his head. 'There is no but. If Fox turns up, maybe, or Barton wants something else, but that's it. There's nothing more we *can* do.'

Sally stared at him. After a long moment, the defiance faded from her face.

'Another job will come along soon.' Rosie's voice sounded too bright.

Jane stood and left without a word. That had always been her way, he thought. No farewells. Back to Mrs Shields and the quiet life that seemed to nourish her. When he needed her, she'd come.

In the afternoon, he wrote out his bill and left it at Barton's house. On the way home, he stopped to see George Mudie. He was sitting at his desk, shaking his head as he totted up the accounts.

'Can't believe how much money you're making?'

Without raising his head, Mudie snorted and took a sip of brandy. 'Wondering how I'll stay in business next month, more like. What about you? No honest work to keep you off the streets?'

'The job with Barton ended.'

'There's one guarantee with crime, it never stops. You know something else will come along soon.'

With a small grunt, Simon lowered himself into a chair, relieved to take the weight off his leg.

'Probably. And you'll have another client.'

'Do you know how many printers there are in Leeds now, Simon? Six. Two of them have opened in the last year alone. God knows why; this isn't a large town. Most of them have new equipment.' He gave a helpless shrug. 'I'm too old to learn another trade.'

'Maybe business will pick up.'

'Maybe pigs will fly. I'm not the best company today.' He

refilled his glass. 'Never mind, the world might look a little better after a few more of these.'

Simon glanced at shops as he passed along Briggate and raised his hat to a few couples he recognised. He knew the empty feeling of one job done with nothing else on the horizon. But he'd done the right thing. No sense in continuing when Barton didn't want to know the truth.

# THIRTEEN

Simon sat on an uncomfortable chair in Nathaniel Gordon's parlour. He'd known the man for years, never particularly well, but the note had asked him to call. All the furniture in the house was made of old, heavy wood, the floors covered with expensive rugs that had grown threadbare and stained with age. Crooked windows with glass that needed polishing. It didn't look like a rich man's house. Gordon had the money for somewhere far better than a mean little home in Briggate below Boar Lane, but this place had been in his family for generations, and that history meant everything to him.

He was an old man now; seventy, possibly even a few years more, known throughout town for the way he dressed: always in the old fashions, as if he'd somehow stepped out of an earlier century: breeches and pristine hose, shoes with shining silver buckles, old-fashioned coats and long, elaborately decorated waistcoats. The only thing lacking was a wig. All of it was utterly natural; he'd been this way his entire life. For two years he'd been a widower and had looked bereft every day since his wife died. Thinner each time Simon saw him, as if he was withering away.

'What's been stolen, Mr Gordon?' Simon asked after they'd talked for a few minutes.

'Nothing,' he answered, and Simon turned his head sharply. 'I thought . . .'

Gordon gave a quick, nervous smile. 'My apologies if I gave the impression I needed your services, Mr Westow. I just wanted a quiet word with you. You were doing some work for James Barton.'

'We were.' A full week had passed since that job had finished. He'd been paid, but he'd had no more contact with Barton or his family. The constable hadn't found Fox or whoever had taken two lives. It didn't matter; nothing to do with him now. 'What do you want from me?'

'Simply to tell you something. I met the Foxes. I thought you might be curious.'

'You met them? Constable Porter might like to hear what you have to say.'

Another fleeting, nervous smile. 'Oh no, this is nothing to do with the present. It happened months ago, back in February. It must have been a week or so before Barton decided to prosecute.'

'What happened?' It couldn't affect anything, but the man had piqued his interest.

'The Foxes came calling on me. Someone must have told them I'd kept my wife's jewellery.'

'Let me guess: Mr Fox knew someone who might be interested in buying one or two of the more expensive pieces.'

'That's it, exactly.' A broader grin this time. 'I'm quite aware that people believe I'm not quite right in the head because of how I choose to dress. That's never worried me.'

No reason it should. He didn't have to please anyone. Gordon had inherited his money, with a grandfather who'd made a fortune as a wool merchant back when the trade roared and a father who'd added to the wealth. Nathaniel had always been happy to do nothing except invest, let the amount grow and live his small life, bothering no one.

'The Foxes,' Simon prompted.

'Yes. He had plenty of charm on the surface, and she . . .' He paused, considering his words. 'She never said much, but she had eyes like a wolf. I wouldn't have trusted her alone with anything valuable.'

'You didn't care for them?'

'Not a jot. I sent them packing before they had a chance to try and weave their spell.'

'I'm glad you did, but why are you telling me all this now?'

'There didn't seem to be any need once they were arrested. After he was pardoned, I wasn't even aware they'd returned to Leeds until the cook told me about Mrs Fox's body being discovered.'

'What changed?'

'Believe me, my dear Mr Westow, this is not an old man's indulgence.' He considered that for a moment. 'Well, perhaps it is, but only a small one. The Foxes were here twice. A short visit the first time, an introduction, you might call it. The real business came when they returned. But Mrs Fox let something interesting slip in conversation. She said some distant cousin of hers lived in Leeds. A black sheep of the family, apparently. They were keeping clear of him because of his reputation.'

In spite of himself, he wanted to know. 'Did she tell you his name?'

'I was curious, so I prodded her a little.' His eyes held a triumphant twinkle. 'I can be persuasive, too. It's Henry Longdon.'

Simon knew about Henry Longdon. A very careful man. He'd never tried to make a fortune from the stolen goods he fenced; that would have made him too noticeable. Instead, he was content to earn enough to live comfortably. Very thorough, excellent at covering any tracks he might have left. There was plenty of suspicion, but nobody had ever managed to trap him. A family connection to the Foxes . . . it might mean nothing, but it was certainly interesting.

'You should tell the constable,' Simon said.

'No.' Gordon was gentle but firm. 'Call it a foible of mine, if you wish. I'm passing this on so *you* can tell him, but you'd have my gratitude if you set my name aside. Perhaps you can say it's a rumour you heard somewhere.'

'Why?' The man was a good citizen. He was wealthy, a man with status in Leeds. Simon had never heard any whisper of trouble.

Gordon gave a tiny cough. 'An uncle of mine had a run-in with a magistrate, shall we say. A very unhappy time, many years ago now. Because of that, I choose to keep my distance.'

Perhaps it was another eccentricity like his clothes. In the end, it didn't matter. But the hint might offer the constable something for his investigation.

'The name just came up in conversation with . . . someone?'

'That's right.' It was right there on the man's face; Porter didn't believe a word, but Simon wasn't saying anything more.

'How reliable is this person?'

'Very. I believe it's true. The one who told me—'

'Whose name you won't pass on.'

'—is honest. I have no reason to doubt it.'

'I suppose it's something,' the constable grudgingly agreed after a few moments. 'Not much, but a damned sight more than we had. It's been a while since I paid Henry Longdon a visit. I'd like to see him off balance for once.' He rubbed his hands together in anticipation and cocked his head at Simon. 'You brought me the information. Do you want to come along?'

Jane relished the freedom of being unmoored. Working with Simon was an anchor, something solid. Without that, she was able to drift. Let the days blend into each other. There were still errands: to the market, the butcher, picking up things Mrs Shields wanted, a visit to the circulating library after she raced through *The Last of the Mohicans*. She found another by the same author, *The Pioneers*, with the same character.

She was sitting outside in the hazy sun, feeling the American wilderness grow around her, when Sally appeared. The girl was wearing her restless look; she needed to be doing something to fill all the empty hours. She grew bored all too quickly.

Today she wanted to walk. Jane had a thin cotton shawl over her shoulders, her boots lifting dust from the dry roads. Sally talked, thirsty for company and hardly pausing for breath; soon Jane shut the girl's words out and let her thoughts roam.

They took the road away from town, heading north past Sheepscar and the Chapeltown barracks. Beyond the few scattered houses in Harehills and the hammering from the quarries near Gipton woods.

As they passed fields bordered by drystone walls the girl finally quieted, drinking it all in as she let the countryside wrap around her. By a stream, Jane cupped her hands and drank water so cold and refreshing that it came as a shock to her body.

She could never feel at ease out here. The land was too open, too wide. She stayed alert every moment; there was nothing here she knew, nothing she felt she could trust. Her urge was to bolt back to Leeds, where brick and stone were solid and familiar.

She turned her head and studied Sally's face. Peaceful, as if this was exactly what she'd needed. Perhaps it was. They sat in silence for a few minutes until Jane stood and dusted off her skirts.

'We should go back. It's a long walk.'

As soon as she saw the haze over the town, Jane felt more settled; the tightness left her chest. Glad to be home. The small cottage in Green Dragon Yard held everything that was important in her life. She was safe there.

The noises of the town engulfed them, sharper now after a few hours away. The ramble seemed to have satisfied whatever urge was tugging at Sally. For now, at least.

The servant everyone knew as Bad-Eye, a disquieting man with one eye staring and intense and the other socket empty, escorted them through to the garden.

Henry Longdon was dressed in a shirt and brilliant white stock, with tight pale trousers and highly polished shoes. No jacket, but an apron to protect his clothes as he moved between the flowers, inspecting, cutting some stems to place in the basket on his arm.

He saw them, straightened and handed the basket to Bad-Eye.

'Put those in water,' he ordered, and untied the apron. 'Well, well, the constable and the thief-taker together,' he said, genial and smiling. 'Should I be worried?' He held out an arm, directing them back to the house. 'We'll be cooler in there.'

In the shadows of the room, Longdon sat and crossed his legs. His eyes sparkled with amusement. 'I'm sure this isn't a social call. You must suspect me of something.'

'I heard something interesting,' Simon told him. 'About your family.'

'Family?' Sudden confusion clouded his face.

'You had a cousin who married a man named Fox.'

'Ah, that's come out, has it?' He sighed. The man had always been a good actor, but this seemed real, the words full of regret. 'Everyone told her not to do it, but she was in love.' He lifted his face to stare at them. 'Besotted, just the way it happens in those terrible novels my wife loves. Now the poor woman's dead. That's what I've heard.'

'Murdered,' Porter said, and the word hung in the air.

'What was her name?' Simon asked. 'I don't believe I ever knew.'

'Harriet. She was born Harriet Amelia Driver, if you want it all. She grew up in Richmond. Her husband was from there, too.'

Fox had told Barton he came from Richmond. At least there was one glimmer of truth among his lies.

Longdon sighed. 'She surprised everyone. She'd been a meek little girl, very studious, always reading and listening. You'd hardly know she was in the room. Fox . . . he brought out something in her. Her family had been honest enough. Not like him. He was a few years older than her, always had his eye on the next swindle.'

'He claimed he was related to high families and knew people at court.'

Longdon barked out a laugh. 'The only court he knew was where he was sentenced. His father was a crook, and Frederick Fox followed in the family trade. He and Harriet eloped. Vanished one night, and the next anyone knew, they claimed they'd run up to Gretna Green and been married.' He shrugged. 'It might have been true, who knows? After that, they drifted away.'

'You must have been gone by then, too,' Porter said.

Longdon nodded. 'I heard in letters. Family gossip. I'd no idea what happened to them. Never gave it a thought. When I read that he'd been caught running one of his little games here, I was surprised. I had no idea they were in Leeds.'

The man sounded believable, Simon thought, and no guile lurked in his eyes.

'They never asked you to sell on what they stole?' Porter asked.

The man stared blandly at him. 'Why would they do that? You know I'm not in the business.'

'No?' Porter said.

'Let's agree you're not,' Simon cut in hurriedly. 'You didn't like Frederick?'

'Not from the first moment I met him. I didn't like the way my cousin was with him, either. When she was little, she was sweet. He drained that from her. As I said, Mr Westow, I didn't know they were here until they were arrested. Before you ask, I couldn't tell you why they returned. I never saw them.'

'Is anyone in her family still alive?'

'A brother. I wrote to him after I heard what happened, but I haven't had a reply. I don't know if he was still in contact with her.'

'She needs burying,' Porter told him.

Longdon nodded. 'I'll take care of it.'

'Do you know why Fox might have been pardoned?'

'No.' The man shook his head. 'The devil's own luck is all I can think. Doesn't the king occasionally select petitions from a pile to reprieve them?'

'Maybe that's it,' Porter said.

As they were leaving, Simon turned back. 'You'll have heard Fox is missing. Do you know where he might have gone?'

A straight, candid stare. 'To hell, I hope.'

'At least we know a little more about their past,' Simon said as they walked back down Briggate. Their grim expressions ensured people kept their distance.

'For whatever it's worth.' Porter's voice was weary. 'What do you make of that reason for the pardon?'

'It makes more sense than anything else I've heard.'

'Nothing in what he said to help us find Fox, is there?'

'He's probably far away by now, if he's still alive and has a grain of sense.' Simon grew thoughtful. 'But what Longdon said makes me keep on wondering why he came back after his pardon. He never went after Barton, just watched him.'

'What about Shackleton?' the constable asked. 'What do we know about him, other than his time in prison, and the fact the Foxes probably rented him that room and Mrs Fox was over there twice?'

'Nothing at all.'

'Inspector Fry's been asking people, and nobody seemed aware he'd come here after his escape from jail in York. They were all surprised to learn he'd been strangled.'

'Another mystery,' Simon agreed and grinned. 'I'm glad it's yours and not mine.'

He grunted. 'One more where we'll never find an answer.'

# FOURTEEN

The soft evening deepened, bringing a small chill to the air. Jane came in from the garden, locking the door of the cottage and setting the lamp on the table.

'I'm going to bed,' Mrs Shields said. 'I've been feeling a little light-headed all evening.' Her skin was dry as paper, eyes rimmed with red.

'Again? You've had that more often lately.'

'It's nothing, child. Growing old and tired.'

'Do you want your smelling salts?' The bottle was sitting on a table by the bed.

'No, bless you. I'll be fine once I lie down.' She seemed a little unsteady as Jane helped her into her nightclothes, finally settling the old woman under the covers and adjusting her cap. A quick kiss on her cheek, waiting until her raspy breathing steadied into a soft, even rhythm of sleep. In the other room, she picked up *The Pioneers* again.

She must have started to doze; the frantic knocking on the door jolted her up in the chair. She blinked, tensing and reaching for the knife in her pocket as she turned the key. Ready to strike, she opened the door.

Two of the children from the camp by the river were standing there, looking at her with wild, terrified faces.

'It's Sally.' The boy was so frightened he could hardly say the name.

'She's been hurt, miss,' the girl said. 'She's very bad. Can you come? Please?'

'Wait a minute.'

Mrs Shields was sleeping; the noise hadn't disturbed her. Could she leave? Jane knew what the old woman would say: go, child, look after her.

She took a deep breath and laced up her boots.

'Show me,' she said as the children caught their breath, then ran through the night behind them, heart up in her throat, terrified of what she'd find. Without thinking, she turned the gold ring on her finger, the one the old woman had given her to bring luck.

'Gently now. Put her down here,' she told them, and the children supporting Sally eased her on to Jane's bed. Getting her to Green Dragon Yard had been a struggle. No shortage of willing hands, but the girl had been unconscious, nothing more than a limp, awkward weight.

Jane darted into the bedroom to check on Mrs Shields, then softly closed the door.

She lit the lamp, raising the wick high enough to give a bright light. The young girl had been right – Sally was badly hurt. Her face was covered with blood, the nose broken. Jane took a deep breath.

She filled a bowl of water from the ewer, soaked a cloth and began to clean Sally's face with small, tender strokes. After that, she'd have a clearer idea of the injuries.

Her blood was roaring in her ears, her chest so tight it was painful. Every nerve screamed at her, but she forced down the panic that kept trying to rise inside. She'd often watched Mrs Shields as she worked, the calm, ordered way she went about each task, and tried to do the same. For a second, she thought about rousing the old woman and have her take charge.

No. She was unwell, she needed to rest.

Jane had to do this herself.

Everything felt urgent, pressing down on her. Sally wasn't going to die. She felt certain of that. Her pulse was strong and steady.

The girl *couldn't* die. She wasn't going to allow it.

'Will she be all right, miss?' one of the children asked.

'Yes,' she answered after a heartbeat. She had to believe, and she wouldn't let them see her fear. Quietly she shepherded them outside, into the darkness. 'You go. I'll send word to you as soon as I know something.'

Sally had grazes and welts all over her face and skull. Some of the hair had been pulled from her scalp. The broken nose was bad. Jane knew from experience how much it hurt. She took a breath, placed her fingers just so, and forced it back into place.

Sally grunted but didn't wake. Jane dampened a tiny wad of cloth to clear the dried blood from her nostrils. Slow work, but the girl would be able to breathe more easily.

Worse was the wound across her cheek, running from hairline to her mouth. Someone had sliced her open with a knife. It hadn't gone deep; that was one small blessing. In the kitchen, she found a jar of white ointment and sniffed it. Something Mrs Shields had prepared to keep away infection. She spread a thin layer over the cleaned skin.

Jane stood back. She knew she didn't have the skill for all this; she'd always been one who killed, not healed. But there was no choice. She pulled off the girl's dress; it was nothing more than a rag now, anyway. Very carefully, she bathed away the dirt and blood and spread more of the white ointment over the wounds. Jane was thorough, pausing occasionally to wipe sweat from her forehead with the back of her hand. Inside, she was frantic, overwhelmed, barely keeping control over everything. It was all in order, she kept telling herself, the way she'd watched the old woman do it.

She pressed Sally's arms and legs: no broken bones. No problem with the ribs.

Jane stood back. She'd done everything she knew. She pulled the covers over the girl's shoulders. For now, rest would help her.

As she opened the door to empty out the water, she saw a girl waiting. Eight or nine years old, a frightened rabbit of a child with large, fearful eyes.

'How is she, miss?'

'Sleeping.' Jane didn't know what else to say.

'Is she going to die?' There was terror lurking around the words.

'No.' She smiled and stroked the girl's hair. 'You can go and tell the others that.' She reached into her pocket and felt for a penny as she glanced up at the sky. Still the deep black of night. 'Buy yourself something to eat in the morning.'

The girl darted away.

Back in the house, she stared at Sally. Had she forgotten something, missed some important sign? Made a mistake? Jane retraced every step, feeling the worry tighten in her chest.

But she'd done it all. She stroked the girl's hand and felt the fingers move to give her a faint squeeze in return.

She settled herself in the chair beside the bed. The screams of the girl from the mill came again as she slept, always unearthly. It seemed to stretch out for minutes.

Dazed, she opened her eyes. Everything was still dark in the room. She listened, hearing Sally's steady breathing, and let her eyes close again.

'Child, I'm proud of you,' Mrs Shields said. She was having a weak morning, supporting herself with two walking sticks. Her skin seemed almost transparent in the light through the window. But her eyes shone bright and there was pride in her voice. 'I couldn't have done better myself.'

Jane beamed, relieved at the praise. She'd done it all properly.

When the old woman woke, she'd given a wan smile.

'I did feel strange last night. But I believe it's almost passed now.'

Then her face had grown more serious as Jane explained what had happened. Sally slept on as the old woman examined her, then nodded her approval and spoke.

'She'll wake later,' Mrs Shields said. 'Do you see how her eyelids are fluttering? That's a good sign. Have you watched her all night?'

'I slept a little in the chair.' No need to mention the dream, though she could still hear a faint echo of the girl's terror. 'Do you think you can watch her for a few minutes? I need to tell Simon and Rosie.'

'Go. I'll look after her.' She smiled. 'Just bring me a small glass of the medicine in the blue bottle first, please, child.'

'Do you know where Sally is?' It was the first thing Rosie asked as she pulled the door open. Her voice was frantic. 'She never came home last night. Simon's out looking for her.'

The horror grew on her face as she listened.

Simon moved around Leeds. Porter had heard nothing about Sally. Inspector Fry had caught a rumour of a beaten girl out near Dale Mill but hadn't checked. It wasn't enough to concern the watch; too many other things needed attention. Walking fast, pain jolting through his leg, Simon hurried over there. A quiet little lane, close to where Kirkstall Road and Wellington Road met. No houses around, nobody to ask. He kicked through the trampled weeds at the side of the path and caught a glint of something in the light. As he bent to pick it up, his stomach lurched. Sally's knife. She'd never give that up without a fight. He placed it in his pocket as he searched all around, urgency clawing at him as every minute passed, but there was no other trace of her.

An hour later, his throat was raw from questions that grew more desperate each time he asked them. He'd looked, but he hadn't spotted any of the children to ask about the girl. Something had happened to her.

As he unlocked the door at home, Simon felt dazed and empty. He saw Rosie's note on the table.

'She stirred,' Mrs Shields said. 'She asked where she was. I gave her a sip of cordial and she closed her eyes again.'

'What do you think?' Rosie asked. She knelt by the bed, staring intently into Sally's face.

'You can see her face and her body are a mass of bruises. Poor girl. I don't know why anyone would do that to her.'

Jane stood quietly, listening as they talked. Sally had woken. She'd spoken. Very slowly, she felt hope rising through her body.

'... it's too early to know.' Mrs Shields shook her head. She began to push herself upright and Jane was there, supporting her, letting the old woman rest her weight against her. A moment for the old woman to catch her breath. 'I had a little turn last night,' she explained to Rosie. 'I'm probably not completely myself yet.' She turned to Jane. 'Could you make me a little of that porridge and bring me some of the elderflower drink? I'm sorry, I don't mean to be a nuisance.'

Sally was going to recover, Jane thought as she worked in the kitchen. She'd suffered; she'd go on suffering for a long time. But most of the wounds would heal.

Simon gave her a quizzical look when she answered his knock, then stood next to his wife to stare at Sally. As if she sensed him there, her eyes fluttered open again. She turned her head to look at them.

'Where am I?' Her voice was slow and wet. From the broken nose, Jane decided.

'You're at Mrs Shields's house,' Rosie told her, but Sally's eyes had already closed.

Simon watched for another moment, his face giving nothing away. Then he tilted his head; Jane followed him into the yard. Warm again, and the air was heavy and dirty; she could taste it on her tongue.

'How bad is it?'

'Someone made sure he hurt her.'

'Who brought her here?'

She told him what had happened. The children knocking on the door, leading her to Sally.

'I was looking for them,' he said when he'd heard the story. 'I didn't see a single one of them.'

'They're frightened,' she told him. 'Hiding.' They knew how to keep out of sight. It was one of the things that helped them stay alive.

Then he asked the question that had been in his mind from the time he arrived.

'Who did it?'

'I don't know yet.'

'What will you do when you find out?'

She kept her eyes on his face. 'I'm not sure.'

He didn't believe her. Simon knew her too well. Jane would be carrying revenge in her heart.

'Do you need anything? Any help?'

That was a question laden with too many meanings. She shook her head.

He'd never imagined Sally as helpless. But looking down at her, at the wounds across her face, the scar she'd carry for the rest of her life and the other injuries he couldn't see, he let his fury rise, bitter and hard.

'She's going to need this.' He reached into his pocket and took out the knife.

Jane weighed it in her hand and smiled. 'I'll give it to her. Where did you find it?'

When he told her, she nodded. 'The same place the children discovered her.'

'Can you look after her?'

'We'll manage.'

'As soon as she's well enough, I'd like her back with us. Home.'

Jane would understand that, he thought. This little house was her home. Her safety. Sally's was with Simon and Rosie. Once she was behind those walls, nobody could hurt her. She'd become a daughter of sorts to them, as well as someone who worked for him. A strange, ambiguous situation.

'She will be,' Jane promised him. 'Once she's able.'

There was nothing he could do here but take up space. Whoever beat her had shown no mercy; it must have been relentless. Maybe her body would return to full health; the young came back quickly. But how would it affect her mind?

Since he'd been stabbed, every step was a reminder of all the things he'd lost. He had to rely on a stick like an old man, he couldn't fight with a knife any more. He couldn't even run. Those were the obvious, physical things. But there was more, hidden away in his mind. The damage had planted a kernel of worry that refused to leave.

Sally had always been fearless. Aware of danger but plunging on anyway. What if she began to hesitate?

He knew he couldn't help her to heal. But he could help discover who'd done this. Jane would search, but he had other avenues he could try.

If he found them, what then? It was the same question he'd asked Jane, and he had no more of an honest answer than she did. First, though, he had to talk to people.

Mrs Shields had gone back to bed, still not herself. She woke shortly after noon, her face brighter than it had been three hours before.

'No need to worry. I'm definitely better now, child.' She lifted an arm and let it glide gracefully back down to the bedcover. 'Still a little weak, but the last of it has passed through me.'

'Are you sure?' Losing her would be . . . Jane couldn't think about that. Not now.

'I'm positive.' She gave Jane a gentle, calming smile. 'No need to fret.'

Jane felt the woman's shrewd gaze. 'You have business, don't you?'

For a second, Jane was reluctant to admit it; her place was here, to tend the girl. Then she said, 'Yes.'

'You go. Rosie's still here. The two of us can take care of Sally.'

Before she left, Jane curled Sally's fingers around the hilt of her knife. She'd feel it. She'd know.

Jane hurried down Briggate, to the corner of Boar Lane where Kate the pie-seller was bellowing her wares. As soon as she smelled the meat, Jane realised she hadn't eaten since yesterday.

'Two,' she said, fumbling in her pocket for the coins.

The big woman stared. 'Come on. I've known you too long. You'd better tell me.'

It spilled out and she saw the fury on Kate's face.

'Please, if you hear anything at all . . .'

'Don't you worry about that, pet. I'll ask around and I'll make sure you know what I learn. We can't have men like that wandering round town.'

She found Dodson sitting on Vicar Lane. The beggar was still wearing a ragged old coat in the summer heat, his wooden leg and tin cup stretched out in front of him. People paid scant attention to beggars, never thought they might hear conversations and secrets; he'd brought her useful pieces of information in the past.

'She's the one who looks out for the children, isn't she?'

'Yes.'

'I'll listen,' he promised.

Davy Cassidy, too, the blind fiddler, when she followed the music down to Vicar Lane.

'Aye,' he agreed, as he started up another tune. 'I'll do that.'

It didn't feel like much. She needed answers, names. At least it was a start. Now she needed to find the children. This was when she needed their help, to start them searching. But Simon was right. They'd vanished.

# FIFTEEN

Simon sat at the kitchen table and stretched out his leg. Rosie was still at Mrs Shields's house and the boys hadn't come home from school yet. The house was quiet, only the soft, regular tick of the longclock in the hall.

He closed his eyes for a moment, but all he could see was Sally's torn face. Before he could begin to brood, Richard and Amos arrived in a tumult of noise. Sometimes it felt as if they'd never been silent since they were born. They tore bread from a loaf and sat across from him, eyes brimming with pleasure as they told their tales of their day, the schoolmasters and the other pupils. Finally, they looked at each other and finished it all with a laugh.

'I have something to tell you.' They caught the serious tone of his voice and sat up straighter, suddenly attentive.

They'd come to accept Sally as a sister. Though she didn't have the same family rules they needed to obey, she'd played games and tumbled with them, run beside them.

He didn't give them much detail; they didn't need the weight of that. Just enough to prepare them for how she'd be once she came back here.

'Can we go and see her?' Richard asked. He glanced at his brother; Amos nodded.

'Not just yet. At the moment she wouldn't even know you'd been. Your mother is helping to care for her.' He paused until they nodded. 'That means the pair of you need to do more here, help to keep everything tidy and clean.'

'How long until she'll be able to come home?' Amos's voice was thoughtful and youthfully light.

'Not long, I hope.' He'd always given them honest, serious answers, never talked to them like children. 'So much depends on how quickly she heals. She's in good hands with your mother and Jane and Mrs Shields.'

For a long moment the news left them subdued. Then they

were hurrying up the stairs to their room, shoes clattering on the floorboards.

The clock showed six when Rosie arrived, drained but hopeful, much of the tension vanished from her face.

'It's good news,' she said as they all sat down to a makeshift meal of bread and cheese. He saw the twins brighten. 'Sally keeps waking,' she went on. 'Only for a few seconds, then she's out again. But that's all welcome, an excellent sign. She's still very confused, not sure about anything. But she's beginning to talk a little more and she moves her head to look at whoever else is speaking. Her eyes are clear.' The relief showed in her smile. 'She's coming back.'

'Why is she confused, Mama?' Richard asked. He was frowning, forehead furrowed.

'That can happen after someone's been badly hurt,' Simon told him. 'The mind is hurting and it needs to' – he struggled for a phrase – 'to find some balance again, for things to settle back into place.'

Darkness came late in summer. He saw the boys settled in their beds and stood in the doorway. Rosie looked up at him.

'Sally really did look much brighter when I left. I wasn't just saying it for the boys.'

'I know.' He squeezed her hand. 'Still a long way to go, though.'

'She's made a start, Simon,' she said as he stood. 'Are you going out to ask questions?'

'I have to.'

Rosie nodded. 'Find them.'

Jane sat with Mrs Shields, watching Sally. The last time the girl had woken, she'd known who they were, where she was, and asked for a drink, smiling at the taste of the cordial. Piece by tiny piece, she was returning.

She complained that she hurt, pain all through her from the beating. Looking thoughtful, the old woman stood and crossed into the kitchen, steadying herself with her sticks. She knew what she wanted, a little from this jar, a pinch from another, a sprinkle from a third, all into the pestle.

'You'll need to crush them, child. My wrists aren't strong enough.'

Jane pounded them together with the mortar, scraped it all into a piece of cheesecloth, tied the neck and placed it in a mug of water.

'Let it infuse,' Mrs Shields said. 'Once she drinks it, everything will ease for a few hours. It will give her a chance to rest so her body can heal.'

'You need to teach me all this.'

'You've watched me enough times; you've learned.' Her eyes shone. 'You really did very well last night.'

'But that . . .'

'. . . was no different from any of this.' She extended a small, thin hand and tapped Jane's head. 'You've seen me do things and you've remembered. You've understood. I have a book of remedies and their ingredients. It will be there when you need it.' She smiled. 'Now, you give her this, and she'll sleep. Then you go.'

'Go?'

'It's right there in your eyes, child. You need to be out there. You have that hunger in your eyes.'

The woman seemed to read every thought in her head. Jane was desperate to find the children; they could help her hunt down the men who'd done this to Sally. But one part of her was reluctant to leave. Mrs Shields was still fragile from whatever had passed through her. What if something happened while she was gone? How could she ever live with that?

'Will you . . .'

Gently, Mrs Shields chided her. 'Don't fuss, child, it makes you sound older than me. I'll be fine. As soon as she's drunk the medicine, you do what you need to do.'

By eleven, Simon knew no more than when he'd left home.

The dramshops and the taverns had brought nothing. No one had heard about a girl being beaten. Nobody cared. Even the quiet conversations at the inns brought no rumours. No gloating, not even a mention.

Standing on Kirkgate, he wondered whether to try one or two more places. The Yorkshire Grey? Maybe not; it was late and he felt drained. Simon turned towards home, his mind drifting as he walked down Sheaf Street. A little cooler in the darkness, but the summer air was still close and sticky.

He sensed something even before they came from the shadows at the side of a building. They moved quickly and easily, with the supple grace of young men. Hats pulled low, kerchiefs tied around the bottom of their faces, knives in their hands.

Simon watched them. He hadn't been in a fight since his stabbing a year ago; his mouth was suddenly dry and he felt the prickle of fear spread across his skin. He couldn't run; with this leg they'd be on him before he managed five paces. No choice but to go against them. He gripped his stick by the shaft and breathed slowly, preparing himself. The knob was good, solid metal; it could cause plenty of damage, and there was a secret inside.

Twice she began to turn back. First at the end of Green Dragon Yard, just as she set foot on the Head Row. What if something happened while she wasn't there? She forced herself on. Then later, down by Bean Ing Mill, to the camp the children had used, abandoned now. She should go home and tend Sally, let Mrs Shields rest.

But the children must be somewhere. They hadn't vanished from Leeds. Finding one would lead her to the others. Jane's eyes flickered around in the darkness, searching for any sign of a fire. Then, hurrying along Dock Street on the far side of the bridge, smelling the wood shavings and pitch from the boatyards, she sensed someone behind. Her hand slipped to her knife. Ten yards ahead, she turned a corner and disappeared into a patch of deep shadow.

He was cautious, each step slow and measured. Jane could see his outline, a black shape against the night. Unarmed, hands at his sides. She waited until he was close, then stepped out and said: 'Who are you?'

His voice trembled. 'Wilfred, miss. I haven't come to hurt you.'

She remembered seeing him with the other children. 'Why are you following me?'

'We saw you looking. I offered to come.'

'You know who I am?'

She could just make out his nod.

He could have been twelve. A year or two older, perhaps, but still as thin as a child. A pair of shoes with most of the leather missing, a grubby shirt and ragged trousers.

'Where did you all go? Why?'

'We heard that Sally was dead,' he said.

The words shook her. Rumours, fears, moving like lightning.

'She's not dead. She was badly hurt, but she's waking up and talking now.' Jane took a step towards him. Without thinking, he shrank back. 'You'd better take me to where you're staying.'

It only took a few minutes, down by the edge of Hunslet Moor. Someone had been keeping watch; they were ready for her. Faces in the crackling firelight. One stepped forward. She recognised Hannah, a girl she'd noticed before when the young men came. A fighter with a fierce expression on her face. Someone who'd already lived too much. She had a blade in her hand.

Jane took a breath and let her gaze move over them before she spoke, loud enough for them all to hear. 'I don't know who told you Sally was dead, but it's not true. I was speaking to her before I came out.' They needed to know that more than anything. There was a buzz of voices.

Hannah moved a pace closer, fists clenched. 'Why should we believe you?'

It wasn't anger burning through her, Jane realised. It was fear.

'It's true. I swear it is. She's alive. She's healing.' Jane stared around all the faces, so many looking lost, hopeless. 'You know me. You know I'm Sally's friend. You saw me stand up and fight beside her when those men attacked you. I'm the one you came to fetch when she was hurt. You trusted me to look after her. You know how badly hurt she was, but she's starting to recover. That's why you should believe me.'

Hannah nodded. 'People kept saying . . . we thought . . .'

'Be patient.' She felt them all watching her. 'A few of us are taking care of her. She's going to need time to heal.' She felt their doubts begin to ebb. 'I'm going to find the men who did that to her. Do you know them? Did any of you see who attacked her?'

None of them had.

'Sally left to go home,' a boy said finally. 'Some of us went to look for more wood for the fire. We heard noises. It sounded like a fight. We ran, but by the time we got there, she was on the ground. The men who did it had gone.'

'Men?' Jane asked. Maybe he'd spotted something after all, and just not realised it.

'It had to be, didn't it?' Hannah said. 'Who else? More than one. The men who'd come for us.'

But Jane was staring at the boy. His mouth became an O as he remembered something.

'Voices,' he said eventually. 'They were shouting. Deep voices. Men.'

'Could you tell how many there were?'

'No.' He frowned as he concentrated. 'I think there were three or four of them.'

Nothing she hadn't already guessed. Had Andrew Barton been one of them? She needed to know the names and faces. To be absolutely certain.

'I want to find them. Anything you can discover about these men might help me. It doesn't matter if it's just a tiny scrap.'

As she started to turn away, the children crowded around, brimming over questions about Sally. How did she look? What had she said? How long before she'd be walking and able to come and see them?

Jane told them what she knew. She spotted Wilfred standing to the side.

'Come to the cottage in the morning,' she told him. 'You can see her, then tell the others.'

As she walked off, Hannah dogged her steps with questions of her own.

'You know where I live. Come with Wilfred tomorrow and you'll see for yourself. I promise.'

# SIXTEEN

The pair knew a little about fighting. They moved apart, ready to attack from different directions. All he could see was their eyes between the masks and the hats. Both of them watching him, looking calm and controlled. Simon tried to swallow, his throat dry.

The one to his left took a chance. A swift dart forward, just a test, but carrying enough power to hurt if he connected. Simon took a step back. He didn't think, just swung the stick low. If he could damage one of them now . . . He heard the crack as the metal hilt connected with the man's knee, and felt the shock rise up his arm. A short, stifled cry as the man fell. From the corner of his eye, Simon saw him try to struggle to climb back to his feet. But he couldn't.

It was satisfying. A small, quick victory that he needed to even up the odds. But it wasn't the whole battle. He turned to face the other man, backing just far enough away to watch his feet. Simon took the stick in both hands, turned the knob clockwise to unlock it and pulled out the sword hidden inside. It was a poor weapon, no real weight to it, but it would make his opponent wary.

Disabling one of his opponents had been luck. It couldn't happen a second time.

'What do you want?' Simon asked.

'To give you a warning.'

He hadn't expected that. 'Warning? About what?'

'The girl got what she deserved. You'd do better to let it go.'

He thought of Sally, lying helpless on the bed. 'If I don't?'

'Then you'll suffer worse than she has.'

Simon's mind was racing as he worked things through. They weren't hired knifemen. These two had helped to give Sally her beating. Locals. A halfway educated voice; smooth, not rough.

But if they imagined they'd deter him, they were very wrong.

'Fine, you've said your piece,' he said. 'Now you can collect your friend and go.'

The man shook his head. 'You still need your lesson, Mr Westow.'

Simon flourished the sword towards the man crawling around and whimpering on the cobbles. 'Take a look. You can see him. Do you think you can do better?'

It was a gamble, but the best choice he had. Could he bluff his way out of this, or would the man feel confident enough to take the risk? He waited, seeing the man's gaze slide over to his groaning friend and back.

'You'd better make up your mind. The watch comes down here regularly.'

He had no idea if that was true, but it might force the man's hand.

A long moment passed where Simon was uncertain what would happen. If the man decided to attack, he'd probably win. He was younger, quicker. All Simon had on his side was experience and desperation and the tricks he'd learned over the years. It probably wouldn't be enough.

The man slid his knife into a sheath on his belt and raised his hands. 'It's over. I'm going to help him.'

Simon stood, sword still in his hand, cautious as the man pulled his friend upright and helped him away. Only when they were out of sight, the awkward shuffle of their footsteps fading into the night, did he feel safe enough to put the weapon away and stand easy again. He rested his back against a wall, waiting until his breathing started to slow and the pounding of his heart gradually returned to normal. But he stayed alert for the smallest movement.

Simon exhaled. He felt weary and battered, as if life itself hurt. This time a single, swift blow had been enough. That and a bluff. But luck wouldn't always be so generous.

Why were they so afraid of him asking questions about the men who'd hurt Sally? What answers were they scared he'd hear?

Names. They'd attacked Sally. The two who'd come for him and who knew how many others. They were protecting themselves. Desperate. He'd find them, each and every one.

He limped home, letting the questions swirl through his head.

The sparks of anger flickered as the weariness rose through his body. He needed time to think about what had just happened, but not tonight. Tomorrow morning he could begin to understand it all.

Quietly, Jane turned the key and eased into the cottage. As she entered, she heard Mrs Shields's soft, musical voice and stood for a moment in the warm darkness to listen. She remembered the comforting sound of the old woman reading to her, the way it had calmed her.

Mrs Shields carried on, turning the page in the middle of a sentence. Sally turned her head, mouth slowly curling into a smile as she saw Jane.

The girl's face was a ruin of bruises and cuts, one worse than all the others. The rest would heal over time, but she'd always have the scar across her cheek to mark her. Change her.

Mrs Shields stopped and closed the book, marking the page with her finger. As she rose, Jane hurried to take her arm.

'It's time I was in bed. Was it a worthwhile night, child?'

'Yes,' she answered. 'It was.'

Jane helped her settle under the covers and closed the door as she left. Sally was still awake, but her eyes looked bleary, beginning to lose their focus.

'Where did you go?' Her voice was heavy with damage and exhaustion.

'To find the children.'

'How—?'

'Someone started a rumour you were dead.'

'Me?' She shifted in the bed, biting down on her lip to stifle a cry of pain.

'I told them you're going to be fine.'

'Will I?' Sally asked with a flicker of fear.

'Yes.' Jane sat and squeezed her hand. 'You will.'

'I've never hurt this much.' She reached out, wincing as her fingertips explored her face. 'How bad is it?'

'It'll fade in time.' Small comfort, she knew. 'You've been hit before.'

The girl closed her eyes. 'Not like this.'

'It's only been a day. You're going to need time to heal.'

'Mrs Shields said you were the one who took care of me.'

Jane shook her head. 'I only did what had to be done. It was the children who found you. They came to fetch me.'

'But . . .' She started to drift, and quickly pulled herself back. 'Thank you.'

Sally seemed sharp. She was thinking clearly. It didn't seem as if there was any damage to her mind, Jane thought with relief, and the body would mend. There were questions she was desperate to ask, but they could wait until morning. Let the girl rest. 'Go to sleep now.'

She blew out the lantern and settled comfortably into the dark. No dreams tonight. No screams.

Saturday morning and people bustling around early as Simon pressed down on the stick as he walked to the coffee cart. No sun today. Just heavy gathering clouds. The air felt like wool in his lungs.

No interesting gossip to hear. No whispers about beaten girls or young men with damaged knees. Rosie had been asleep when he arrived home last night, and he'd left her snoring quietly when he slipped out of bed and dressed. Ample time to tell her about the fight later. It was still high summer, and light had arrived quickly: from night to pale dawn before he reached the end of Swinegate.

He drained the cup, relishing the bitter taste, and placed it on the trestle before turning for home. He hadn't gone ten paces before he sensed someone following him. Two more steps and he turned, brandishing the stick.

It was Jane, almost invisible in the drab old dress she wore for work, a plain, threadbare shawl gathered over her hair. He felt a sudden panic, a chasm opening up in front of his feet; she never came out here to find him without a powerful reason.

'Don't worry. Nothing's wrong.' She must have seen the panic on his face, and spoke as soon as she fell in beside him. 'Sally's talking more. Her mind is fine.'

He exhaled slowly, but felt his heart still racing. Thank God for that, he thought. 'Have you asked her about the attack?'

'Not yet. But Mrs Shields says people often can't recall things like that.'

Rosie joined them at the kitchen table as Jane recounted what had happened the night before: Sally, the children.

'How's Mrs Shields?' Rosie asked.

'Much better.' Jane smiled.

'I'll come to the house later.'

'I told two of the children they could visit and see her,' Jane said. 'Seeing them might help her remember.'

'I was out asking questions last night, too,' Simon began, and told them about the few seconds the fight had lasted, the second man's hesitation, watching the emotions cross Rosie's face.

'That stick was worth whatever you paid for it,' he told her. 'But I don't know why they did it. Nobody had anything to tell me.'

'They're scared someone will talk,' his wife said. 'You have a reputation.'

Once, perhaps. But that was before the stabbing almost killed him. Had it lingered? Was that why the other man had chosen not to fight?

'I'll try to find out who's suddenly damaged his knee,' he said. 'If I can discover a name . . .'

It would be their way into this.

'Which knee was it?' Jane asked.

He thought for a second. 'The left.'

'I'll ask the children to keep their eyes open for anyone limping badly,' Jane said.

It could be something. But there had to be hundreds like that in Leeds, he thought, from accidents in the factories and the streets.

'How were they dressed?' she asked.

Simon tried to picture them in his mind. It was dark, he hadn't been watching their clothes. Still . . . 'Quite well, I think. Definitely not rags. The one who spoke had some education in his voice.'

'Maybe Sally will recall some of her attackers' faces when I ask. One of the boys thought he heard four men, maybe more.'

'If she tells you anything . . .' he began.

'I'll make sure you know.' Then she was gone. Just Rosie sitting across from him, the boys beginning to stir upstairs.

'Last night,' she said.

'I was lucky. I know that.'

They went through it moment by moment, the quick blow, his gamble, everything he'd relived all through the night.

'Luck runs out, Simon. You can't rely on it forever,' she said when his voice trailed away.

'I know,' he replied with a snort. 'Believe me, I know that all too well. What else can I do? The only other option is to give it all up. Stop being a thief-taker. And what then?'

They'd gone over that time and again during his long months of his recovery.

Catherine Shields had been up early, eyes sparkling, still using her sticks but barely needing them, moving around the cottage quite steadily. Recovered, Jane thought with relief.

Sally woke before the children appeared, blinking in the light. By the time they arrived, she'd eaten a little porridge, and Jane had gently washed the girl's face and combed her tangle of hair.

Hannah began to speak as soon as she was standing by the bed. Wilfred stayed a pace behind her, bashful and silent, eyes taking in everything in the room. Jane sat in the corner and watched carefully. Five minutes later she herded them outside again.

'Do you believe me now?'

'Yes.' Hannah gazed down at the ground. 'I'm sorry, miss.'

'Now you can go and tell the others that Sally's healing,' she said. 'You remember what I need you to do?'

'We do,' Wilfred replied.

'There's something more. A particular man.' She gazed into their eyes as she described the injury, needing to be certain they understood. 'His left knee. If you see him, follow him and send someone to fetch me.'

She gave them a handful of coins, everything she had in her pocket. The children would eat today. Maybe it would make a difference. But this was only one day. What about all the others that stretched out ahead? She wasn't Sally, she couldn't look after them all.

Inside, the girl had pushed herself up. Jane rushed to support her, to take the strain.

'Are you sure you feel ready to sit up?'

Readiness had nothing to do with it. Sally needed to prove something to herself. She breathed slowly, forcing everything down. 'I have to.'

'You don't. Not yet. It's going to take time . . .'

'I have to find them.'

'No.' She surprised herself with the firmness of her voice. 'You can't even stand yet. We don't know when you'll be able to walk. You're not ready.'

'Soon,' Sally promised. 'Very soon. I want to find them.'

Them. A perfect time for the question: 'How many were there?'

'Four.' Suddenly, she frowned, looking doubtful. 'I think it was four. There might have been another, too. It's blurred.'

'Can you remember any of it?'

'Just . . .' The silence stretched out before Sally quietly shook her head in frustration. 'No. Only glimpses. Little flashes.'

But that was a start. She remembered something. Jane had expected an emptiness, something pushed down too deep ever to return.

'What about faces? Can you see any of them?'

Sally's eyes snapped wide, astonished by the memory. 'Yes.' She turned her head to look at Jane. 'One of them. He was in the group that attacked. The one who vanished.'

'Barton's son?' Jane asked in disbelief. 'Are you sure it was him?'

'Yes.' The word hissed out of her. Definite. Defiant. Her fingers began to explore her face. 'I want to see what it looks like.'

For a moment Jane considered refusing. Then she brought a small looking glass from the dresser and handed it to the girl. Sally stared for a long time; her expression showed nothing.

'My nose. Did you . . .'

'I put it back in place.'

A nod, and she traced the cut on her cheek, up and down, up and down, before she returned the mirror.

'That's never going to disappear, is it?'

What could she say? The girl already knew the truth.

Suddenly Sally looked drained, as if her determination had been stolen away. Jane lowered her on to the pillow and Sally closed her eyes. She'd carry that scar for the rest of her days.

# SEVENTEEN

Jane worked in the garden, the front door propped open with a brick to hear everything inside. Mrs Shields was busy in the kitchen, preparing a rabbit for the oven, as if she wanted to prove she'd completely shaken off her brief illness.

She cut flowers and placed them in a basket, letting her thoughts linger on Andrew Barton. Had Sally really seen him or was it that the face remained in her mind from an earlier time?

She'd find him and make sure of the truth. If he'd been involved, he'd hand her the other names. Jane wouldn't give him the chance to refuse.

As soon as Rosie arrived, she'd hurry away and tell Simon. He was searching too; he needed to know.

She heard the footsteps on the other side of the wall, coming along Green Dragon Yard. Her hand slid to her pocket, curling around the handle of the knife. Old habits returning.

But this was no danger. She raised the hand in greeting as Rosie appeared, looking like a grand lady paying her social visits in a dove-grey gown set off by a pale-yellow shawl and plumed hat.

A moment to tell her everything and see her settled by the bed, then Jane asked, 'Do you know where Simon was going?'

Rosie shook her head. 'Out asking questions. That's all he told me.'

She'd have to trust her senses, to see how sharp they were these days.

It took Jane more than half an hour of prowling the streets, the sultry closeness in the air leaving her skin damp and prickly.

She finally caught up with him on Boar Lane, heading towards the courthouse. With his limp and his stick, he was easy to spot. She weaved through the crowd on the pavement, sliding and ducking until she was next to him.

'Has something—' he began, but she shook her head.

'I might have a name.'

His mouth hardened as she told him.

'What do you want to do?'

'Talk to him in a place where he can't run. He'll give me the names of the others.' She felt his stare burning into her. 'After we have those, Sally can decide what she wants to do.' Jane lifted her gaze to meet his eyes. 'That's her right.'

'Do you want my help?'

'You can go and talk to his father.'

They walked up Briggate together. A coach came roaring out of the Talbot yard, not even pausing as it hit a woman and sent her spinning to the pavement.

Some people began to scream and shout as others rushed to help. Jane slipped between them and knelt by the woman. She was dazed, crying from the pain. Blood was smeared across the flagstones where she'd hit her head, and her right leg splayed out at an impossible angle.

'Help her inside.' She looked around, pointing at one strong man, then another. 'You and you. Be very gentle.' She pointed. 'Her leg's broken.'

The woman shuddered with fear. Jane stroked her hair.

'Don't worry. They'll find a doctor for you. He'll take care of you.'

The woman blinked, fearful. 'Am I . . . Will they . . .?'

'No,' she assured the woman. 'Your leg will stay, it will all be fine again.'

Someone gathered the parcels that had scattered when the coach hit her. Jane stood as the men returned with an old door and eased the woman on to it. The crowd parted to make way for them as they disappeared into the inn. A few more moments and everyone had dispersed.

Simon watched her: the easy way she took charge, how the others had listened when she gave orders. How she'd gently assured the woman. So different from the person she'd been only two years before. Back then, she'd burned with fury at him when he'd stopped her taking revenge on a man. He'd had to; it would have killed her. The anger had ebbed away, but she'd kept a distance between them ever since, a reserve. Seeing her now, he realised she'd grown and spread her wings and left the child in her behind. She'd been calm, in control. A woman.

As they continued up Briggate, they agreed on their approach. He'd see Barton and ask to talk to the son. Andrew would deny everything, and the father would be indignant. Jane would hide outside, ready to confront the son when he hurried out to talk to the other men who'd taken pleasure in hurting Sally.

The same ones who'd come after him; he'd have put good money on it.

She drifted away among the trees and bushes, vanishing in the blink of an eye. Simon walked down the short drive to hammer on the door.

James Barton took his time, apologising as he entered the sitting room.

'Business, I'm afraid, Mr Westow.' He cocked his head, a curious glint in his eye. 'Have you heard some news about Fox?'

'No.' That seemed like another age. 'This is different. I'd like to speak to your son.'

The gaze grew suspicious. 'What about? Last time you accused him of things he denied.'

Simon dipped his head. 'He might be able to help. A girl who works for me was attacked by a group of young men a few nights ago. They damaged her.'

Before Barton could speak, Simon plunged on.

'Late last night, on my way home from asking questions about it, two young men found me on a quiet street and told me to stop. They both had knives and tried to use them.'

He took a breath. 'I see. Why do you believe this has anything to do with Andrew?'

'I don't know that it does,' Simon replied. 'I'm hoping he might be able to help me identify the men responsible.' He paused. 'One of them might never walk properly again.'

Barton ran his tongue around the inside of his mouth. 'You and your . . . people live in a violent world, Mr Westow.'

He nodded; if it left the man a little fearful, that could be useful. 'That's part of the trade. Believe me, I'm not suggesting your son had anything to do with this. Simply that I'd appreciate anything he can do. There are times we need help, too.'

The only sound in the room was the slow tick of the clock standing against the wall as the men stared at each other. Would

Barton refuse? Simon felt the balance beginning to tip that way. Then a curt, decisive nod.

'Let's have him down here and see if he can answer any of your questions, shall we?'

'I'd be grateful.' Even if there wasn't likely to be much, whatever the young man said, that wasn't the point. He was here to plant some doubts and fears.

'I haven't heard him moving around this morning.' A shake of his head. 'I don't remember what time he came home last night.' He called for the servant and sent him to wake Andrew.

'You asked about Fox. Nobody's heard anything about him. He's long gone from Leeds, if he's still alive,' Simon said.

'Do you understand what happened?'

'No.' How could he, when he only had half the pieces of the puzzle?

The servant's shoes clattered on the treads as he ran down the stairs and pulled the door wide.

'He's not there, sir. His bed hasn't been slept in.'

Barton didn't try to keep the fear from his face. His son had gone again.

'You know where his friends live,' he ordered the servant. 'Go and see if he's with any of them.' As the man disappeared, Barton turned to Simon, his desperation clear. 'Perhaps you'd better tell me exactly what's going on, Mr Westow.'

He listened, but his head kept turning at every small sound.

'Do you believe this girl?'

'That's why I wanted to speak to your son.' It wasn't an answer to his question, but the man didn't seem to notice.

'I see.' Barton gave a bitter sigh. 'My son likes his drink. That's hardly a secret. He's a sot, but since he returned after he went missing, it's been worse. Out with his friends every night, coming home later. My wife and I have talked to him.'

'Did he listen?'

'No,' he replied slowly. 'He's . . .'

'What?'

'I've seen his face sometimes, when he doesn't realise I'm looking, and he seems . . .' Barton weighed his words. 'Sad. Angry. Lost.'

A volatile mix. 'Has he said more about the time he was gone? Anything about the woman he was with, where they were?'

'No,' he admitted. 'Nothing at all. We tried, but he became so furious that we decided to stop.'

'Did he still deny meeting Fox?'

'You were here when he gave his answer to that. I believed my son, Mr Westow. Wouldn't you believe yours?'

'Yes,' he admitted. But he'd make damned sure Richard or Amos was telling the truth. He glanced at the man's face. Life was crumbling all around Barton. He needed to hold on to something.

They waited, time creeping past until they heard a door close. Barton flinched, as if he already expected the worst. The servant came in, panting, his face slick with sweat after dashing around town.

'Well?'

'No, sir. He wasn't with any of them. None of them saw him last night.'

'I see.' A nod and the man was dismissed. Barton closed his eyes for a second, then turned to Simon. 'It seems we both want to find Andrew. I'll pay you to do it.'

'Are you sure?'

'I don't know what's happened to him or what he's done, Mr Westow, but it has to be something bad. Find him for us.'

He left with the names and addresses of Andrew Barton's friends. He'd take Jane with him. She could see their faces, remember them. If Sally's recollection was true, and Andrew Barton had been one of her attackers, some of these others could have been with him.

If one of them had a damaged knee . . . He stopped himself. This wasn't the time for indulgence and settling scores. He'd just been hired to trace a missing young man who'd been gone overnight, and every hour was vital.

Outside, he whistled a short call and began to hobble towards the street. A quick salute as he passed Mudie's printing shop, then Jane was beside him, pulling her shawl over her hair.

He explained as they walked. She listened carefully, her face showing nothing.

'Last time he vanished with a woman,' she pointed out. 'He might have gone back to her.'

'It's possible,' Simon agreed. But it didn't feel right. 'We don't know her name. Or if she ever existed. The only proof he was with anyone is what Andrew Barton himself said, and we already know he's a liar.'

Five names, five addresses. Maybe they could tease something out of them.

He talked to the men while Jane stood back, a ghost disappearing in the room. They all carried the sleek shell of money, but she could see how the news about Barton's disappearance shook them.

Jane had seen two of them before; they'd been among the men who attacked the children's camp. One glanced at her as if she might be familiar, then looked away without recognition. She paid close attention, setting them aside for the future.

The first three had little to offer. They were the ones Simon had talked to the last time Andrew vanished. The only insight was that Andrew had always drunk a great deal, but it had become heavier after his return; that confirmed what his father had said. Each night he'd go stumbling home, awash in rum and brandy. A sad, desperate man, she thought. But one who liked violence too, as long as nobody fought back.

'Why did he change?' Simon asked, but the young men didn't seem to know.

The fourth was different, a quieter, more thoughtful young man. Malcolm Ridley possessed none of the brashness that characterised the others. Like them, he came from a good family, no need to work all the hours God sent to put food on the table and a roof over his head. His fingernails were clean, his hands soft, and his voice was quietly musical when he spoke.

'I tried to ask Andrew once why he drinks so much,' Ridley said. 'The curious thing is that he never seems to enjoy it.'

'What do you mean?'

'He takes no pleasure in getting drunk. It seems like something he needs to do.'

'Why? Is he trying to forget something?' Simon asked.

The young man shook his head. 'I don't know. When I asked,

he told me it was a way to find forgiveness. I couldn't understand, so I asked him to explain. He was already in his cups at the time. All he did was turn silent. He's trying to turn himself into a souse.'

'Do you have any idea where—?'

'No,' Ridley said sharply. 'But if he's vanished, you ought to be worried about him. If the mood catches him, who knows what he might do . . .?'

Simon glanced at Jane. Would Barton kill himself?

She stood completely still, staring down at the floor, listening intently.

'Are there any places he likes?' Simon asked. 'What about the woman he said he'd gone off with last time?'

'He never said another word about her. There were a few times I wondered if he'd made her up. I don't know why he would, though.'

Andrew Barton was the only one who could tell them the truth about that.

'What about places he goes?' He needed *something*. Somewhere to begin.

Ridley shook his head. 'I don't know. Do you have John Dale's name on your list? He isn't one of the drinking crowd. I know that sometimes he and Andrew go walking together. He might have a few thoughts.'

Dale's name was the last one there. The only man among the group with a job, dressed in a plain black suit, covered by a long, stained apron, sitting at a desk in his father's spice warehouse on the Calls. As a clerk led them past all the sacks, Simon felt the smells tug and itch at his nose.

It was a little better in the office, with the door closed and the window open to the stink of the water.

'It doesn't take long to get used to the scents, Mr Westow,' he said with a smile. 'It still catches me occasionally, though.'

'Andrew Barton,' Simon said.

'He's gone again?' he said after he heard the news. 'I saw him a few days ago. I don't know what happened to him when he disappeared, but he's never looked happy since he returned.'

'Did you ask him?'

'No.' His eyes widened, as if the question had taken him by surprise. 'It's his business. If he'd wanted to tell me, he'd have said something.'

'I understand you two are close. You go walking together.'

'It's been a few months since we took a long walk, Mr Westow.' He frowned. 'Close? I'm not sure about that. We both enjoy walking. For the pleasure of being out there and breathing clean air. Believe me, after a week in this place, it can feel glorious. Andrew and I talk, but he's never revealed any deep secrets, if that's what you're hoping to hear.'

That would have been too much to hope.

Dale was thinking, diving into his memory. 'Last time we went must have been late in the winter, not long after that ugly business when that man tried to steal from his father. Andrew seemed uneasy then.'

'Uneasy?' Simon repeated the word. 'In what way?'

'He used to be pleasant company. Never much of a care in the world. He'd laugh all the time. We'd walk, stop somewhere and have a drink. But that last time, he was different. All the joy he used to have had vanished. He was tense, hardly spoke a word while we were out. We'd barely been out for an hour before he suddenly wanted to turn back. Usually we were out all day.'

'He never suggested going again?'

'Vague promises, nothing more. I've run into him, and he's always polite, but he turned distant. As if he had things clawing at him.'

Simon's voice became more urgent. 'Do you have any idea what was troubling him? Was there any talk among his friends?'

'None that I heard. But I'm not a part of that drinking set.' He waved a hand at the office. 'I have work to keep me busy.'

'Does Andrew have any favourite places? Anywhere you went often?' Simon asked.

'I've been trying to think about that. We went out towards Towton a few times. It's on the way to York, not far from Tadcaster. There was a big battle there a few hundred years ago. Andrew had read about it.' The man shrugged. 'It was just fields and a stream to me, but he seemed to find something there.' He paused, caught by a memory. 'There's a church close by, old and very small, in a strange place called Lead. It's a tiny building, but he always made sure to spend some time there when we were up that way. I'm sorry, that's all I can think of.'

'It's helpful, thank you,' Simon told him. Somewhere to begin.

'You heard it all,' he said to Jane as they walked up the Head Row towards Green Dragon Yard. 'What do you think?'

The fact that Andrew had changed around the time Fox was arrested had to be important. Could he have been involved in that?

'I don't think we'll find him,' she said. 'Do you?'

He knew she was probably right. The worry crept through his body. They'd need the devil's own luck to discover Barton alive.

Sally was still resting when they arrived. The shutters were thrown back, light streaming through the windows. Jane heard Mrs Shields moving softly around the kitchen.

No pain on the girl's face. That was a good sign.

She sat, took hold of the girl's hand, then ran her fingers over Sally's forehead. The girl opened her eyes and smiled.

'I was awake. I must have drifted off. Were you working?'

'Andrew Barton's gone again.'

Sally pushed herself up until she was sitting. Still moving slowly and carefully, but not as strained. Small grimaces. Such an improvement from the unconscious girl they'd helped here, looking as if she might die. The bruises across her face were at their most vivid, the cuts all scabbed over. As Jane told her about Andrew Barton, her eyes were suddenly curious and eager.

'When?'

'Last night.'

'What are you going to do?'

'That's for Simon to decide.'

A final light squeeze of the girl's fingers, then Jane stood and drifted outside to join Simon and Rosie.

'He seemed to like this small church. We need to look at it,' he said.

'Could you go?' Rosie asked.

'I've barely recovered from the trip out to Temple Newsam,'

Simon said. 'It would ruin my leg.' He turned to Jane. 'What about you? You'd recognise him.'

She'd certainly know him again. She'd seen him with Fox, gone up against him with a knife. But if she found him, what would she do? They'd been hired for this, but he had to pay for the pain he'd inflicted on Sally. How could she balance those things?

'Be at Barton's house in half an hour,' Simon said, then hurried away, leaning heavily on his stick.

'We won't find anything there,' Jane said. Andrew had been gone too long, and the place had been no more than a guess.

'I don't imagine you will,' Rosie agreed. 'But we still have to look. It sounds like we don't have anywhere else to try, doesn't it?'

'His friend said there's a battlefield he liked, too. Somewhere called Towton. I don't think it's too far from the church.'

'You could look there, too.'

Jane glanced back at the cottage. 'What about Sally?'

'She's going to be fine. A week and she'll be up, and soon after that she'll be nearly as good as new. Her mind isn't damaged, you've seen that.'

The thought made her smile. The kind of comfort she needed. But as she crossed through into Green Dragon Yard, any pleasure fled. She could feel it in her heart; this tale with Andrew Barton would have no happy ending.

A chaise this time, bigger, more stable than the gig. James Barton was a good, steady whip, safer than Sally. He was dressed for the part, wearing a light summer riding coat and high boots that were polished to a brilliant shine. Jane still hated being perched on the seat, so high off the ground, but at least she didn't feel she might tumble off at every turn.

Barton was lost in his thoughts and fears as the horses sped between the high banks and hedgerows. He hadn't tried to talk, and Jane was grateful. She wouldn't have known what to say to him. He didn't need to hear the things that she knew. Silence was easier, more comfortable. Nothing more than a pale grey sky above them, the clatter of hooves and the rattle of the wheels the only sounds.

They'd already travelled ten or twelve miles from Leeds, moving at a brisk pace over the uneven dirt road; it would have been a long walk out and back again in a day. Quite possible, though; Jane had heard of men on the tramp for work who covered forty miles between dawn and dark. Maybe the rhythm of walking soothed Andrew.

Barton tugged on the reins and pointed. 'Over there. If the man back at the crossroads was telling us the truth, that's the church.'

It stood alone, as small as she'd been told, set back about two hundred yards from the road, in the middle of a field. No other buildings, just mounds of turf and a few stones poking up from the ground, covered with moss.

She slid down, grateful to have her feet on the ground again.

'I'll stay here,' Barton said. She could hear the tremor in his voice, desperate to know but terrified of what he might find.

Jane crossed a rickety plank bridge over a beck and followed the rough track where feet had trampled the tall grass in the field. Nothing felt quite real and she turned, half-expecting to find herself alone. But Barton and the chaise were still there.

Over in the trees, birds were calling. Somewhere in the far distance she could hear cattle lowing.

The wildflowers stood as high as her waist; their different scents rose into the air as she brushed against them.

The church looked so small, so unlikely, out here on its own. She wondered at the stones, the mounds that surrounded it, as if there had once been other buildings that had fallen to nothing over the years while this remained. People must have lived here, worked and laughed and come to this place to pray. Where had they all gone? How long ago did it happen? Why?

All abandoned, except for this. People still came; someone had made the path through the grass. That could have been Andrew Barton, she realised with a start.

At the church door, she stopped for a moment, resting her hand on the wood. Sometimes, in places like this, there was an instant when she believed only a thin veil separated her from the past. If she could rip it apart, she'd be able to see these people who'd once walked here. Talk to them, hear about them. They'd be as alive as the characters in the novels she read:

those Americans, Charles returning from exile, Ivanhoe and Lion-Hearted Richard. In her head she knew it was all a fancy, but her heart still believed. She took a deep breath, then the door slowly creaked open as she pushed it.

Inside it was a single room, barely more than four walls and a roof where missing slates let in the sun and the rain. It had its own smells, perfumes of the past, of neglect and hope and faith. A series of stone slabs lay in a line on the floor, coats of arms roughly carved on them, half-covered with dirt, all the sharpness of the cuts worn away by the centuries. No signs Andrew had been here, but she'd never expected to find any.

The windows were gone. A single bell outside to call people to service, but no congregation to hear it. They were all ghosts now.

It was quiet, and a sense of comfort and peace wrapped around her. She could understand why Andrew Barton liked to come here. Perhaps it brought him some peace.

She'd seen what she needed; there was nothing to keep her. Yet she was reluctant to leave. The church seemed to weave a delicate web of magic around her. As she pulled the door closed, she stroked the weathered stone of the arch.

Barton was sitting rigid in the chaise, staring straight ahead, a man trapped in his terror. He never turned to watch her approach.

As she stepped on to the bridge, a stone turned under her foot and she stumbled, gasping as she grabbed for a tree branch to stop herself falling.

Without that, she'd have never spotted him.

She tried to steady herself. The bough started to bend and suddenly Jane was staring into the beck. The wavering image of the body lay right there under the lapping stream.

Andrew Barton.

First Mrs Fox in Kirkstall, now the young man here. Both of them lying dead in the water.

She dashed to the gig, heart racing, wondering how to tell a man that his son was no longer alive.

There was no need for words; he read it on her face.

# EIGHTEEN

Simon hailed Charles Granger, hurrying towards him as the man stopped and turned.

'Mr Westow, you look well.' His expression changed as he realised what he'd said. 'Apart from the leg, of course.'

Simon laughed. 'Nothing to be done about that. How's business?'

Granger ran the factory he'd inherited, a business that made hessian sacks and shipped them around the country. He was in his middle twenties, thrown into the thick of it all before he was ready after his father died suddenly of a heart attack. Simon had known the older man, saddened to read of his passing. But death came for everyone.

Back before he had responsibilities, Charles Granger had spent most of his nights carousing around the inns and beershops. He'd left that behind, but he'd gone around with some of the same men as Andrew Barton. Like the ones who could have beaten Sally and who attacked him.

'I haven't seen any of them in months.' He shook his head when Simon asked. 'My life is the factory these days. When I'm not there, I'm at home.'

He'd married just a year before, a business alliance rather than true love, and his wife had given birth to a son a few months earlier. The man had his heir; duty done.

'One of the men who came for me might have a damaged knee.'

'Good God,' Granger said, incredulous. 'Did this happen in town?'

'No more than a few yards from here. I'd appreciate it if you could ask a few discreet questions. It might be someone you used to know.'

The man gave a reluctant nod. 'If I run into any of them. These days, though, I can't promise . . .'

'Of course. I understand.'

Simon spoke with a few others as he moved up Briggate, stopping by the market cross near the Head Row.

A moment turned into five minutes as he watched the surge of people and traffic. Andrew Barton. He thought about what John Dale had said, that the young man had changed around the time Fox had been arrested. He'd been the only one to notice that. Simon knew he needed to talk to the Bartons again, and go back to Andrew's friends with more questions.

Perhaps the young man would simply reappear, the way he had last time. But something told him that wasn't the likely outcome.

'Waiting for an answer, Westow?' Porter appeared next to him.

He chuckled. 'Hoping for one, perhaps. Do you have any?'

The constable shook his head. 'Nothing more than problems of my own. How's that young girl who works for you? I heard what happened.'

'Improving,' he said cautiously.

'Looking for the ones who did it?'

'Among other things.'

A hand raised in farewell, and he hobbled across the Head Row.

In George Mudie's printing shop, Simon sat and stretched out his leg as he watched the man working. All the walking had tired him. After ten minutes, Mudie stopped and poured himself a tot of brandy.

'You've got something on your mind, Simon. It's not like you to be so quiet.'

'I know.'

'You have your hands full,' Mudie said after Simon unburdened himself. 'You're trying to do three things at the same time.'

'They're connected. Two of them, at least: find the people who came for me and the ones who hurt Sally.'

'Very likely,' he allowed after a moment. 'But you're being paid to search for Barton's son.'

'All I've found so far is one faint clue to where he might have gone.'

'One's better than none. Maybe it will bring you something.'
He stood, grimacing as pain shot up his leg. 'We'll see.'

Barton dashed past her and plunged down the bank, straight into the water. It rose over the top of his boots as he thrust his hands under the surface to reach for his son.

He began to tug Andrew from the beck. The head surfaced first, lips pale, life gone. Then the chest.

The man looked up, helpless.

'You'll have to help me. Please. He's too heavy.'

A moment and Jane scrambled down the bank. Her boot heels dug into the dirt. She placed her hands under the arms of the corpse, gritted her teeth and pulled. She didn't look at Andrew's face, just used her strength to try and drag him on to land.

No rope marks or redness around his neck. Andrew Barton hadn't been strangled. She saw no sign of a knife wound. But from the moment she spotted him, she'd never believed this was murder. He'd come out here to kill himself.

Why would he do that?

Finally they had the body up by the road and Barton knelt by it, torn between emptiness and the need to howl out his grief.

Jane had seen the dead before, far too many of them. Life departed, and they became nothing more than a sack of bones and decay. Their pain was gone, left for those still alive. She watched as Barton cradled his son, tears running down his face. Jane didn't try to break the silence. She didn't know any words that might comfort him, if they existed at all.

A final, punishing effort as they lifted Andrew into the chaise. Barton covered him with a rug, all the respect he could offer out here. Up on the seat, he flicked the whip above the horse and they began the journey back to Leeds. She knew they should have told someone, the constable of the nearest village. But she wasn't about to try and tell Barton anything; he wouldn't have listened.

They'd covered a mile before he spoke. He sounded dazed, trying to make sense of something beyond comprehension.

'He never mentioned that place to us. Not once.'

She knew the man didn't want to hear her voice. He was

speaking to himself, searching for a way to let his sorrow to find its way to the dead. Jane glanced at the emptiness on his face. He was a man whose soul was shattered.

'Andrew liked to sleep late, but there were days he'd wake very early, the same time as the servants. He'd leave the house and he wouldn't return until well after dark. When I asked him about it, all he ever said was that he'd been out. Nothing more than that.'

The silence fell again.

'I should have . . .' he began, then ended again as words failed him. They passed through Aberford without anyone giving them a second glance. Just another vehicle on the road. Barton kept the horse at a swift trot towards home, guiding it without thought, his hands and eyes working while his mind roamed through other places and times.

He never glanced over his shoulder at the body. The smell of water from the stagnant pool filled the chaise. The scent of death.

Barton lapsed into his silence and regrets. Eventually Jane looked up and saw the haze over Leeds. The darkening of the sky that meant they were close to home. All around them, dusk was gathering.

Barton drew up outside his house. For the first time, he turned to look into her face.

'Thank you,' he said, and took a shallow breath. 'I . . .' he started, then shook his head. He was lost inside, trapped in a place that terrified him. 'Can you ask Mr Westow to call on me tomorrow?'

He called for a servant and she slipped away, first to Swinegate to tell Rosie what had happened, then hurrying through the streets until she reached Green Dragon Yard, through the gap in the wall and into the house.

# NINETEEN

Andrew Barton's death hadn't become public property yet. Nobody mentioned it at the coffee cart outside the Bull and Mouth on Sunday morning. No hum of gossip in the air as Simon made his way up Albion Street.

Another warm day, with enough of a threat of rain to make his skin prickle; he was happy to step into the coolness of Mrs Shields's cottage.

Sally was awake, sitting up and eating porridge. Bruised and damaged, but her eyes were bright. Really on the mend, he thought with relief.

'I'm on my way to see Barton,' he said to Jane. 'Rosie told me what you said to her last night, but I'd like to hear it all from you.'

The words came hesitantly; she was reluctant to live it all again, to see everything gone from the young man's face. He listened attentively, watching Sally and wondering what she made of the death. Justice? Her expression gave nothing away.

'Did he kill himself?' Simon asked.

Jane raised her head to stare at him. One sorrowful word: 'Yes.'

He glanced again; there was no triumph in Sally's eyes. No pleasure at hearing the fate of one of her attackers.

'I know there are no words for what you and your wife must be feeling.'

What could you say to a man who'd lost his son? How would he feel if Richard or Amos had been pulled from the river?

Barton looked decades older than the man he'd seen just the day before.

'Thank you,' he replied. But it was nothing more than formality, as if he hadn't really heard the words at all.

'You wanted me to come and see you.'

The bells at St John's Church had been pealing as he walked

past, loud enough to drive all the thoughts from his head. Maybe that wasn't a bad thing, Simon decided as he stood in the silent room. It had stopped him brooding too hard.

'Yes.' The man blinked. 'I did. I want to employ you again, Mr Westow.'

Simon frowned. There'd been no crime, nothing for a thief-taker. 'Employ me? What do you think I can do?'

Barton drew in two long breaths before he found the answer. 'I'd like you to find out why it happened. I accepted the things my son told me, even though I knew they were lies. I need you to discover the truth.'

He didn't know how to respond. He hadn't expected anything like this.

'I've never . . .' he began, then stopped as he wondered if it was possible. Barton needed to understand what had happened. But . . . 'I don't know if I can,' he said. 'I don't know if anyone can.'

'Would you be willing to try?' Barton asked. The pain showed in his voice. 'I'll pay you well.'

Simon took a long time to make his decision. 'I'm willing to try. But you have to understand that I can't promise more than that.'

People were spilling out of the parish church as Simon passed. He'd been walking for an hour, trying to see how they might discover the reasons behind Andrew Barton's death. He'd just come from Grey's Court, standing in the stink of the night soil and staring up at the room where Daniel Shackleton had been murdered. Somehow or other, he had a part to play in all this. What was it? The same with the Foxes; they might be gone, but their shadows loomed large over Andrew's death.

The last time he tried he'd had no luck trying to untangle this case. Maybe this time would be different. Perhaps a search would uncover the pair who attacked him. The ones who beat Sally, too; very likely he'd already talked to some of them when he questioned Andrew's friends.

Jane sat on the edge of the bed, perching close to Sally in the warmth of a Sunday afternoon.

Simon and Rosie were standing, filling the room. Together, the four of them discussed how they could find out about Andrew Barton's death.

'I need to talk to his friends again,' Simon said. 'Dale, the one who told us about the church, he might have some ideas. Or Bradley.'

'Was he courting?' Sally asked. 'Sweet on anyone?'

'Nobody ever mentioned anything like that,' he told her. 'There might be someone in the past.' He turned to Rosie. 'Talk to his mother. She might know, he could have talked to her about it.'

'Not today,' she said. 'You're going to have to give her time, Simon, she's just lost her son. You know,' she said thoughtfully, 'his friends all claimed he liked to drink. Were there places he favoured, ones where he might have had credit?'

Jane listened. So far, this was work for Simon and Rosie. Nothing for her. But there were things she could do. She could discover exactly who'd inflicted the beating on Sally.

She had her eye on two of the young men Simon had questioned. One of them had definitely been among the four who attacked the children. Another might have been there. Andrew Barton too, she thought, but he was dead now.

They were going to answer her questions and give her the truth. If they hadn't done the damage to Sally, they knew who did. They'd tell her; she'd give them no choice.

The silence grew in the room. Sally broke it.

'Fox.' She gave a small, dry cough and tried to reach for the cup of cordial by the bed.

'He's gone,' Rosie said, handing her the cup. 'We have no idea if he's dead or alive.'

'Andrew was involved with him.' The girl sipped, and her voice grew clearer. 'Jane saw them.'

'The only one who can tell us about that is Fox.'

'Can we find out what happened to him?'

Jane smiled to herself. Porter and the watch had looked and spread the word from town to town, but the man had vanished. What chance did they have?

'We can try,' Rosie said. 'We have to follow up on everything. I don't believe we'll succeed, but . . .'

But, Jane thought. Such a small word to say so much.
She needed to be out there, doing something, anything, instead of all the talk.

John Dale had just returned from church when Simon knocked on his door. It was a prosperous house, set out along Woodhouse Lane, beyond Queen Square, with a view over Leeds and its hazy sky.

'My parents said we're welcome to use this room,' Dale said as he entered the parlour. 'I heard a rumour about Andrew before the service this morning. Someone saw his father coming back into town yesterday with a terrible look on his face. Is it true?'

'He was by that church you told me about. His father pulled him from the beck.'

He saw the young man flinch at the thought. His skin grew pale.

'He drowned?'

'Yes.'

'You know, that water always fascinated him. He said that the blood from the battlefield at Towton must have run along it. He called it the death stream.'

What could he make of that?

'Did he ever talk about killing himself?'

Dale shook his head. 'Not to me. He never revealed that much about his thoughts. But I know he had his dark moods.' A moment's reflection. 'I suppose that was usually when he wanted to walk. As if the miles could get rid of the feeling.'

'Did it help?'

'Sometimes.' He pushed his lips together and sighed. 'Forgive me. The news has shaken me, Mr Westow. It really has. I can't believe Andrew's not here.'

'Do you have any idea at all why he might have done it?'

'No,' Dale answered after a long, thoughtful pause. 'If he told anyone what he was thinking, it wasn't me. I can't imagine Andrew confiding in anyone. He kept his feelings to himself. But there had to be something, what with his drinking growing heavier. But this . . .' He shook his head. 'I never saw this in him.'

Simon had more questions, looking for reasons, anything the young man might have said about what tormented him so badly. Some clue to take him further.

'There was one thing,' Dale began hesitantly as Simon pushed himself up from the chair and leaned on his stick.

'What?'

'Something Andrew said. It was months ago. Probably about the time his father had that man arrested.'

'What was it?'

'That he'd felt as if he'd betrayed his family.'

'Did he explain what he meant?'

'No, that was it. I asked, but he moved on to something else as if it didn't really matter. I'd forgotten about it.' He looked up. 'I'm sorry, that's all.'

'It's something. Thank you.'

'As I said, Andrew was very good at keeping secrets. There were times during the spring when a few of us wondered if he had a woman. But when we asked, he'd never say.'

This could be something. Any small clue at all . . . 'Was there ever an indication who she might be?'

'None. It wasn't anyone from one of the local families, I'm sure of that. She probably never existed. None of us ever saw him with anyone.'

One more mystery about Andrew Barton, Simon thought as he trudged along the road, and no nearer to finding any answers.

She knew where the young men lived; she'd been in their houses when Simon asked his questions. Jane was waiting when Charles Ibbotson came out and strode off into the darkness. The night was deep black, only the lamps on the passing coaches and the light leaking through windows to show the way.

She was still there in the deep shadows when he emerged from the Rose and Crown two hours later. He was swaying a little, walking beside another man who shuffled awkwardly on crutches, his left leg heavily bound.

They stopped at a house on the Head Row, talking quietly for a minute before the injured man went inside and Ibbotson moved on. Jane noted the door as she passed; information to give to Simon in the morning.

She caught Ibbotson by Rockley Hall Yard. Hurrying, letting her footsteps ring loud so he turned and saw the knife she was holding.

'In there,' she ordered.

He raised his hands, eyes never leaving the blade. 'You can have my money.'

'I don't want it.'

His body stiffened. 'Then—'

'You were there tormenting the homeless children.'

He stayed silent.

'Weren't you?'

'Yes.' His voice was a husk, terrified. All his bravado fled when he was on his own.

'There was another attack. A young girl.' She brought the knife closer to his face, sliding the flat of the blade along his skin.

He pulled back.

'Was that you?'

She smelled the acrid scent of urine. He'd pissed himself with fear. Good.

'Well?'

An age seemed to pass before he hung his head. 'Yes.'

She'd expected him to beg, to plead. But he stayed quiet.

'There were others with you. Who were they?'

He was quick to give her the three names, as if he hoped that might save him. One she didn't recognise, then Henry Harrison, and finally Andrew Barton.

Ibbotson still had his eyes on the ground. 'What are you going to do? Are you going to kill me?'

'No,' she told him and he raised his head in surprise.

'I thought—'

'I'm not here to pass sentence on you. You know who gets to decide that. But you'd better warn the others that her judgement is going to come. Tell them that she knows who you are. First, though . . .'

'What?' It was a frightened cry.

She looked at Ibbotson, seeing if she could summon up the smallest trace of sympathy for him. No. He believed money let him do whatever he pleased. It meant he imagined he could torment feral children and drag them through hell. That beating a girl turned him into an important man.

Suddenly he was learning that money gave no protection at all. It was just an illusion.

Almost like a caress, she slid the edge of the blade along his cheek. She'd honed it so fine that he wouldn't feel it until the blood began to run. Now he would carry the same scar as Sally.

'That's the beginning of what she owes you.'

Jane turned and walked away. No hurry. Ibbotson was a broken man. He wasn't about to come after her.

'So those are the names,' Sally said. But the girl had no light of revenge shining in her eyes. Her hand, a series of scabs, moved to rest on Jane's arm. 'I don't know how I can thank you.'

'You don't have to.'

A grateful nod and then worry filled her face. 'Who's looking after the children?'

Wilfred and Hannah had been waiting outside the cottage when Jane went out early that morning, eager for news they could carry to the others.

'She's still asleep,' Jane told them. 'But she's mending, I promise you that. It takes time.' Jane had emptied out her pocket, all the coins she'd taken from their hiding place in the house to go shopping. 'Take it. Buy some food for everyone.'

'Thank you, miss.'

'I'm trying to help them,' she said now, and saw relief pour over Sally's face.

# TWENTY

Simon stood on the Head Row, gazing at the house Jane had described to him earlier that morning.

He'd slept poorly, no more than fits and starts, one of those nights when the heat snatched rest away. Up before light, he'd been the first customer at the coffee cart on Briggate, lingering long enough to feel the town come awake around him. Boilers were fed in the factories, machines began to thump and grind, smoke poured from chimneys all over Leeds. Another few minutes and the first tiny smuts began to fall. Soon enough he could taste them in the coffee, and hobbled back to Swinegate.

Now he was standing here, wondering whether to hammer on the door or leave it until later. He'd escorted Rosie to talk to Mrs Barton and see what she might learn about Andrew.

There were things he ought to be doing, work to earn the money Barton was paying him. More important things than this. Finally, he forced himself to leave, glancing back over his shoulder as he walked. He'd return.

For now, it was time to talk to all the fences who handled stolen goods. Some remembered Fox's name because he'd been pardoned, but hadn't done business with him; like Henry Longdon, they were astonished that he'd come back to Leeds. By the start of the stifling afternoon he'd grown weary of asking questions and hearing the same answers.

Mrs Marsh squinted in the dusty light of her shop. The air was musty, nothing had been cleaned in all the years Simon had known the woman. Her trade was mostly honest, always busy on Monday morning as the wives around Holbeck pledged what they could for money to last the week, in again to redeem everything on a Saturday night after their husbands were paid. Sometimes, though, she dealt in stolen items. Jewellery, mostly.

She seemed ageless, a heavy, shapeless woman, but sharp-eyed, with a keen sense of what things were worth and the profit she might make.

'Was it a man and wife?' she asked.

'Yes.' All the tiredness left him and he felt a prickle of hope. 'Why, were they ever in here?'

'They were,' she told him. 'I remember them clear as day. He acted like he was the one in charge, all very superior.'

Simon smiled; that sounded like Fox.

'What name did they use? What were they trying to sell?'

She snorted. 'They called themselves Fox. The first time they were here, they brought me cheap stuff. I told him that, too. Not worth my time.' The woman took a pinch of snuff from a small tin on the counter. 'He was annoyed, but she seemed amused.'

'When was this?'

'Some time in June,' she replied. 'I don't know exactly when.'

That was when Barton had hired him again, after he'd spotted Fox following him around Leeds.

'You said the first time. How many others were they here?'

The woman was slow to reply. 'Two,' she said finally. 'They came back a few days later.' Another hesitation, then she seemed to make up her mind and plunged on. 'They brought better goods that time. Some little baubles that were worth money. Hardly a fortune, mind, but I bought them. Sold them on easy enough.'

'Both of them came?'

Mrs Marsh shook her head. 'Just him. The last time, it was the pair of them again. It was a Saturday night, I remember that. It's always the busiest time of the week in this trade. They came about an hour before all the wives were set to turn up and take back what they'd had to pledge.'

The Foxes had vanished from Leeds on a Saturday.

'Do you remember when this was?' Simon asked.

'The middle of June,' she replied. 'I'm sure of that. Right around my daughter's birthday.'

The hairs rose on his arms. The Foxes had last been seen on a Saturday in the middle of June. She might have been the last person in town to have seen them.

'What did they bring?'

'More jewellery. Rings, bracelets, a brooch. Wait there . . .' she bustled off into a back room and returned holding an elaborate silver brooch with a deep red stone, maybe a ruby, at its heart. 'I liked that, I decided to keep it for myself,' the woman told him with a blush. 'All the rest was as good as this, too. Got good money for it all, too; I'd have been a fool to turn it down.'

'Did they say why they were suddenly selling so much?'

She turned a withering look on him. 'No, they didn't, and I'm not enough of a damned fool to ask a question like that, Simon Westow. This was the best stuff they'd brought. Enough of it that they came close to cleaning out the money I keep about me.'

'A good sum?'

She gave a sharp nod. 'Enough,' she repeated.

From time to time the rumours circulated that Mrs Marsh was a wealthy woman; he'd heard them for years. There was nothing in her appearance or the shop to show any money, but Simon believed it. She was canny and cunning.

'Did they say much?'

'Hardly a word. When I was counting out the money, she was looking at it like it was a feast.' She chuckled. 'You should have seen her. Any hungrier and she'd have been trying to gulp it down.'

As he walked back towards Briggate, he felt as if he could put together a tale of the Foxes' last few hours in Leeds. They murdered Shackleton and decided to run. Sold all the jewellery they'd gathered to give themselves travelling money and vanished into the night.

Not far enough, though. Jane had discovered Mrs Fox's body in Kirkstall, just three miles from town.

Found the day after Andrew Barton disappeared from his friends at Kirkstall Abbey. Since then he'd been drinking more heavily than before. Had he been involved in her death? Was it guilt that had made him drown himself?

A tale, yes, but so ragged it was in pieces, and so many other ways to tell it.

Rosie might still be with Mrs Barton, but he needed to go there and ask the woman to see if any of her jewellery was missing. If so . . . there was only one person who could have stolen it.

\* \* \*

A sound woke her. Small movements in the kitchen. Knife in hand, Jane crept through, only to see Mrs Shields, dressed and busy with ingredients for her ointments and medicines.

'I can do that for you,' she said, and the old woman turned with a start, suddenly turning pale as her hand moved to her chest.

'Oh child, don't do that. I almost jumped out of my skin.'

But she said it with a quiet laugh and tender smile. Jane helped, learning, until Sally began to stir. The girl was hungry, wolfing down the porridge and bread, back to the appetite she'd had before the beating.

Her eyes were alert, her face alive. Jane helped her from the bed and took her arm, feeling the girl clutch tight as she rose to her feet. The effort and strain showed on her face: squinting, mouth tight. Sally waved her off, kept still for a few seconds, gathering her strength before she managed two halting steps, eyes tightly closed as she took quick, shallow breaths.

She stopped. Very carefully, she turned, moving stiffly back to the bed.

'Enough.' She exhaled the word and Jane steadied her as the girl sank back down, panting and nodding to herself. 'Longer next time.'

Jane had been the same when she was hurt. She'd pushed herself hard. Made herself do more. At times, she saw much of herself in the girl. The desire for revenge would be burning inside, waiting for the chance to flame bright.

Before that, though, she had to heal.

Onions, carrots, beans. Meat from the butcher on Timble Bridge. Back through the courts and yards to come out just below the junction of Boar Lane and Briggate.

Kate was in her usual spot, shouting her wares, beaming as she spotted Jane.

'Here you are. Two meat pies, still warm for you,' she said, and took the three pennies. 'How's the lass?'

'She's starting to walk again.' To stumble, at least, but it was a beginning that would grow better.

The woman's eyes flashed. 'One of those children she looks after said it was very bad.'

'It was. I found the men who hurt her.'

'What are you going to do?'

'That'll be up to her.'

A few minutes with Dodson the beggar, handing him one of the pies after dropping coins in his tin cup. He'd heard nothing of interest, no stray words about anyone named Barton or Fox. But how much of an answer could they ever find for the troubles that plagued someone's mind?

On the way home she stopped by the Market Cross at the head of Briggate. Davy Cassidy was playing his fiddle. Jane closed her eyes and let the music carry her off for a few minutes. A small piece of calm in the day.

'Mr Westow,' Barton said, surprised to see him. 'If you're looking for your wife, she left no more than five minutes ago.'

'No,' Simon said, and saw the confusion in the man's eyes. 'I'd like to speak to you and your wife. Together.'

'Why? Have you found something?' His voice was hopeful, his expression crestfallen when Simon shook his head.

'Not yet. But I need to ask another question.'

Two minutes later the three of them were sitting in the parlour. James Barton seemed lost, disconnected from the world, but his wife had the face of a woman locked in torment. Red, ugly with grief, eyes rimmed. She glared at Simon, as if he'd been responsible for her son's death. He'd have preferred to wait a few days, but the man had asked him to find some answers.

'We know the Foxes left Leeds on a Saturday.' He paused until he was certain he had their attention. 'Before they went, they sold some jewellery to someone who deals in stolen property. She said that there were good items in there. Believe me, I know this is the worst time I could ask, but please, I'd like you to look and check if anything of yours is missing.'

She stood, moving away with a slow tread.

'We're burying Andrew tomorrow,' Barton said into the quiet room. 'The vicar decided he must have had an accident and gone into the water, so he can be buried in consecrated ground.'

What could he say? The sorrow hung heavy all around the house, a pall so strong it might never lift. They waited until the door opened again.

'There are three pieces I can't find.' Her eyes moved to her husband. 'Do you remember the brooch your brother gave me five years ago, the one with the ruby?'

Very like the one Mrs Marsh had decided to keep for herself. No real surprise. The parts were beginning to slide together. A garnet gold ring had gone, too, and a simple, thin gold bracelet she hadn't worn in years.

'Why did you need to know, Mr Westow?' Barton asked.

'At least one of them sounds like an item they sold.' He didn't want to tell them what that meant; better if they thought it out for themselves. Simon gave a small bow. 'Thank you.'

Barton caught up to him outside the front door.

'Do you think Andrew stole them? Is that what you were trying to say?'

'I don't know,' Simon replied. He'd choose his words cautiously. The man wouldn't want to accept the truth. Not yet. His son's death was an open wound.

After the fog in his mind cleared, Barton would understand. The image of his son would crack and tarnish. Let that happen in its own time.

'I tried to talk to her,' Rosie said after Simon settled in the kitchen and rubbed the sweat off his face. The boys had gone down to the river with some of the others from school, enjoying the long days of summer.

'Any joy?'

She shook her head. 'You were just there, you saw her for yourself. All I could do was listen while she talked about Andrew. I didn't attempt to ask any questions; I don't think she'd have understood them.' She sighed. 'Poor woman.'

'We have to try. Barton wants us to find answers.'

'If we can. Andrew's dead. Some things you can't explain with words, Simon. Whatever made him kill himself, it's over now. Mr and Mrs Barton are the ones who'll have to carry the weight and try to understand. They're the ones who'll keep suffering.'

That was true, Simon thought. His own parents had died before he was old enough to fully understand they'd gone. He could barely recall them, couldn't see their faces in his own. He'd been sent to the workhouse, spent twelve hours a day labouring in the mills as soon as he turned six. He'd had no place for grief as he grew up.

'How are we going to find out what happened?'

'I'm not sure we ever will.' Everyone who could tell them was dead. Andrew, Mrs Fox . . . maybe Mr Fox was, too. He sighed. 'But we're being paid, and Barton needs it, so we'll keep trying.'

Where to look, though?

# TWENTY-ONE

Sally stood again, gritting her teeth and swallowing hard as she pushed herself up from the bed. Jane watched as she paced slowly and stiffly across the room, reaching to touch the wall, then back again.

Quarter of an hour later, she made herself do it again. Then every five minutes for the rest of the hour.

'That's enough for today,' Mrs Shields told her finally. She rubbed ointment on Sally's wounds and made her drink from a mug. 'Sleep now. It will help.'

Jane picked up her book and slipped outside to read in the July warmth, quickly losing herself again in the American woods with Natty Bumppo and *The Pioneers*. At first, she'd wondered if she'd been gone too long, but within three pages she was there once more, a part of it all.

Later, as dusk fell, Jane took a handful of coins from behind the loose brick where she kept her money.

She pulled the shawl up over her hair.

'Going to see the children?' Catherine Shields asked quietly. She was sitting by the bed, her own book open on her lap.

'Someone has to help while Sally's poorly.'

It wasn't a task she'd expected, not one she wanted, but someone needed to do it. Years had passed since she'd been a child out there, but the memories stayed sharp.

The money she gave wouldn't last longer than a day or two. But without it, some would probably die, even in this weather. She could afford it. Even more than the coins that could feed them, they'd be clamouring for news of Sally.

Early morning brought thick clouds, the heat building until it seemed to press down on his chest. The threat of rain made Simon's skin prickle as he stood by the coffee cart. He was sweating in his wool coat, palms slick as he gripped the metal knob of his walking stick.

No real gossip. It was that season when little happened and time felt sluggish. The Bartons would never forget this day, though, when they lowered their son into the ground.

He'd wondered about going and decided against it. Let them keep their dignity, and their anguish private.

That left him . . . with nothing to help his search.

There was one man he could go and see, the visit he'd put off the day before. The man with the damaged knee. But at eleven, just as the bell at St John's Church began to toll for the dead, he walked past the door on the Head Row for the fourth time, still undecided whether to knock.

For the love of God, Simon told himself, if he was that unsure, it was better to leave it. He marched away. Knowing all the while that he'd return and face the same indecision.

Jane watched the girl move again. With each pace, Sally seemed to grow a little stronger.

Mrs Shields beamed with pleasure at the way the patient was healing. Even faster than she'd hoped, Jane knew. The broken nose would be somewhere close to its original shape. But the scar on her cheek would remain; the men had left their mark on her.

Wearing an old dress Jane bought for her at a clothes stall, with a hand to steady herself, she stepped outside, blinking in the light as she settled herself on the wooden bench with a deep sigh. The muted sounds from the Head Row seeped in, and the air was filled with the stink and smoke of the factories. She breathed it in like the freshest scent she'd ever known.

'Do you remember the names of all the men who hurt me?' she asked after five minutes.

'Of course I do.'

'I want to know all about them. Where they live, where they go.' She looked thoughtful, making her plans. 'When the children come again, I'll ask them to do it.'

Her little army. The ones nobody ever noticed or remembered.

'What are you going to do to them?' Jane asked.

'I'm not going to kill them.' Her voice was slow and considered; she'd given this some thought. 'They're all from money, aren't they?'

'Yes.'

'They've already done this to me.' She gestured at her body. 'I'm not going to risk hanging for them. If I killed them, their families would make sure I was found.'

'Then what else?'

'I'll give them something they'll see every time they look in the mirror. Make sure they remember me for the rest of their lives so they can regret it every single day.'

'I already did that to one of them.'

Sally gave a cold, satisfied smile. 'That's what gave me the idea.' Her fingertips traced the wound on her cheek. 'I'll never have the chance to forget. Why should they?' Her gaze moved to the book next to Jane's hand. 'Is it a good story?'

'Very good.'

'What's it called?'

'*The Pioneers.*' She held it up, pronouncing the letters as she traced them.

'What's it about?'

How could she describe it to someone who knew nothing about geography or history?

'It's a story set in another country. America, on the other side of the ocean. The main character is called Natty Bumppo and he knows a lot of Native Americans. They're the people who lived there before the white men came.'

Sally wrinkled her nose. 'Natty Bumppo. That's a strange name. What does it mean?'

'I don't know,' she replied. 'Maybe they use it over there.'

'Could you read some of it to me?'

The request took her by surprise. The girl had never shown any interest in books or stories. Perhaps she'd enjoyed the soothing sound when Mrs Shields read to her. More likely she just needed something to fill all the empty time.

'I'm halfway through. You won't know what's happening.'

'I don't mind. Please?'

Before she could start, Wilfred and Hannah arrived through the gap in the wall at Green Dragon Yard, loud and overjoyed to see Sally out in the sun. Jane tucked the book under her arm and went back into the house.

\* \* \*

The rain never arrived on Tuesday. The oppressive feel lingered into Wednesday, the sense of a torrent growing more and more imminent, as if the heavens could open at any moment. The only talk at the coffee cart was Andrew Barton's funeral. Simon already knew the truth; he didn't need the rumours. He drained the tin cup and made his way home.

He'd barely closed the door before the rain began. Hammering on the roof and windows, a deluge that bounced high off the flagstones and the cobbles. Loud, overwhelming. As he watched through the window, a stream formed along Swinegate, swirling and spreading over the cobbles until it claimed all the dirt and the rubbish and bore it away.

A quarter of an hour and it stopped as suddenly as it began. Water still rushed along the street, but as he opened the door and stood outside, the air felt cleansed, all the grime washed away from Leeds. The air was cooler and the wet town appeared to shine.

An illusion, of course. A few minutes and it would pass. But for this one short moment he could enjoy it.

Simon had barely settled at the table and opened the *Mercury* when he heard the knocking on the door.

Mr Barton had been caught in the weather. His cape dripped water on the kitchen floor, clutching his hat between his hands. He opened his mouth, then closed it again, as if he wasn't sure where to begin.

'Give me your coat,' Rosie told him. 'You're drenched.'

'Yes,' he said as he shrugged it off. The man looked dazed, Simon thought. He blinked and looked about him. 'I suppose I am.'

'We're both so very sorry about your son,' she continued. 'Your wife . . .'

He gave a grave nod and a sigh that seemed to fill the room. 'Thank you.'

'Has something happened?' Simon asked. It must be something important for him to trudge here through the downpour with the pain of the funeral overflowing in his heart.

'It has . . .' he began, then hesitated again, confusion flickering across his face. 'That is, I think it has.' He plucked at something on the sleeve of his coat. 'There were only a few of us for the burial yesterday. That was my wife's request. She wanted it to be small, very private.' He left a long pause while he summoned the words. 'Once it was done, I happened to turn toward the gate, where it opens on to the road.'

'The lychgate,' Simon said, wondering what was coming.

'I'm sure I saw Fox standing there, watching us.'

'Fox?' How? The man had to be dead or gone. Nobody had seen him since he'd left Leeds.

'Are you sure it was him?' Rosie said softly.

'No.' Barton kept his voice low, as if the event was some strange wonder. 'I'm not. Seeing him was the last thing I expected. It took me by complete surprise. He held my gaze for a second. I closed my eyes and when I looked again, there was nobody there.' He swallowed, then raised his head to look at them, unsure of everything. 'I don't see how it can be. But it certainly seemed like him.'

Simon was quiet. He didn't know what to say. Had Barton experienced a moment of madness, some vision conjured out of grief, or had it been real? Could Fox have returned? It didn't seem possible . . . but they'd never found any trace of him.

'What do you want me to do?' he asked.

'I want you to search for him, Mr Westow.' Barton was pleading, the ache a weight in his voice. 'Believe me, I know what this must sound like to you, but I honestly believe I saw him. I'm not a stupid man. I spent all last night asking myself questions. I'm convinced Fox is here again.'

'I can try.'

'He's the one who knows what happened. He can tell me why Andrew killed himself. I need those answers. My wife and . . . we both need them. Please, Mr Westow.'

How could he promise to find someone who might be a ghost? What if the man had returned? Barton wanted to believe that. What would he do if they found nothing? Could he accept that as the truth?

Simon glanced across at Rosie. Her face showed nothing, but she gave a tiny nod.

'Tell me what you remember about it. What was he wearing?'

# TWENTY-TWO

Porter sat back in his chair, staring at the ceiling of his office and rubbing the bristles on his chin. Not much more than an hour and a half since the rain had lashed down and the refreshing coolness had already vanished, a stifling heat returning; the windows were open wide to try and catch a thin breeze.

'It sounds like grief to me, Westow.' He shifted his gaze to stare out at the sky. 'Or imagination. How likely does it seem to you?'

'Not very,' Simon admitted. 'But we never did find a trace of Fox. You sent letters to the constables of the towns around Yorkshire.'

'And I heard nothing back. If you want my guess, Fox is dead somewhere and the animals have feasted on him. Good luck to them. Barton wants someone to blame for his son committing suicide.'

That was very likely the truth of it, and the man had seen a phantom constructed of desperation and sorrow. But Simon had agreed to search; Barton would be paying his fee . . . and there was the small chance that Fox had really been standing by the lychgate to watch the burial.

'Can you ask your men to keep their eyes open for him?'

A nod and a small chuckle. 'Don't expect too much. None of them are that good at raising the dead.'

Jane frowned as she listened to Simon. How could Fox have simply reappeared, completely unnoticed? It didn't seem possible.

'Do you believe it?' she asked.

'I don't know,' he admitted. 'I truly don't. Barton does. That's enough.'

Sally was standing, wearing a cotton dress and old woollen stockings. Mrs Shields had brushed the girl's hair, patiently working through all the tangles to leave it shining. The bruises and cuts were beginning to fade on her face, though the black eyes and nose were still swollen.

Jane glanced at her. The strain was showing on the girl's face, knuckles white where she held on to a chest of drawers to keep herself upright.

'Did anyone else see him?' Jane asked.

'Barton says not, and when he looked again, there was nothing. He's not a fool; he knows it might have been his imagination. But he wants us to search. You saw him, you'd recognise him.'

'Yes.'

'Will you help?'

She hesitated. There was probably nobody to find. She glanced at Sally, seeing the girl's encouraging smile.

'Yes,' Jane said. 'I will.'

Simon hurried around the town, searching out the petty thieves, the fences, anyone who might be able to help. Describing Fox, offering money for solid information on the man. The chance of a few easy coins caught their attention, but nobody had seen Fox.

It had to be Barton's fevered dream, his wishful thinking. Simon knew that, but now he'd agreed, he was going to pursue it all until he was certain there was nothing left to find.

There was little more he could do during the day. Pass the word and hope. Tonight would be different, once the drinkers and the dangerous were out on the streets.

He walked up the Head Row and stopped outside the injured man's front door again, leaning on his stick. Simon stood and gazed for a full minute, then hobbled away again. If the man was there, what did he hope to find? The name of the one who'd decided not to fight? Maybe it would be better to let it lie. He'd done some damage; perhaps that was enough.

Sally was improving, maybe the world was starting to look brighter again, returning to the way it ought to be. He sighed and turned for home, ready to rest until darkness came.

The morning's downpour felt like a memory. Rain had scoured the streets clean, but a few hours later the cobbles were covered in horse dung once more as Jane picked her way across Albion Street. She stayed alert, eyes always moving. She didn't expect to see Fox, but there was always the small chance.

Very few whores out during the day. Their real trade arrived with the night. But two or three could still spread the word, and the promise of money would make them eager. On Vicar Lane, she squatted beside Dodson the beggar and talked to him for a few minutes, hearing about this and that, telling him about the books she'd read, then putting coins in his old cup as she left.

Jane passed the word to the people she knew. The more who were looking for Fox, the greater the chance of finding him. Was he here at all? Since the day Simon found the body at Grey's Court, she'd had no sense of the man in Leeds, never felt a trace that he was in town. Two people had been strangled. He couldn't be stupid enough to return, could he?

She saw three of the children standing on a corner, looking for a likely purse to cut. If they were caught, they'd be crammed into a ship and sent to the other side of the world. No mercy from the courts. They spotted her and stepped back. She told them about Fox, what he looked like, how he moved. A coin each and she sent them on their way to tell the others to begin looking.

Nothing more to do until evening. Three pies from Kate, one for each of them, sitting outside the cottage in the warmth. Sally walked before she ate. The steps were still slow, but growing stronger and she managed five full minutes before she sat and tore into the food with a deep hunger.

'You were going to read to me yesterday,' she said as she took a drink of cordial.

'The children came.'

She turned a curious eye to Jane. 'Would you do it now?'

The girl was quiet, keeping still as she listened. Her eyes closed, but she wasn't sleeping. Jane kept glancing over at Sally, watching the expression on her face change with the turns in the story.

After an hour her throat was dry, her voice growing scratchy. She closed the book.

'I liked that,' Sally said. She had a note of wonder in her voice. 'Is there really somewhere like that?'

'America? Yes.'

'He makes it all seem real.'

Jane smiled. 'A good book can do that. Mrs Shields taught me to read.'

'I'd like to learn. I don't know if I can, though.'

'Why not?'

'It seems like a lot. I don't know if I can manage all that.'

Jane smiled. 'People do it all the time. Simon's sons can read.'

'Yes, but they were little when they started.' Sally stared at the ground. 'Maybe that makes a difference. Would you try to teach me?'

The question caught her off-guard. The girl had always seemed content without knowing; she'd never seen the need for it. It wasn't long since Jane had learned, then started to devour words. Maybe it took time for the appetite to develop.

'I can try. I don't know if I can teach anything.'

A short lesson to start, dipping a toe in the water, until Sally began to look weary.

'Can we do more tomorrow?' she asked.

'Yes.'

Sally pushed herself up. She'd come back quickly from the broken, unconscious girl the children had found on the road. She was healing well. Another two or three days and she'd be ready to move back to Simon's house. Once that happened, would she still want to learn to read?

Jane sat on the bench, took out her knife and whetstone, and put a keen edge on the blade.

At dusk, she slipped out through the hole in the wall, along Green Dragon Yard and through the courts and yards. Plenty of noise from the inns and beershops, but she kept moving.

Alice Kearey. That was the woman she wanted. A mother of sorts to the whores. Out here longer than most. Strong, a survivor.

It took time to find her, standing by the entrance to a court off Briggate, a sharp, wary look in her eyes.

'Not seen you in a while.' She was smoking a pipe with a short stem, her teeth stained and brown. Scrawny, with a lined face that made her look old before her time, a shawl covering curly dark hair that held the first streaks of grey. 'You must want something.'

Jane told her. 'There's money for good information.'

A snort. 'What do you call good, pet? Any of the women here could make up a convincing tale. We do it half a dozen times a night.'

'He calls himself Fox.'

'Names can change faster than the weather.'

'He seems to keep to his.' She placed three pennies in the woman's hand. 'Tell everyone. Please.'

Other places, other groups of prostitutes. Down by the Hol Beck, back across the river to the bottom end of Mabgate where it met Quarry Hill.

She made her way home in full darkness. Only light leaking from behind the shutters to guide her. Suddenly she was aware of something, a small sound on the edge of her hearing. She stopped; it continued for a moment. Someone was there. She could feel the heartbeat in her blood.

Jane slid a hand into her pocket and grasped the knife handle. Drew it out and held it by her side, ready. Who was there? One of the men who'd attacked Sally? Someone who saw a woman alone as easy prey?

Easy to slip off into a ginnel, to vanish as if she'd never existed. Jane breathed quietly, listening. Soft footsteps, someone trying to move quietly. She heard them go past. But even if they'd glanced down the entry, they'd never have seen her.

Then she was out again, behind him. Now she was the hunter. A glimmer of light from an upstairs room captured the shape for a second; from the size, the way the figure moved, she was following a man.

His shoe caught a pebble; it skittered down the street, loud enough to make him stop. She edged closer. He never turned, not aware of her at all.

A few moments and he moved again. More cautious now, slower, pausing to cock his head and listen. But she was silent; all he heard were the sounds of the night: a voice off somewhere, bellowing and angry, a trace of song from behind a window, the hungry cry of a child.

They were drawing closer to town, through the streets of Quarry Hill and down towards Timble Bridge. A chained dog barked and surged at the man. In a panic, he jumped two steps back.

Her chance.

She raised her knife and pricked the back of his neck. Suddenly he was completely still.

'Keep walking.' Her voice was a whisper close to his ear. 'Round the corner.'

The animal stopped its racket, its growls turning to a few angry snarls.

'Drop your knife.' He didn't move. Another prod of the blade, enough to start a trickle of blood. Jane felt the last few days weigh heavy on her and suddenly she had no patience for this. All she wanted was to be at home, to fall into sleep. Finally, the quiet clatter of metal on the cobbles. She kicked it away, well out of reach and lost in the night.

The fear came off him in waves. He was terrified, he didn't understand how this could have happened. Bested by a woman.

'What's your name?' At first, he didn't reply. She sliced along the back of his neck. Felt him flinch and heard his gasp. 'What's your name?'

'Young,' he replied finally. 'Carter Young.'

She'd never heard it before.

'Why were you following me?'

'I wasn't—'

Another cut, just enough to stop the lie before it could flower. 'Why?'

'I was hired.'

Why would anyone pay to have someone go after her? 'Who?'

'All I know is his name is Fox. Never seen him before today.'

Fox. She kept the surge of fury buried inside, breathing quietly and evenly.

She forced him to tell it all. The chance meeting in a dram shop late in the afternoon. The promise of money to stop her or Simon. Young knew a prostitute who told him someone had been round offering money for the act. He'd found Fox up by Mabgate.

'How did he want you to stop me?' Even before she spoke, Jane knew the answer; she just wanted to hear him say it.

'He didn't care. Kill you if I could get away with it.'

'How much did he offer you?'

'A guinea.'

That was what her life was worth. A single guinea.

'Did he show you the money?'

Young shook his head. 'He told me to be in Brice's beershop tomorrow morning after it was done and bring some proof. He said he'd come and pay me then.' His voice quavered. 'A guinea can buy a lot.'

'You thought it would buy my death.'

A hesitation, then: 'Yes.'

'Give me one reason why it shouldn't buy yours.'

She knew she was talking too much. Trying to stave off the moment when she'd need to decide. Killing him would prove nothing. All it would bring were questions she didn't need. A disfigured enemy sent a loud message.

Before he could pull away, she darted in. A deep cut down one palm, the blood welling up, then the same to the other. Finally, a slice with the sharp blade along his bottom lip until it was only attached at one end.

Jane stepped back, out of his reach. But he was too busy, staring at his hands in horror even as he reached for his face. Trying to staunch all the blood and hold on to his flapping lip.

'This was a lesson you won't forget. Come after any of us again and we'll kill you. Do you understand that? Do you?'

She waited until he nodded, distracted by the blood and the pain. Then she turned and marched off into the darkness. Her heartbeat was racing, thudding so hard she felt it might break through her ribs.

Fox.

# TWENTY-THREE

'Fox.' Simon rolled the name around his tongue. Jane had found him at the coffee cart, listening to people wondering about a man called Fox. Not that any of them had seen him. Just his work was paying off. He'd been out the night before, back into the beershops and dramshops. Asking his questions and finally going home with nothing at all. Maybe the man had only existed in Barton's grief, he thought.

Now, listening to Jane tell him everything as they walked up Briggate, he knew it was real. Fox was back.

'The man who came after you—'

'He'll be staying out of sight for a long time.'

'Fox promised to pay him for killing either of us?'

'A guinea.' She spat out the words.

'Did he show this man . . .'

'. . . Carter Young . . .'

'. . . the money?'

'No. Told him where to be this morning and he'd pay him then.'

'Where was it?'

'Brice's beershop. I already looked. He was never likely to appear.'

By now, he imagined Fox would be lucky to still possess a guinea. He'd used words and promises. But why would the man offer to pay someone to kill *them*? What was the sense in that?

'Do you understand it?' he asked.

She shook her head. 'Why wouldn't he just get the man to kill Barton?'

'I don't know,' Simon said. 'I really don't know.' He thought for a moment. 'Come with me.'

'The master's down at the grave,' Barton's servant told them in a hushed voice. 'He's started going in the morning.'

They found him in St John's churchyard, standing by a pile of dirt that would gradually settle back into place.

His head was bowed, hat grasped in his hands. The lines in his face had turned into valleys, with deep shadows under his eyes from sleep that refused to come. A voice like a low, rusted croak after Simon spoke his name.

'Have you seen Fox?'

'No. But you were right. He's definitely in Leeds.'

That made him pay attention. 'He is? How do you know?'

Simon looked at Jane. She gave a small shake of her head, so he told the story.

'Why would he do that?' Barton frowned, confused. But no more than they were.

'I wish I knew. But he might convince someone to try for you.'

Barton shuffled, a few paces to his left, then back. Finally, he turned and exhaled.

'Find Fox. Do that and it all stops. Find him and discover why my son took his own life.'

'Are you going home from here?'

'Yes.'

'Will you stay there?'

'That's my intention.'

A last nod and he walked off. Simon nodded for Jane to follow and see him safely back to the house. Barton disappeared through the lychgate and out of sight. He'd never acknowledged Jane was there, Simon noted. But she was the one who'd found his son's body. In his mind, maybe he laid some blame on her for the death.

Find Fox before he persuaded someone else to come for them. Someone better than Carter Young.

The man had to be staying somewhere. But there were too many lodging houses and rooms in Leeds to begin searching through them all.

They'd set things in motion. People were looking. Now they had to wait, to be patient and that the promise of money would make sure people kept their eyes sharp.

'You're so much better, child.' The old woman beamed as she watched Sally's awkward walk. 'It's been quicker than I'd expected after the way you were when you arrived. You're ready to go home.'

Jane saw the relief on the girl's face.

'I don't know how to thank you. Both of you. You . . .' She searched for the words then gave up, shaking her head instead. The eagerness shone in her eyes. Going back to the attic room at Simon and Rosie's would mean she was almost well.

'Just be careful,' Mrs Shields warned. 'You still need to give your body time.' Her fingertips traced the line of the cut across Sally's face. 'This will always be there. But you'll forget about it.'

'No, I won't. I'll remember.' Her voice was hard. 'I'll always remember.'

They kept a slow pace from Green Dragon Yard down to Swinegate. Jane walked beside Sally, there in case the girl stumbled or grew weary. But always with a hand on her knife, all her senses aware of the people milling about them. Watching, taking in the faces.

But with their shawls drawn over their hair, they were invisible.

'What about reading?' Jane asked. 'Do you still want another lesson?'

'Yes,' she replied. But she sounded as though she hadn't given it a thought, caught up in the excitement of going home. 'Could we do it tomorrow?'

'Of course.' But would tomorrow become the next day, then the one after that?

'Rosie can help you, too. Simon. Rich and Amos.' No shortage of people in the house to teach her.

'I know . . .'

Maybe she'd keep going. Maybe not. It was probably a distraction, something to relieve the boredom.

By Boar Lane they stopped to see Kate the pie-seller.

'Fresh in, not even five minutes ago,' she said, staring at Sally's face. 'You took a proper battering, pet.'

'I know.' A blush glowed through the bruises that coloured Sally's face.

'Have one of these.' A grin. 'It can't cure you, but at least it'll fill your belly. No charge for you, today only. But you tell anyone and you'll feel the rough side of my tongue.'

'One for me, too,' Jane said; she handed over the coins.

'This is a good batch.' Kate turned back to Sally. 'You watch out for yourself.'

Eating as they strolled down towards the river, then along Swinegate. The house stood on the corner, and she saw the last stiffness leave Sally's body as they drew close.

Home. It would help to heal her.

'Almost cut off his lip?' Constable Porter nodded in admiration. 'She's quite a one.'

'I know.'

'So Fox has come back.' He let out a long breath and rubbed his chin. 'He has to answer for two murders.'

'I've put the word out,' Simon told him.

'If you find him, let me have him, Westow.'

'I have a few questions of my own first.'

'Just make sure you turn him over to us in one piece.'

'I will, and if you find him . . .'

'I'll give the two of you five minutes together.' He paused and ran his tongue around the inside of his mouth. 'Want to make it interesting?' He rummaged in his pocket and brought out a sixpence. 'I'll wager you this my men track him down before you.'

It cut against the grain to bet on work. But if it made everyone look harder, why not?

'Done.'

Nothing to do but walk and wait. Twenty minutes later, Simon stood on the Head Row, leaning on his stick and breathing heavily as he looked at the house where the man he'd injured lived.

It was time. If he didn't do this now, he might as well turn away and never come back.

He rapped on the wood, waiting until the landlady turned the key and opened the door a few inches. Just wide enough to let her assess him.

'Who are you?'

He took off his hat and made a small bow. 'My name is Simon Westow. I believe the man who has his rooms here hurt himself the other night.'

'Took a bad fall,' she told him. 'Why? What is it to you?'

'I wanted to ask after him.' He held up the stick and smiled at her. 'I might be able to offer him some advice.'

'Does he know you?'

'We've met.' That much was true, at least.

For a moment he wondered if she'd close the door in his face. Finally she decided and pulled it back.

'Up the stairs. I've heard him moving around.'

Everything was clean, the wood polished, not a speck of dust to be seen as Simon knocked lightly on the door.

Uneven steps, and then he was facing a young man who stood awkwardly, leaning heavily on the stick in his left hand. Dressed in a shirt and stock of brilliant white and a jacket that fitted close against his body, he was a gentleman of fashion. But one who couldn't stand tall with a damaged knee.

'Yes?' he asked. He looked at Simon with a sneer. 'What do you want?'

He'd taken the man by surprise. 'You mean you don't remember me . . . friend?'

'No . . .' he began, and then he realised. His face changed, suddenly pale. He tried to back away and close the door, but Simon took two paces forward. He was inside, and the young man was still retreating.

A moment to close the door behind him and take in the room. Bright, airy, smelling of tobacco and the jug of coffee on the table.

'I . . . how did you find me?'

'People tell me things. Don't worry, I'm not here to hurt you.' A short glance at the man's leg. 'I came to talk. Fetch some cups and we'll sit at the table.

'Are you in much pain?' Simon asked as the man lowered himself to the other chair and eased out his leg.

'The physician said you did something to it. He explained, but I didn't follow.' The corners of his mouth slipped down. 'He claims it will ease in time, but I'll have problems for the rest of my life. I'll always need to use a stick.'

'I won't apologise, Mr . . .'

'My name is Collins.'

'Mr Collins. You know who I am.' A flicker of a smile. 'I hope you do, since you and your friend tried to kill me.'

'We only intended to warn you. To hurt you a little and discourage you.'

'I see. Why would you want to do that?'

The man's hand shook as he raised the cup to his lips and coffee spilled on the table.

'The girl got what was coming to her.'

'Did she? That was as bad a beating as I've ever seen.' No need to raise his voice. Collins's eyes were enough to terrify him. 'She'll have a scar on her face. You and your friends gave her that, then left her to die.'

He shook his head. 'I . . .'

'If you're going to say you weren't there, it doesn't matter. You became a part of it when you went after me.'

'I'll spend the rest of my days paying for that.'

'We always pay for our mistakes.' Simon tapped his own damaged leg. 'Tell me, who was with you that night?'

For long, strained moments he wasn't sure if the young man would answer. If he didn't . . . no violence or threats. He'd try persuasion or simply leave.

'Billy. Billy Harding.'

Good. He had that information. 'Did you both take part in beating the girl?'

Collins shook his head. 'We weren't here. At a ball in Ripon. Billy's cousin.'

Simon didn't understand. 'Then why would you threaten me?'

'Charles heard you'd been asking questions. He said that since we missed the fun, we could be part of it by warning you off.'

'Charles.' He racked his brain for the name. 'Ibbotson?'

'Yes.'

Simon drained the cup. No better than coffee from the cart. He pushed himself upright. He'd found what he came for.

'Good day to you, Mr Collins. I wish you a speedy recovery.'

The man's expression was a mixture of relief and disbelief that it had ended so peaceably. Let him wonder, Simon thought as he walked up the Head Row.

Billy Harding. It shouldn't take too long to find him.

Charles Ibbotson. He remembered the man.

# TWENTY-FOUR

The cottage felt strange, Jane thought. Too empty, too spacious. She'd grown used to Sally being here and now the difference was stark.

Jane moved a hot pan from the stove for Mrs Shields, the scent of elderflower cordial filling the kitchen. A final look around before she placed the basket over her arm, pulled the shawl over her hair, and started for the market.

This was a domestic day. There was nothing more she could do now in this search for Fox. Simply stay aware of danger and keep her knife close and sharp.

Onions, potatoes and long beans. One final stop for meat. She'd just come out of the butcher's shop on Timble Bridge, counting coins to be sure she'd received the proper change, when she felt someone watching her.

Hitching up the basket, she slipped her knife into her hand and began to walk. A short lane led to the gates of the burial yard. As good a spot as she was going to find in the middle of the day. She turned, ready.

The boy held up his hands, mouth open wide in fear as he suddenly faced the blade. A child of seven or eight, hair clumped and matted, face sharp with the cunning he needed to survive. The words rushed out of him.

'Hannah says can you come, miss. She thinks she's seen the man you wanted.'

She followed, heart pounding as questions rippled through her mind. Could it be Fox? That would be too simple, too easy.

Over Leeds Bridge, hurrying along Water Lane. Past Marshall Street, with its big factory, to the end of Kellets Row, close to the mill ponds. The girl was sitting on a low wall, so still that she was barely noticeable. As Jane approached, she stood and moved a few yards, out of sight of the street.

'Is it him?'

'I don't know.' She glanced back at the street. 'It could be.

All we have is what you told us.' Her face clouded. 'He had someone with him. A woman.'

A woman? She wondered for a moment. That didn't feel right. No reason she could name, nothing more than her sense of the man. Still, he was somewhere in Leeds, and this was the first hope they'd had of him.

'Which house?'

'The third one along with the strips of paint peeling off the door.'

'He's in there now?'

Hannah nodded. 'One of the boys saw him earlier and came to fetch me. I started to follow him. He met the woman this side of the bridge and they came back here.' Her eyes narrowed. 'I think it was about an hour ago.'

Jane took coins from her pocket and gave them to the girl. Another penny for the boy who'd found her. She calculated: back to Green Dragon Yard with the basket, find Simon. It would take time.

'Can you keep watch for another hour or two?'

'Yes.'

'Sally's gone home.'

The girl smiled. 'I know. One of the others saw you both going to Swinegate.'

Simon stared at Kellets Row. Back-to-back houses, no more than a few years old, but the bricks already smoke-blackened. Jane stood beside him; she'd found him walking with the constable and given him the news.

Porter was on his way with men from the watch. The law wanted Fox for murder; he'd let them do the rough work of dragging the man out of the house.

'You said you haven't seen him yourself?' he asked.

'No.'

All of them were hoping the man behind that door was Frederick Fox, that they could write an ending to the story. But the chances were slight when there were so many men in Leeds. Still, if it was him . . . He sighed. Lady Luck wouldn't just be smiling down on them. She'd be giving them a wide grin.

He stayed by the corner after the inspector and two members of the watch arrived and marched to the house behind Porter. The knock echoed, then the men disappeared inside. Only one entrance. No easy escape if Fox was really in there.

Three minutes and the men trooped out again. Porter dismissed them and shambled along the flagstones, hands pushed into his pockets.

'It's definitely not him. Married with a child. A mechanic at the Round Foundry.' He shook his head. 'We're back where we began.' His gaze moved to Jane. 'Next time just make sure it's Fox before you come for us.'

'Don't pay any attention to him,' Simon assured her as they crossed Leeds Bridge. Below them, the river stank with chemicals from dyes and waste. A pair of dead rats floated downstream. The wharves were busy, barges moored two and three deep with men scurrying across planks with the cargoes. 'You did the right thing. If that had been Fox, he'd have been cock-a-hoop and singing his own praises. Keep them looking.'

'The children have never seen him,' Jane said. 'All they can do is guess.'

'Yes. Next time we'll wait to tell Porter. Make sure it's the right man.'

She nodded; at the Head Row she turned towards Green Dragon Yard. He strode on, stopping at Mudie's printing shop. No reason to go there, but nowhere better to be.

'Did you honestly believe you'd find him so quickly, Simon?'

'Not really. But . . .'

'If wishes were horses, beggars would ride. Ever heard that?'

Simon chuckled. 'He's here somewhere. He already conned one man into going after us.'

'Is he still alive?'

'He won't want to be seen for a while.'

Simon saw the man's expression change; Mudie didn't ask for more.

Another few minutes and he left. Safe enough among the crowds on the street.

The house felt different. Full once more, alive. A burble of conversation from upstairs. Richard, Amos, Sally, all eager and speaking over each other. In the kitchen, Rosie was stirring a pan, the rich smell of meat filling the room. With the girl here, it felt like home again.

'Did Jane find you?'

Simon nodded. 'It wasn't Fox.' He raised his eyes, looking up to the ceiling. 'It's like having a family back, isn't it?'

Rosie laughed. 'I thought exactly the same when she came in. Do you know the first thing she wanted? Some bread, even before she went upstairs.'

'How did she manage the steps?' Two sets, going all the way up to the attic.

'Slowly. But she was steady.'

Walking from Mrs Shields's house, climbing the stairs . . . only a short time since that had looked impossible. But young bodies made fast recoveries, even if she'd carry some scars forever, probably far more of them inside. He'd had a raw childhood in the workhouse, bullied day after day in the factory. But at least he'd had somewhere to sleep and his meals. Both Sally and Jane had needed to survive on the streets every day, to find food, to remain one step ahead of death. They were tougher than he'd ever be. In some ways, older than he'd ever been. He heard Sally laugh upstairs. The sooner she was busy again, the better. He needed her skills, and with little to fill her time, she'd be restless, bored with the world. For now, though, the boys could keep her entertained.

A breeze began to blow after dark. Jane felt it rippling her skirts as she walked up and down Briggate, back talking to the whores in the slim hope one of them might have seen Fox. But not a single one of them knew him.

The man was still out there. She knew it, she felt it in her blood. Somewhere in Leeds. Whatever he was planning would come soon, she was certain of that.

The first fat drops of rain sent her scurrying for home. The streets were suddenly quiet as she ran. Far off to the west, rumbles of thunder boomed, growing louder each time. Lightning lit the world for a brief moment and the rain grew heavier.

Jane was soaked by the time she locked the door behind her. She spread her clothes over the chair to dry and stuffed newspaper into her boots. Towelling her hair with an old piece of linen, she caught sight of herself in the mirror before she pulled on her nightdress.

A woman now. She knew it, she'd known it for a few years, but each time, the sight took her by surprise. Thunder exploded overhead, making her jump as the windows rattled.

'Child, are you home?' Mrs Shields called.

'I'm here,' she replied, and went to her.

The storm lingered, lightning flashed and thunder rolled, with the rain lashing down outside. She felt safe inside these four walls.

Not inside her own mind, though. The girl returned to her dreams, carried from the mill with a scream that cracked the world open. She sat up in bed, struggling through the fog of sleep as it echoed through her head. It was all her imagination, she *knew* that, but still real enough to terrify her. Why did it keep returning?

She settled back down, heart still racing, and closed her eyes. Fox. What could they do about Fox?

The rain had cleared long before Simon woke and made his way to the coffee cart on Briggate. Cooler, with a breeze, but the air was smudged with early smoke from the factory chimneys; around him, voices hummed with news of a dead body. But it was all too vague: a young man, someone said; another claimed he'd heard it was some old devil. That didn't tell him a damned thing.

'Yes, there's a body,' Constable Porter said when Simon had climbed the steps at the courthouse. 'But it was Elias Cutler. You know him? Hadn't been well for a while, according to the neighbours and went off in his sleep. I'd have sent a message if it was anything to do with Fox.'

No closer to finding the man. He felt the frustration eating at him. Where else could he look?

At home, Sally was eating a heel of bread in the kitchen, eyes bright. Rosie stood in the hall, adjusting a hat in the mirror. She was wearing her favourite plum gown; going visiting, he decided.

'I'll tell the women about Fox's return,' she told him. 'He's going to need money. He might be after some jewellery.'

Simon nodded, feeling a flash of anger for not thinking of it himself. Work she could do that he couldn't. Perhaps she'd discover something, some little thread they could pull.

With a sigh, he settled on the bench. Sally was watching him.

'What are you going to do today?' she asked.

He had no answer for her. Nobody else to ask. He'd been out again last night, caught in the rain as he moved between the beershops and the inns, stuck in the Talbot watching coaches come and go until the downpour eased and he could walk home. Nobody knew anything about Fox. He was here in Leeds, but he was invisible.

Yet somebody knew where to find him. Who?

'What do we know about Fox?' he asked.

'He knew that man Shackleton,' Sally said. 'The one who was strangled in Grey's Court.'

'Fox or his wife murdered him.' But it was something. A woman had rented the room; that could only have been Mrs Fox. Why?

Shackleton and Frederick Fox had met in York prison. What reason did they have for wanting him here? Why kill him when he came? They'd never discovered much about the man. It was time to dig for more.

'Do you want me to help?' Sally's voice was hopeful. He smiled; she was eager to work again.

'A few more days,' he said, and saw disappointment flood her face. 'You'll be busy soon enough, I can promise you that.'

Jane read for a while, then closed the book. She was close to the end of *The Pioneers* and she didn't want it to finish. She'd become a part of that world, felt she was deep in America. The author made it all so real.

There would be other books to carry her away and other places to visit, but she wasn't ready to leave this one quite yet. She laced up her boots and raised the shawl over her hair.

'A walk, child?' Mrs Shields asked.

'Some air.'

She wandered wherever her feet led her, and let the thoughts play and jangle in her mind. Somewhere near Central Market,

Davy Cassidy was playing his fiddle. She stayed clear of Kate the pie-seller, Dodson and any of the familiar faces. Lost inside her own head as she covered the streets on the other side of the bridge, following the canal towpath east as far as Thwaite's Mill.

The river rushed over a weir, loud and fast to power the water wheels and the machinery. A slick scent from the seeds crushed to make lighting oil. Set on an island between river and canal, it was a world apart. All round, the leaves were bright green, the underbrush ragged.

Jane stood, absorbing it all, blocking out the heavy thunder of the wheels. After a long while she turned back, not even sure why she'd come out here. There was nothing she especially wanted to see. Only the pleasure of walking. Perhaps this was as close as she could imagine to the America of her book.

The familiarity of Leeds grew around her. The chimneys and the dirt and the stink that felt oddly comforting. She bought a pie from Kate and wandered off to sit at the bottom of Pitfall, staring at the river and the people passing above her on the bridge.

# TWENTY-FIVE

People remembered Shackleton as the man who'd been a murderer and been sentenced to hang. Others recalled the man who'd somehow managed to escape from York gaol. But the Shackleton who'd come back to Leeds only seemed to exist as a rumour to most.

Simon knew it wasn't just talk; he'd seen the body. Two hours of asking questions and finally a man said, 'Go and see Silas James. He can tell you, if anyone can.'

He knew the name, but he'd never met the man. He ran a small shop on St Ann's Lane at the top end of Quarry Hill. The door stuck for a second, then creaked as he pushed it open.

Half-empty sacks of flour and dried peas stood on the carefully swept floor. The windows were clean and shining. A carefully shaved shopkeeper in a long, starched apron smiled at him.

'Can I help you, sir?'

'I'm looking for Silas James.'

The man gave a nod of his head. 'At your service, Mr Westow.'

Interesting; the man knew him. Simon chuckled. 'I trust you'll excuse me for not knowing you.'

'You're a familiar face in Leeds.'

'I'm flattered. I was told you might be able to help me.'

'I was wondering how long before you'd call.' The man spread his arms in a gracious gesture. 'You want to know about Daniel Shackleton.'

Even more curious. 'How well did you know him, Mr James?'

'I'm married to his sister.'

Now Simon understood why he'd been directed here. 'Did you know him well?'

'There was a time when we saw him often. That was long ago. He'd come to try and borrow money.'

'Did you lend it to him?'

James sighed. 'At first. After I told him I wasn't about to

support him any longer, he started to threaten me.' He cocked his head. 'I threw him out. He stayed away. That was all before he killed that man.'

'What about after his return to Leeds?'

'Once. He came to see Noelia. My wife,' he explained as Simon raised a questioning eyebrow. 'He only stayed for a few minutes. She gave him a little money. Against my wishes, but he was family.'

The tie of blood could run deep.

'Had he come asking for help?'

'He took what she offered,' James said. 'But he claimed he'd been invited back to Leeds by the man who'd been pardoned.'

'Fox.' That confirmed the connection. 'Why? Did he say?'

'No. Nothing more than sly little hints. That this man Fox had some plan in mind which would bring them money. I heard all this from her. I didn't see him myself. He was careful to visit while I was working.'

'Was he specific about this plan?'

'Only that it couldn't fail.' He shook his head. 'But nothing ever could, in Daniel's eyes. At least, until it fell apart. One of life's believers. Unfortunately, he always believed in the wrong things.'

'When did he last come and see your wife?'

'A week before he was found. He told us a room had been arranged, but he had to go to Wakefield and finish some business before he could take it.'

'Anything more than that?'

James pursed his lips. 'No. As I said, he only came to see her once.'

'Why didn't you come forward after you heard he'd been murdered?'

He kept a genial face, but there was a chill in his voice. 'We're respectable people, Mr Westow. My wife listened to me and we agreed to say nothing unless someone came to us, the way you have.'

'You didn't pay for his funeral.'

'No.' He drew out the word. 'I believe that men like him are best forgotten.'

All the memories would fade soon enough.

'There's nothing else at all?'

'He never told us any names and he was never specific. That's as far as I can help you, Mr Westow.'

Another piece of the puzzle. James had given him the information readily enough, as if he'd rehearsed what he was going to say; he seemed to have been expecting the visit, glad to get the burden of family off his chest.

Fox wanted Barton's wealth. That would be revenge enough for coming so close to death. He had a plan of some sort that never happened. Why? What about the connection? The only possibility was Andrew, the son.

Could that explain his suicide? Guilt was often a heavy burden for a man to carry. Too heavy, sometimes.

There was one other thing in what he'd heard: Shackleton's visit to Wakefield. That was something to pass on to Porter and the inspector.

With a hand on the doorknob, Jane stood outside the cottage in Green Dragon Yard, hearing voices inside.

She reached into her pocket and drew out her knife. The muffled conversation continued. One swift movement and she was past the threshold, staring at Mrs Shields reading with Sally.

The girl offered a bashful smile. 'Everyone had gone and I didn't have anything to do on my own. I thought you might be able to give me another lesson. Mrs Shields is helping me.'

She'd walked from Simon's house, she explained, stopping a few times to rest and catch her breath.

Mrs Shields turned to Jane and shook her head. 'I told her she needs to be careful, to give herself time. But she's as bad as you, child; she's not going to listen to an old woman.'

They sat outside, shaded by a wall, and Jane guided Sally through the start of the new book she'd borrowed from the circulating library: *The Crusaders* by Louisa Stanhope.

'A woman wrote it?' Sally asked in astonishment.

'Why shouldn't she?'

'I never thought about it.' She pointed to the title page. 'I know *The*. What does that other word say?'

\* \* \*

Billy Harding was elusive. Gone to stay with an aunt, someone said. Off somewhere on business, another told him. One thing was certain: the man wasn't in Leeds. So much for that idea.

But there was one name left. The one who'd sent the pair after him. Charles Ibbotson. He remembered speaking to the man after Andrew Barton's disappearance, coming away with the sense of a leader, one who could direct the others. A thinker. That made sense. He'd take his time before approaching Ibbotson.

All of that was an indulgence. He was being paid to find Fox and he was still nowhere close.

Jane walked back to Swinegate with Sally. The girl tried to hide it, but she was weary; the strain showed in the tightness on her face. Close to the bottom of Albion Street, they turned as they heard a shout. Hannah and Wilfred with three of the other children, all waving their hands with pleasure as they ran towards them.

They crowded around Sally, filling the air with their chatter. The girl was beaming, her tiredness evaporated. As they all talked, Jane slipped away, disappearing into the crowd.

How long would Sally's sudden desire for words last once she was fully recovered and active again? How much of it sprang from boredom, the need to fill the hours? The girl still had so much of the child inside, flitting from one thing to another without realising it.

Time would tell.

'The women all know about him now,' Rosie said as she unpinned her hat and examined her face in the mirror. 'None of them will give him the time of day and the word will be all over Leeds tomorrow.'

She turned, satisfied.

'Have any of them seen him?' Simon asked.

'No. But if he's hoping for a glad ear or to prise any jewellery from them, he's out of luck now. I'm going to change.'

One avenue cut off. But they were still no closer to finding him.

# TWENTY-SIX

The wind blew overnight, rattling tree branches and sending green leaves tumbling to the ground. By morning it had passed, leaving the weather cooler, offering a reminder that autumn would soon be on them.

The coffee cart was doing brisk business, men happy to put something warm in their bellies to begin the day. Low murmurs of conversation but nothing to interest him until someone spoke quietly into his ear.

'I hear you're looking for someone.'

Simon turned. A man he didn't know with a squat, solid body. He was wearing clothes long out of fashion, but he carried himself well, back straight and proud. Grey hair spilled out from under his hat, and he had a heavily lined, weatherbeaten face with a cunning expression.

'Where did you hear that?' There was something about the man, the type you wouldn't trust an inch.

'Around. People talk.' He shrugged. 'I'm Alexander Brady.'

He spoke the name as if he expected it to be familiar. Simon smiled. 'You seem to know who I am.'

A nod. 'As you can see, sir. If I said I've come down from Richmond, would that make things clearer?'

'It might. It depends on why you're here.'

'Perhaps you've heard of a family named Driver. They live up around there.'

He was sure he'd heard that name before. His mind began to race. Then it clicked. Mrs Fox. Born Harriet Amelia Driver.

'Their daughter's dead, if you're looking for her.'

'Dead and buried, murdered by her husband, as I understand.'

'That's not certain, but he's the likely one,' Simon agreed.

'The family put up a reward for his capture,' Brady said. 'Enough to make it worth my while coming down on the coach to find him.'

'A thief-taker.'

The man gave a small bow. 'Among other things. I make a living where I can.'

The family must have been offering a fair sum to make the man travel across Yorkshire.

'When did you arrive?'

'Yesterday afternoon.' He pointed a thumb over his shoulder at the Bull and Mouth. 'I'm staying there. Your name came up as soon as I began to ask questions.' His eyes narrowed. 'I thought we might combine our talents and share the money once we find him.'

'I already have a client, Mr Brady.'

'There's no need to tell him, Mr Westow. This could be our little secret, one that puts money in your pocket.'

Simon smiled. He'd trust Brady no further than he could throw him.

'I've given my word.'

Brady snorted. 'What does that mean? Men break their word all the time.'

'Do that and you lose your reputation. If you're really a thief-taker, you'll know that's important.'

'All that matters is finding the man. I'm here for Fox and the reward.'

Simon put the mug down on the trestle. 'I wish you well of it. Good day to you.'

Competition, Simon thought as he walked away. But Brady had no contacts in Leeds. He didn't know the town or understand the people. He looked the type to blunder wildly through everything. One more problem among all the others.

'I'll have my men keep an eye on him,' Constable Porter said. He sat in his office, windows open wide, the piles of paper weighted down on his desk. 'The last thing we need is some stranger muddying the waters.' He glanced up. 'I don't suppose you've come up with anything, have you?'

'Only that Shackleton had reason to go to Wakefield before he died. Interesting, perhaps, but nothing to do with Fox. He's still here in Leeds, staying out of sight.'

'We'll find him, and sooner rather than later,' the constable said. 'You think this Brady has a chance of success?'

'Not unless it's blind luck.'
'Never much chance of that in this place.'

Jane had been out in the night, going round the whores again to ask if Fox had visited. Nothing. If he was out in the darkness, none of them had noticed him. Not a waste of time, she tried to tell herself as she started on her way home.

From the corner of her eye, she caught a shape moving. A sense of someone there. She brought the knife from her pocket and slipped into a deep pool of shade. A few moments and he'd edged into her vision.

Wilfred. The boy from the camp. He held up his hands as Jane stepped forward, blade flashing in a glint of light.

'Were you looking for me?'

He nodded dumbly, never taking his eyes from the knife.

'Do you have information?' she asked. 'Have you seen Fox?'

'No.' His voice was cracked and dry. Scared. 'I . . .'

'What?'

He blurted it out. 'I've seen you; I thought you could teach me what you do.'

'Me?'

'Yes. Maybe I could learn to be a thief-taker.'

She looked at the boy, so meek and retiring. He didn't look the part. But that might be an advantage if he had some iron inside.

'Why do you want to do that?'

'I thought it might stop me being scared.'

'You ought to talk to Simon Westow.'

The boy shook his head. 'Not him. I know you. I'd ask Sally, but I'm afraid she'd laugh at me.'

'She wouldn't do that.'

'She learned from you. She said so. Will you teach me?'

He sounded too earnest.

'Be outside the cottage tomorrow morning,' she told him. 'I'll show you what it's like.'

He was there, waiting in the early light, eager to learn. Jane looked him up and down. His clothes were rags.

'First thing,' she said. 'You need clothes. Dark trousers, a coat. Boots. A knife to defend yourself.'

'I have one.' He produced a stub of a blade, only good for peeling apples.

'We can do better than that.'

She'd taken a little money from behind the loose stone in the wall for this. The stalls in Central Market provided most of what he needed. The blade came from the knifesmith on Kirkgate. He turned it over and over in his hand.

'Now you're ready to learn,' she told him. 'Just stay with me and listen.'

No luck in her search during the morning, but she'd never expected much. They crossed the Wellington Bridge, over into Holbeck. Nobody there had seen anyone like Fox. She worked her way back towards Leeds on the south bank of the canal, Wilfred right behind her, listening intently as she asked more questions in the streets around Meadow Lane. This was the real grind of her work. Keeping going when you found no answers. It was what he needed to see, all the frustrations, always hoping for a word, a hint from someone; all too often that was enough to set her on the trail. None of that today.

'Have you had enough?' she asked as they finished.

'No, miss.' He sounded determined.

'Come back tomorrow.'

Jane shook her head as they all sat at Simon's kitchen table. He could see the frustration on her face.

'He's got to be somewhere,' Rosie said, frustration cracking her voice.

'We'll find him,' Simon said, then told them about Brady.

Sally sat thoughtfully, watching their faces. The bruises on her face were fading, the scabs starting to peel from the cuts on her cheeks and hands.

She still had the hunger in her eyes. 'How does he think he'll be able to find Fox if you can't?' she asked.

'He's cunning,' Simon replied. 'Or he thinks he is. He doesn't know Leeds, but . . .'

All it took was one stroke of luck.

'I could follow him,' Sally offered. 'I'm well enough for that.'

He smiled at her. 'Could you manage a whole day?'

The girl opened her mouth to speak, then exhaled.

'Very soon,' he promised her. 'Very.'

Tonight the darkness felt like a friend. Simon stood in Bay Horse Yards talking to Big Jake, the man everyone called the Robber. He lived up to his nickname, big and intimidating and violent when he needed to be. Somehow, he'd escaped a sentence of transportation twice, but it hadn't changed his ways. They were outside the circle of light cast by a lamp, nothing more than faint shapes, hidden a few yards from all the inn's laughter and noise.

'I haven't spotted Fox,' Jake said. He had a hard man's rasping voice, full of suspicion. 'Are you sure he's back?'

'There's no doubt.' He thought of the man Fox had sent after Jane.

The Robber nodded as he took in the information.

'What's in it for me if I find him?'

'A cut of what I make for it. Easy money.'

The man chuckled. 'I'm always wary when someone mentions easy money. There's something about it. It's never easy and it's never much.'

Simon laughed; true words. But Jake knew people who'd never talk to him.

'Just keep your ears open.' He hesitated. 'There's another man looking. His name's Brady. Not local.'

'Fox is popular. Must be more to it than I thought.'

'Let me know if you come up with anything.'

He slipped away into the night.

All through town. Speaking to one man here, another there, the same thing he'd done for the last few nights. Hoping one of these seeds would flower. He didn't trust Jake, but he was out of choices.

By the time bells started to peal for Sunday services, Simon had been up and working for hours. He'd started at the coffee cart. Brady wasn't anywhere to be seen, and the harassed clerk in the Bull and Mouth said he'd left the day before. Curious. Had he realised Leeds held nothing for him, or moved somewhere cheaper?

Simon walked slowly around town. He'd had a disjointed night, pain from his leg stabbing through him almost as soon as he settled down to sleep.

No reports from the men who'd been watching for Fox. With a sigh, he crossed the Head Row, along North Street and up the drive to Barton's house. The man was almost ready to leave for church, a solemn look on his face, a Bible cradled in his hand.

'Have you found him, Mr Westow?'

'Not yet,' he replied, and saw Barton grimace. 'Have you seen him again?'

'All the time. In here,' he said and tapped his head. 'Whatever he was trying to do to me, he's succeeded. He'll never let me go until he's caught.'

Barton pushed back his jacket to reveal a knife in its sheath.

'My wife's nerves are in tatters. The doctor has given her something, but it hasn't helped.' He glanced at the walls around him. 'She hasn't left the house since Andrew's funeral. This man hasn't just taken Andrew, he's robbing us of our lives, too.'

'I'm searching for him.'

'But . . .'

'Nobody knows where he is. Plenty are looking.'

He escorted Barton down to St John's, the bells too loud for conversation. Perhaps that was just as well, Simon thought; he had nothing to comfort the man.

Jane stayed fifty yards behind them, Wilfred following her. She'd been hidden outside Barton's house long before Simon arrived.

She imagined the man would go to church; that was the reason she'd come. Fox wanted Barton. Why else would he risk returning to Leeds? He was after some kind of revenge. If she watched Barton, she could keep him safe.

Once Barton and Simon were safely inside the church, she checked the area all around. No sign. As the service ended, she trailed them to Barton's home. Still no sense of Fox, but she stayed for another hour, alert for the smallest indication of the man.

He'd come, sooner or later. Deep inside, she knew it.

Finally she left, following the Head Row past the entrance to Green Dragon Yard, down to Swinegate and Simon's house.

'You were behind us? I never felt you there,' Simon said.

He saw Jane smile.

'We need to watch over him. You said so.'

She was right. It was time. But the problem was the same as the last time he'd considered it.

'There aren't enough of us.'

'I can help,' Sally said. 'I can sit and watch his house.'

'What if he leaves?'

She bristled. 'I could still manage.'

Could she? he wondered.

'I can be there, too,' Rosie said quickly. Simon knew she'd had too little to do lately.

The idea could work. Sally was eager for something to do. She ought to be well enough to sit and keep watch. If she and Rosie were up at Barton's house, then he and Jane were free to search for Fox. They were circling; he felt they were slowly coming closer, but still so far to go.

# TWENTY-SEVEN

People in their good Sunday clothes left the late service at the parish church by East Bar at the bottom of Kirkgate. The beggars sat with their pots where the families would pass, feeling full of Christian charity.

Jane waited off in the shadows with Wilfred tucked close by her. From somewhere near the top of Kirkgate she heard Davy Cassidy's fiddle, a lilt played sweetly enough to bring tears. It should be a good day for him, too.

The air was comfortable, the cloying stickiness vanished on the only day in the week when factory chimneys weren't throwing out smoke.

'It's time,' Jane said quietly, and the two of them crossed the street to see Dodson, the old soldier with the wooden leg. He was sitting on a scrap of blanket, the false leg stretched out in front of him, counting out the coins in his cup. Jane added three more and he looked up to thank her.

'People are generous,' he said, and she heard the gratitude in his voice. He was a good man; she'd known him a long time. He cocked his head towards Wilfred. 'You've brought someone to meet me.'

An introduction. The boy was confused, not knowing what to do, so he lowered his head and made a small bow.

'Any word on Fox?'

'I've heard one or two talking as they pass,' he replied, and she felt a small surge of hope. Dodson shook his head. 'I think it was because someone's been asking questions.'

The possibility crumbled. 'That must have been Simon.' She described Fox; she'd seen him, she remembered him well.

'There are so many men like that,' he told her as he shook his head.

Jane knew it was true. Dozens, hundreds who were similar, and no marks to distinguish him.

'If you . . .' she began and he nodded.

'Of course. I'll tell the others, too.'

The beggars saw people. They relied on them, they developed a sense, a wariness that could keep them alive. They remembered faces and the way men walked, the snippets of conversation of passers-by.

'I've seen that man before. Does he help you much?' Wilfred asked as they moved up Kirkgate.

'Sometimes. He used to be a soldier, lost his leg fighting the French.'

'How?'

Jane smiled. 'You should ask him. He likes to talk.'

A crowd had gathered around Davy Cassidy, worshippers on their way home, caught by the blind fiddler's music. For two minutes he let the melody sing and fly before softening the notes to a gradual silence.

Some left. Others moved forward to put money in the hat and thank him for the beauty of the music. He nodded, said a word or two as he made tiny adjustments to the tuning of the violin.

'That's still a little bit high,' Wilfred told him as he pointed to one of the strings.

'You heard that too, did you?' He laughed, turning his head as if he could see the boy. 'It should be an A, but it's a wee bit sharp.' A turn of a small screw and he plucked the string. 'That's better. Do you play, then?'

'Me?' Wilfred sounded horrified. 'No. Never.'

'Just a good ear, then. And I'd say you were here with Miss Jane.'

She didn't know how he managed it; maybe she had a scent about her that he recognised.

'He's helping me,' she said. 'We're still hunting for Fox.'

He nodded. 'I've been hearing the name a time or two lately.' He pursed his lips. 'Someone said it not one hour ago.'

Jane was suddenly alert. 'What did they say?'

'Someone called another man Fox. They stopped for half a minute to listen, then moved on.'

She felt as if someone was squeezing her tight; she could hardly breathe.

'Do you remember anything else?'

'The man who spoke had a deep voice.' He thought for a second. 'A heavy tread when he walked away. He must smoke cheroots, I could smell it on him. I don't know about the man who was with him. He didn't say a word.'

'How long ago was this?' She heard the eagerness in her question.

'It might have been an hour. Probably no more than that.'

'Which way did they go?'

He pointed with his bow. Up Vicar Lane.

Six pennies in the hat; worth it to have heard all that. There must be other men named Fox in Leeds, but this was the right one. She *knew* it.

They were so close.

'What are you thinking?' Wilfred asked.

'That it won't be long now.'

Simon walked with his wife and Sally. He could see the girl still hurt, the grim, determined set of her face and her silence as they moved through town. None of her usual curiosity; she concentrated on putting one foot in front of the other. Before they came out, she'd spent ten minutes sharpening her knife on a whetstone.

Her expression eased as she settled on the ground from where she could watch the house, and he turned to Rosie.

'When I saw him back from church he said he'd be home the rest of the day. But if he leaves . . .'

'We'll follow,' she told him. 'If Fox shows himself, we'll stop him.'

He caught sight of Brady on Call Lane, talking to a man with a pony and cart who kept pointing. Asking directions.

He raised his hat. 'Searching for something, Mr Brady?'

The man turned, a sharp look of annoyance on his face. The man in the cart flicked the reins and moved on.

'Where's Hunslet?'

'At the end of this street, turn to your right and go across the bridge. Everything to your left on the other side is Hunslet,' Simon told him. 'If you go the other way, you'll be in Holbeck.'

The man nodded. 'I thank you. Do you know Bowman Lane?'

'Keep going straight from the bridge for a hundred yards and you'll see it.'

Someone must have told him about Joe Rawlings. The man who boasted he knew all about crime in Leeds and ran most of it from his ironmonger's shop on Bowman Lane. All in his head, but his fancies didn't trouble anyone.

As Brady ambled away, Simon called, 'Rawlings won't have his shop open on the Sabbath. But he lives upstairs. The door is to the side.'

The man's footsteps hesitated for a fragment of a second, then began again. Simon allowed himself a smile. Whatever information Brady was seeking, Rawlings wouldn't have it. Let him find that out for himself.

Matty Harker's house was tucked away off Beck Street, where Timble Beck came down to join the river.

'Mr Westow,' he said in surprise as he opened the door. It was a shabby place, slowly falling down around him but Harker didn't seem to notice. Or he simply didn't care.

'It's been a long time, Matty.'

The man nodded. 'Since before you were attacked. I heard you were working again.'

'That's why I'm here. What about you? Still in the same line of business?'

'This and that.' He gathered small crumbs of information, keeping them close until someone was willing to pay a price. It wasn't much of a living, but his needs were few.

'I'm after a man named Fox. Does it mean anything?'

Harker frowned. 'Didn't he leave Leeds? I know the constable was looking for him. You must be aware of that.'

'He's returned,' Simon said. But if the man didn't know, he had no information worth buying.

'He killed Shackleton, didn't he? Him or his wife. That's the rumour.'

'It looks that way.'

'Did you know Shackleton had a friend here? A woman.'

'No.' Was it true? The man had kept that quiet. When he'd been out asking questions, nobody had mentioned any woman. But Harker had often been right in the past. 'When was this? Before or after he came back? Who is she?'

He knew the urgency of his voice was betraying him, but he didn't care. This could be important.

Harker gave a slow smile and rubbed a thumb across his fingertips.

Her name was Betsy Watling and she lived in a little court off Workhouse Row. That was all Harker knew. A couple of scraps, but if it was true, worth the money Simon had just given him.

The old workhouse stood on the corner of Vicar Lane and Lady Lane. God only knew how old, but it was still in use, even with large gaps in the mortar between the stones, and roof slates that seemed to be held on with prayer.

He knew the place very well. His eye picked out the window that had been closest to his bed when he was a boy. He'd spent hours staring out it, dreaming of a world that had to be better than living inside those four walls.

He'd walked out when he was thirteen, ready to find his own way. Ever since then, he'd been expecting the building to collapse or be torn down. Once a year, someone raised the idea of demolition, but every time it faded to silence.

Workhouse Row ran by the side of the grounds, facing a high brick wall. A couple of questions and Simon knew exactly where Watling lived.

Better to use a woman's touch to start her revealing about Shackleton and Fox. Rosie would be perfect. Jane was too blunt, not an ounce of subtlety about her, and Sally was too young.

'We'll go down together,' he said as he slipped in beside her and Sally to watch Barton's house. 'I'll talk a little and let you ask the questions. You know what we need to find out.'

Rosie nodded then looked around. 'What about once we're there?'

'As soon as you start talking to her, I'll leave and come back here.'

Sally was still a shadow of herself; he was slow. Together, they weren't likely to scare a soul. But they'd keep guard.

But there was little for them to do. Twice he saw Barton behind the window, shuffling around like an old man, head bowed. But the man never came out, and no sign of anyone else lurking and waiting.

When Rosie returned, moving with quiet grace, he stood and stretched.

'I can stay,' Sally offered, but he shook his head.

'Tomorrow. There won't be anything else today.'

She took a few stumbling paces, reaching for a tree branch to steady herself, before she began to walk a little more easily. Simon watched her carefully. Healing swiftly, but she was impatient; none of it could be quick enough for her. At the Head Row she left them, going to visit Jane, she said.

'Do you think she's ready?' Rosie asked, watching the girl move away from them.

'Probably not, but she'll go her own way,' he told her. 'You know what she's like.'

Would Sally be safe enough alone? That was what Rosie had meant. But it was the tail end of a late summer Sunday afternoon and couples were still parading around town. Trouble didn't look likely.

He took his wife's arm and they began to stroll home. 'Now, what did Betsy Watling have to say? Was it worth a few pennies?'

She heard the fires crackle and roar and saw the smoke rising from the tops of the chimneys. Monday, and the mills and factories woke from their Sunday sleep.

Jane had risen early. The terrifying dream had come again, the girl's scream tearing the night apart as if it was never going to leave her. She'd lit the lamp and sat for half an hour, reading more of *The Crusaders*. But it didn't pull her in the way the stories about America had done. It felt like a makeweight. Something to ease the tendrils of a bad dream away.

Sally had surprised her yesterday, arriving to ask for another reading lesson. She'd expected the urge to pass very quickly. Jane did what she could; she was no teacher, but the girl had been attentive, quick to grasp things and recognise more words, as if she'd made a decision that she was going to master this. Why, Jane didn't know, and Sally said nothing. Meanwhile, Mrs Shields had watched, nodding her approval.

Finally she'd walked back to Swinegate beside her, seeing the drawn face as the mask slipped and the weariness and pain showed.

Good sleep hadn't returned; she was just waiting for the first hint of dawn as an excuse to be up and out. Wilfred would come around later, but first she'd find Simon at the coffee cart.

He didn't realise Jane was there until she was standing at his side. That invisibility was her skill, her weapon.

'Matty Harker told me about someone who knew Shackleton,' he said quietly as they walked down Briggate. 'A woman. Rosie saw her yesterday.' He waited for a reaction, but she stayed quiet. 'You remember he and Fox were in prison together in York.'

She nodded. 'Yes. He escaped.'

'This woman claimed that Fox told him to come to Leeds at the start of the summer if he read about a pardon. He had a plan to make them both some money, if Shackleton didn't mind murder.'

'But . . .' She blurted out the word, frowning.

'Yes. That meant he must have thought one was coming. Or hoped it would.'

He'd scarcely been able to believe it when Rosie told him. Was this some fanciful story? Could it really all have been arranged? Who had the money and the power to take care of that? Why would they do it for someone like Fox?

'Do you believe it?' Jane asked.

'Honestly? I don't know,' he said after a few moments. He'd kept turning the words over during the night, still no closer to an answer than when he'd first heard it. 'But it's all we have.'

'Fox's plan must have involved Barton,' she said with a frown. 'Why didn't he act on it though? All he did was follow him.'

'You saw him with Andrew Barton. They probably had a scheme of some kind.'

She nodded. The son must have been a part of it, but now he'd never be able to give them answers. The only one who knew all the answers was Fox.

'How do we find him?'

He still couldn't answer her question, and they both knew it.

'I'd like you to watch Barton today.'

He had other plans for Rosie and Sally.

'If Fox comes?'

'Take him alive if you can. But make sure you stop him.'

Another nod and she vanished as silently as she'd arrived.

At home, Simon sat at the kitchen table. Richard and Amos had been up early and bustled out, off to walk in the country for the day with four of their friends. They were old enough, and a group of six would deter trouble, Simon decided when he gave his permission. Let them enjoy themselves; soon enough they'd be back to their lessons at the grammar school.

The air was thick with flour and the room had the sweet, domestic perfume of bread baking in the oven.

'I need you to go back and talk to the women,' he told Rosie. 'Find out who they believe might have had the influence to promise a pardon and what it might have cost.'

'If the Watling woman's story is true, do you mean?'

'What do you think? Is it?'

'She believed it. But even if we manage to come up with a name or two,' Rosie asked him, 'what does it matter?'

'Maybe it doesn't. Until we know, we can't say.'

'What about me?' Sally asked hopefully. The damage to her face was healing, but still obvious when anyone looked.

'Go and talk to the children.'

Her movements were stiff; she'd done too much yesterday. Today would tax her, too, but she was the only one who could do this.

'To ask them to look for Fox?'

'Yes.'

'I already have.'

'Remind them.' He understood that they all needed to find food, their first thought was survival. But they could be the best chance. Eyes open, the ones nobody noticed . . . Simon brought a small purse from his pocket. Coins jingled. Barton would cover the cost. 'Pay them.' Not much, but enough to ensure nobody would go hungry today. 'Tell them there's a reward for whoever spots him.'

Sally weighed the purse in her hand. 'What do you want them to do if they see him?'

'Stay close and send someone to find you. They need to keep their distance and out of sight.'

'They know how to do that.'

# TWENTY-EIGHT

'The devil you say.' Porter looked stunned.

'That's what the woman told me.'

'I don't believe there's an ounce of truth in it. There's nobody here who could arrange a pardon from the gallows.' He snorted. 'He must have been hoping. Condemned men all do that. That's what I've read – they hope and pray a lot. Think they'll be chosen.' He gave a slow shake of his head. 'No, I don't buy a word of it. Do you?'

'I don't know.' He had to agree, though; it seemed impossible.

'Don't be so bloody stupid, Westow.'

'I'm trying to find the truth.'

'Truth?' The constable barked out a laugh. 'The only way you'll manage that is getting hold of Fox, and none of my men have seen hide nor hair of him. I wish you well with the search.'

'Someone's coming out,' Wilfred said softly.

Jane stirred. She'd been sitting, lost in thought about Fox. She rose, watching Barton close the front door of the house before shuffling down the drive. The death of his son had turned him into a man who had become old long before his time. All the confidence and pleasure had gone from his stride.

The boy gave her a questioning look, but Jane shook her head. Not yet; Barton was moving slowly. Finally she pulled the shawl over her hair and slipped out and on to the noise and bustle of the road, with carts and coaches and people hurrying past.

Barton was twenty yards ahead. Jane glanced around. No sense of Fox. Nobody looked at them. A woman and a boy were invisible in the throng.

He turned through the lychgate at St John's Church, halting for a moment to look around, then on to his son's grave. It was the most important place in the world to him; Jane remembered the look on his face as he waded into the water to pull out the body. That was the moment his world had cracked apart.

'What should we do?' Wilfred asked.

'We go in and keep watch. Stand over by the wall, out of sight.'

She led the way and they stayed in the shadows. A few yards away, the life of the town continued. In the churchyard, things were quiet. Jane kept glancing around. A feeling had begun to rise in her: something was going to happen.

From the corner of her eye, she caught sight of something by the gate. Someone. A man, standing and looking before turning away. Fox. She felt a spark through her body.

'You stay with Barton,' she ordered Wilfred hurriedly. 'He'll go home from here. Follow him.'

'Where—'

But she'd gone, the figure of Fox sharp and clear in her mind.

She saw him again, standing by the Head Row, shifting his weight from foot to foot, impatient as he waited for a line of carts to pass so he could cross.

Jane stayed a few yards behind, shielded from his view by a large man and his wife. She kept her hand close to the pocket in the dress, ready to grip her knife. As soon as people began to surge across the road, she moved. Keeping to the other side of Briggate, ten yards behind Fox now. She was giving him some distance, but staying close enough to follow every turn and catch him in a moment.

Jane swallowed. Suddenly the day felt hot. Her heart was beating a tattoo in her chest and a flutter of fear ran through her body. This was definitely Fox; she remembered his gait from the times she'd followed him, almost rolling from one foot to the other.

He turned down Wood Street. She crossed Briggate and cautiously followed. It was darker down here, blackened bricks rising up to cut off the light. Quieter, too; every noise carried.

Jane stayed close to the wall, creeping along, while Fox let his footsteps ring. He'd done nothing to disguise himself. Perhaps the crowd was enough, she thought.

He turned down a small ginnel that had no name. It led to a tiny court, a place she knew, but this was the only way in or out. If she tried to enter, he'd be able to see her. If she waited here, Fox would spot her as soon as he came out.

Just a moment to decide. She didn't panic, mind working quickly, weighing everything, before she walked on, down the rest of Wood Street to Vicar Lane. At the corner, she stopped and looked back.

Had Fox realised she was following him and led her there deliberately? He'd shown no sign of it, but that meant nothing. She could stay; he'd have to come out sometime. If Fox was here, Barton was safe. The man would go straight home, she felt sure of that. Wilfred could watch him there; she'd shown him what to do.

Not many people passed along Wood Street. Jane stood on Vicar Lane, peering down it. A few of those who cut through gave her curious looks; most ignored her. An hour passed, then most of a second, and her imagination began to work: had she missed him somehow? Had he really turned down that ginnel? Had the figure even been Fox?

Then he was there again, striding towards her. With a jerk she pulled back, scarcely daring to breathe as she turned away.

He walked past her, so close that she could smell him, sour and sweaty. If he was aware of her, he hid it well.

Her heart was thudding, fear roaring through her veins and making every nerve sharp. She gave him five yards and began to walk. Slowly, enough to let him pull a little farther ahead yet still keeping him in sight.

Jane tried to swallow. She paused at the horse trough, splashing water over her face. When she looked up again, Fox had vanished.

A sudden panic. Disbelief. Her eyes were lying; this wasn't possible. She'd glanced down for no more than two seconds. How could he disappear? She must have missed something.

But as she peered frantically around, there was no sign of him. Jane dashed down the street.

There was a tall, scarred door where she'd last seen him. She tried the handle. Locked. Jane looked up. The building stood three storeys tall. Nothing to show if it was offices, or if people lived there.

Jane stood on the other side of Vicar Lane, keeping to the

shadow of a doorway. People jostled her as they passed, carts and coaches rattled and banged up and down the road. She stared up at the windows. No movement, no sign of life behind them.

Fox must have gone in there. That had to be it. It was the only place.

She almost missed Hannah, the girl from the homeless camp, as she passed. A short whistle and Hannah turned in surprise; she'd never spotted Jane. A few quick instructions and Hannah scurried away.

She came running headlong towards him, her hair wild, eyes wide. No weapon in her hands; that was the first thing Simon noticed. He braced himself, but the child stopped herself, bent over, panting and gasping.

'It's Jane.' She could barely speak, drawing in a breath before she could carry on.

'What?' A thin line of terror ran through him. 'What's happened to her?'

'She's seen Fox.' Another pause. 'On Vicar Lane. He went in somewhere. She's there.'

Simon fumbled a penny from his pocket and passed it to the girl.

At first he didn't notice Jane; she seemed to blend with the stonework. Then she gave a small wave and he realised she was just three yards away.

'Where?' he asked.

He watched her nod towards a brick building. 'Over there.'

'Is it definitely him?'

'Yes.' She explained how she'd seen him and followed, the ginnel off Wood Street.

'Who's watching Barton?'

'Wilfred, the boy who was with me. But we know Fox is the danger.'

He nodded; she was right. Simon gazed at the building. No idea what was inside. Nobody had come or gone, Jane had said. He could try the lock picks, but not in the middle of the day on a busy street.

He needed Porter and his men.

'Stay here until I come back,' he said. 'If he leaves, keep with him.'

Constable Porter shook his head as he stared at the door.

'We've no idea who's behind there,' he said. 'Ready to find out, Westow?'

Jane had been in the same spot when Simon returned with Porter. He glanced around now and saw she'd faded away.

Porter hammered on the door, stood back and waited. He tried again and they heard footsteps inside and a woman was facing them. Somewhere close to fifty, well dressed, with sharp, raw features and an educated voice.

'These are lodgings for gentlemen,' she explained, when Porter told her about Fox. 'They all have keys to the door.' She pursed her lips, the wrinkles clear around her mouth. 'But I have nobody who looks like the man you described. He couldn't have come in here. You saw I keep the door locked.'

'Have any of them lost his key lately?' Simon asked.

She cocked her head and narrowed her eyes. 'Yes. Mr Perkins. Why?'

Simon looked at Porter.

'Is there a yard behind your house?' the constable asked.

'Of course there is,' she replied, as if he'd asked a stupid question. 'There's a gate that leads into a court. Why?'

They had their answer. Fox must have realised Jane was behind him. He'd been too clever for them. Very well prepared. What other tricks did the damned man have up his sleeve?

'Have you had any problems?' Jane asked as she slipped into the undergrowth beside Wilfred.

The boy turned quickly, wide-eyed and startled. The knife wavered in his hand. Jane raised her arms.

'No need to worry,' she told him. 'It's only me.'

A sigh and a terrified smile. 'I was frightened when you didn't come back.'

'It's fine,' she said. Wilfred was shaking a little, and the blade looked heavy and unwieldy in his thin fingers. 'What about Barton?'

'He stayed in the churchyard for a long time and then he came home.' The words erupted in a childish rush.

'Did he speak to anyone?'

The boy shook his head. 'He hasn't come out again.'

Barton was probably inside for the rest of the day. But she'd wait and watch.

'Where did you go?' Wilfred asked.

She told the story and wondered how it had ended. Fox had slipped through a locked door. He'd never seemed to realise she was behind him.

They must have caught him.

Wilfred stayed quiet. Jane let her thoughts and imaginings rise.

Suddenly, she heard a noise and rose, the blade ready in her hand. Simon. Never as quiet as he liked to believe, she thought with a smile.

'We didn't find him.'

As he told her, she understood. Fox had played with her, led her on. When had he first known she was there? In Wood Street? Or was it earlier, as soon as she left the church?

He possessed more cunning than she imagined. She remembered the first day she'd come to watch Barton and the way Mrs Fox had appeared from nowhere. She'd had no sense the woman was there. Now the man . . . Had she lost some of her skill? He was better than her; he'd proved that. Played with her in the same way she'd seen fishermen ease in the fish they'd hooked.

'Fox won't be back today,' Simon said. 'He won't take a risk like that.'

'Yes,' she agreed, but her voice was empty. He'd beaten her, without even trying.

'You did the right thing.'

Jane nodded, but she couldn't find any comfort in the words. She hadn't been good enough.

# TWENTY-NINE

Simon watched Jane's face. She was brooding, even quieter than usual. After all this time, he knew her well. She'd feel as if she'd failed; she'd probably spent the night going over each and every detail.

But she'd brought them a little closer to Fox. Now Porter was convinced he was here. That would help; he could light a fire under his men to make them search.

The children were searching, Sally had told him when he returned last night. The bruises on her face were gradually fading, the scabs mostly gone. Her eyes were clearer and brighter, but her movements were still stiff and pained as she walked.

He'd noticed her talking quietly to Jane at the far end of the kitchen table. No more than a few words, but they'd seemed satisfied.

'If we see Fox again, we're not going to follow him,' Simon announced. He saw the shock on their faces. He hadn't even told Rosie about this. 'We're going to stop him.'

'Stop him?' Sally spoke into the silence. 'Do you mean kill him?'

Simon shook his head. 'Not that. He still has too many questions to answer.'

'What if he won't give up?' Jane asked.

'Wound him.' He rubbed his chin. 'Don't kill unless there's absolutely no choice . . .'

He'd said it. The death sentence.

Jane took three pennies from her pocket.

'Do you know Kate the pie-seller?' she asked.

'Yes,' Wilfred told her.

'Go and buy two of her pies.' The boy was listless, unable to keep still, feeling cramped by the quiet routine of keeping watch.

Once he'd gone, Jane walked around, checking that nobody else had an eye on Barton. After yesterday, she couldn't trust her senses. She had to see.

Not a soul. She was satisfied now. Yesterday evening, she'd tormented herself with failure. How had it happened? Why? Was Fox really better than her?

Sleep had finally arrived last night, but it only brought the screaming girl back to tear through the darkness. Each time she managed to slip towards rest, the girl would arrive. Again and again, until Jane slid out of bed and into the yard, trying to shake off the tendrils of the nightmare.

Outside, the night was welcoming, warm and soft around her. Jane stood, letting the thoughts slowly vanish from her mind until she felt she could sleep without visitations.

A few hours. Enough. She sat again now, still and silent until Wilfred returned and the smell of pastry and warm beef filled the air.

Barton came out as they finished eating; they followed him to the churchyard. Jane kept glancing around, feeling her pulse race, but there was no Fox today. When the man finished, they trailed him home again.

'There's no need for you to be here,' she told the boy. 'He won't come out again today.'

'I want to stay.'

Jane studied him. 'Are you sure? You've seen what I do for yourself. Most of it is hours of sitting or standing.' She offered a kindly smile. 'I can see it on your face – you don't enjoy this.'

'But yesterday you went after Fox—'

'I did, and he must have known I was there.' The admission hurt, but it was the truth.

'He'd have seen me straight away, wouldn't he?'

'Very likely.' She wasn't going to lie to him; that wouldn't help at all.

His face fell. 'I don't know if I can do this.'

'You've barely tried. It's too early to know.'

'What do you think?'

Jane gave him a thoughtful look. 'Come to the cottage tomorrow morning.'

He nodded, then hurried away. A day, maybe two, and he'd give up. Some had the quality; others didn't. In the meantime, she could use another body to help.

Alone, she settled back into the undergrowth. One more hour and she'd leave. Sally wanted to come by later for another reading lesson. The request as they sat in Simon's kitchen that morning had taken her by surprise. The girl seemed determined to learn. Something had shifted inside her.

Simon sat in Mudie's print shop, the scent of ink as familiar as breathing after all this time.

'Everybody's looking, but nobody's caught him,' George Mudie said. He sat down on the other side of the desk and poured himself a tot of brandy. The front window was smeared with dust and dirt, softening the light. 'Is that right?'

'Yes,' Simon admitted.

'Sounds like he's slippery.'

'Very. Clever, too.'

'You need to be ruthless, Simon.'

A nod and a sigh. He'd come hoping for a little sympathy, but there was none here. He stood, pushing himself up with his stick.

'Are you going to find him?'

That was the question.

'Yes.' He had to believe it.

Jane walked back from Swinegate through the late evening light. She'd gone with Sally, a stroll that was an excuse to make sure the girl reached home safely. The lesson had bumped along. Jane had no faith in herself as a teacher; there was still so much she didn't know.

Sally had spent the morning in the children's camp, the rest of the day on some elaborate game with Richard and Amos.

'I'm going to find the ones who beat me,' the girl said as they moved down Albion Street.

She watched Sally's face, her eyes and the set of her jaw. Her mind was ready, but she still needed a little longer for her body to heal before she went into any battle. 'Very soon.'

On the way home, Jane kept one hand on her knife as she

walked. Fox had left her doubting herself and kept the questions floating in her mind. Had her skills trickled away?

She was alert for any sound, pricking her ears at a soft scuffing of pebbles behind her. She drew out the blade, holding it down against her leg. For a long moment, the only sound was the swish of her skirts as she walked.

Then he came in a rush.

In an instant, Jane turned. Took a pace to the side, feet apart, braced.

He was slow and ungainly. She felt his arm slicing through the air, aiming for where she'd been and finding nothing.

She slammed her knife hilt into the back of his neck to send him sprawling. The fall jarred his weapon from his grasp, a tinkle of metal fading into the darkness.

Jane knelt on his back, one hand tight in his hair to pull his head back, the flat of the blade tight against his throat.

'Who are you?'

He didn't answer and she ground his face into the flagstone. He stank of rum, struggling to move underneath her.

'Who are you?' She repeated the question, tightening her grip on his greasy hair until he grunted.

'Luke.'

Jane wasn't breathing hard. This had felt like nothing, a simple moment's work to take him down. Now the thing she needed to know: 'Who sent you?' Fox? Who else could it have been?

'Who?' he asked. He was quivering with fear.

'Was it Fox?'

'Nobody. I saw you . . .' She heard the truth in his voice.

Nothing more than a drunk who thought he could rob and rape her. For a moment, all the frustrations and fears of the last day welled up inside. One simple slash across his throat and she could let him bleed and die. Not a soul would see. She'd be the only one to know when word of murder flew around in the morning.

'Are you going to kill me?' His voice was quivering.

Jane took a breath and looked down. She could see the terror in his eyes, wondering how he'd done this to himself and what was going to happen. Wondering how deep the anger ran inside her.

She stayed silent and kept him hoping for mercy until the feeling had passed through her. Just a man. Not somebody paid to kill her. Slowly, she lifted the knife from his neck and heard him exhale. Smelled the acrid odour where he'd pissed himself.

She was quick. A fast, single cut to mark him and make him pay. Some justice to remind him of his mistake.

She rose, slipped the knife into her pocket and away. At the corner she heard him start to wail as he reached around and discovered his ear gone.

Better than killing. Let him carry his shame forever.

The man didn't visit her dreams. But the girl did; her screams rang out inside Jane's skull. As they faded, they carried her somewhere. Deep into the woods she imagined from *The Pioneers*. Tangled and green, but with no way home.

No peace. Not yet.

A cooler Wednesday morning. Grey clouds hung over the haze from the smoke and machines as Simon stood near the coffee cart. Someone mentioned that the night watch had found an ear somewhere, but not its owner.

Nothing for him. Sally stood on the other side of the road, shawl pulled down over her hair, angled to hide her healing face. But the scar on her cheek would always stand out.

He saw her eyes dart around, keeping watch as he talked to a few men he knew. Soon enough he began to amble home and she arrived out of nowhere; her skills hadn't rusted during her recovery. She answered his questioning look with a shake of her head. Nobody seeking him out. He hadn't expected any trouble, and this made a good way to ease her back into things.

'Barton sent his servant,' Rosie said as soon as he came through the door. 'He wants to see you as soon as possible.'

'Fox?' he asked. But what else could it be?

'He's frantic.' She pinned a hat on his head. 'I'll come with you and talk to his wife.'

The man was pacing, walking a circle in the middle of the room. His face was panicked, exhausted and colourless. Barton had shrunk from being a vital man just six months ago to a shell of a human. Another reason to see this all ended soon.

'He was here,' Barton said without any preamble. He turned

towards the window that looked over the front of the house. 'Out there.'

'When?'

'In the middle of the night. I don't sleep well. I was up and I glanced out. We had a good moon, and I saw him there. He was staring at me, plain as day.' He sighed. 'I'm not sure if it was real or in my mind. You have to catch him, Mr Westow.'

'We will.'

'I could make out his face. His eyes were laughing at me. I woke my wife, but when I brought her down, he'd gone.'

If he was ever truly there.

'Have you ever seen him outside your house before?'

'I think . . .' he began, then stopped and shook his head. 'I don't know. A glimpse maybe, at the corner of my eye.' He raised a hand to touch his temple. 'I thought so, but I can't be certain.'

Five more minutes of talking. The more Barton spoke, the more Simon knew it was all in his imagination. His son's death was taking him apart, piece by piece. Would finding Fox and seeing him in court stop things? Impossible to know.

'What did his wife have to say?' Simon asked as he and Rosie made their way down Briggate. He'd tried to spot Jane keeping guard over Barton's house, but she'd kept safely out of sight.

'She's terrified.'

'Does she . . .'

'Of course not. She knows it's not real. Half the time, he does, too. That's what she said. Last night was bad. She told me he seemed so certain about it.'

'Has the doctor seen him?'

'She's asked, but he said he wouldn't let a physician through the door because he can't catch Fox for him.'

'Let's hope we can,' he said.

'They just left,' Wilfred said. He moved back into the undergrowth, the way Jane had shown him.

'We'll check around the house.'

No sign anyone else had been there, everything the way it had been when they'd looked first thing in the morning. They'd seen the servant dash away and return, then Simon and Rosie arriving, worried looks on their faces.

If it had been anything important, Simon would have given her a sign.

Twice her thoughts had flickered over the man who'd attacked her last night. She felt no anguish, no regrets. Then she moved on and forgot him. He wasn't worth more than that.

By late afternoon, Barton hadn't emerged.

'There's nothing more for us here today,' Jane said. 'We might as well leave.'

Wilfred stood; he'd been chafing all day, bored by the lack of action. As they walked off, she asked him: 'Do you still want to do this?'

His face reddened. 'You spent money. The clothes. You bought me food.'

Jane smiled, suddenly feeling as old as Mrs Shields. 'That doesn't mean anything. You're not under any obligation to me. You needed something better to wear, and you had to eat, didn't you?'

'Thank you. For all of it.' He stared at her, then turned and ran off.

Would Wilfred come back? Tomorrow would tell. She should know better by now. The endings she read in books were rare in life.

The tapping on the door didn't surprise her. Sally for her lesson. They worked together while Mrs Shields sat in her chair and read. From time to time, Jane's eyes moved to her, glad to notice the quick smile or tiny nod of approval.

'Can you walk back with me?' the girl asked as they finished. The fierceness in her eyes that had been missing had returned.

'If you want.'

'I was with the children today.' She kept her voice low, glancing around as she walked, as if she expected danger.

'Have any of them seen Fox?'

'No.' She turned her head to look at Jane. 'One of them saw you last night.'

Slowly, thinking, she drew a breath. 'What did they say?'

'He. A boy. I'm the only one he's told. He watched the man come for you.'

'Just someone who saw a woman on her own. Easy prey.'

'What did you do? The boy ran off as soon as he heard the man cry out.'

'Took his ear.'

Sally nodded; she understood. 'I'm almost ready.'

'I'll be with you. You know that.'

'There's no need for Simon to know about it.'

Jane kept secrets well. There was so much she'd never told him, far more than the girl could ever guess. Things she'd done that he'd never wish to know about.

Simon was out in the night, asking his questions and learning nothing more about Fox. As he was leaving the Pack Horse, the glee club was singing loud in the room upstairs; as he headed towards the Turk's Head on the other side of Commercial Street, a hand tugged at his sleeve.

A face he'd seen several times before, although he didn't know the name. The man smiled, raising his hands to show they were empty.

'You ought to go and see Henry Longdon,' he said. All around, people were talking and laughing. No one paid them any attention.

'I've already talked to him.' Longdon. Mrs Fox's cousin.

'I know. I saw him earlier today. He said you should call tomorrow. Take Porter.' He tipped his hat and moved into the throng.

Maybe things were finally moving, Simon thought as he made his way home. God knew they needed it.

# THIRTY

'It doesn't sound likely, Westow.' Constable Porter had been complaining ever since they left the courthouse. He had proper work to do, he said, none of this visiting. But he was here, intrigued when Simon told him what had happened in the Pack Horse. 'Why couldn't he just send you a note?'

It was definitely strange; he'd thought that during the night. But what was there to lose beyond a few minutes? Another cloudy day, with the air oppressive and stifling, thick with smoke and soot. Summer, but the only way to know was the heat.

When the servant showed them through, the fence was sitting at his desk, furiously writing. He held up a finger for them to wait and Simon saw Porter grimace with annoyance.

Another few seconds and the man put down his nib and smiled.

'I'm glad my message reached you,' he said.

'Damned strange way to do it,' the constable said.

'It worked, didn't it?'

'Why do you want to see us?' Simon asked. It had to be Fox. No other possible reason.

'I know where he was.' Longdon pursed his lips.

'Was?'

'The night before last. The hotel down by Eye Bright Place.'

'The Western?' Porter asked and the man nodded.

'Why didn't you say something sooner?'

'I only found out yesterday. A gentleman mentioned it to me.'

'Who told you?'

'Someone who was here on business.' He smiled. An honest enough answer that admitted nothing.

'Is he still there?' the constable said.

'I've told you everything I know.' He turned to face Simon. 'If you hadn't come first thing, I'd have sent word. I hope you find him.'

'If he'd said something last night . . .' Porter said as they hurried out along Boar Lane. 'You keep watch on the place while I find some of my men.'

Simon stood, feeling the excitement rise in his chest. If Fox was still there, the chase was over. The hotel was a nondescript building, the painted sign over the door beginning to fade. There'd been a well there once, an old man had told him. A place where the water was supposed to be good for the eyes. Long since dried up or covered over. All that remained was the name.

A few people came and went from the Western, but no Fox. He smiled as he saw Brady, the thief-taker from Richmond, hurry past without giving the hotel a second look. He didn't know. Simon stood on the opposite corner, eyes on the door, only starting to move when the constable appeared with the inspector and two men from the watch. He followed them into the building.

Clean inside, the floors swept, a pair of armchairs recently upholstered, and the smell of beeswax where the woodwork had been polished. An eminently respectable place. One that was housing a murderer.

'Yes,' the clerk said, flustered as the constable and inspector loomed over him. 'Here, see?' He stabbed an ink-stained finger at the ledger. 'He arrived two days ago. I remember him. He looked dusty, as if he'd been travelling, and he had one small valise, that was all.' He looked hopefully up at the faces and Simon felt his hopes of finding the man wither.

'When did he leave?'

'The next morning.' He pointed at the page again. 'You see the mark? That means he was all paid when he left.'

'Did you talk to him?' the inspector pressed the clerk. 'Did he say anything?'

The man shook his head. 'Just wanted the room then handed the key back the next day.'

Outside, Simon sighed. Close, but far too late. Porter was still questioning the clerk, but he knew the man had nothing to give them. He raised his head and looked around, close to laughing with frustration. Where was he hiding?

\* \* \*

Jane sat patiently, wondering if Barton would come outside today. Wilfred had returned, looking abashed, waiting by the cottage behind Green Dragon Yard.

'I want to try again,' he said.

'Come on, then.'

They'd barely settled in the spot that gave a good view of the house when the boy lifted his head and hissed: 'Someone's coming.'

Good; he'd heard it. Jane had caught the sound a few seconds before, already reaching for her knife. Another moment and she let go of the hilt.

Sally.

She kept the shawl around her face, so it covered the scar on her cheek. 'The children are searching. They know where to find me.' She stretched out her legs with a small wince of pain. 'Simon had a tip on Fox.'

She'd noticed him as he came out of the hotel and he'd told her everything.

They were drawing closer, Jane thought. Only a jump or two behind the man. Fox had to make his move soon. He'd had so many opportunities, plenty when he and his wife were on Middle Fold. He must have made some sort of arrangement with Andrew Barton, but never tried to kill the father.

Why? That was the thing she didn't understand. Perhaps it didn't matter, as long as they caught him. The images of death came into her mind: Mrs Fox, lost and beyond help in the water. Barton pulling his son's body from the beck.

By noon she could see that Sally was growing restless, needing to be off. Jane sent her with Wilfred to buy food. A sound in the distance caught her ear. Davy Cassidy's fiddle playing a tune. Jane half-listened, sitting up as a female voice joined the melody. She wondered who he'd found; they sounded natural together.

The others returned. They hadn't finished eating before Barton came out, breathed deep and began to walk.

'You and Wilfred follow him,' she told Sally. 'He'll be going to see his son's grave.' That should be simple enough. 'If you see Fox . . .'

'We'll stop him,' Sally said. Her eyes were as hard as her voice.

Once they'd gone, Jane checked around the house. Nobody. She caught a glimpse of Barton's wife through a window. Standing, staring at nothing. Life must be empty inside those walls, she thought. A place without hope or future. Time standing still, as though a clock had stopped ticking.

Simon asked at the hotels. Fox wasn't there. Too many lodging houses in Leeds for him to check every one of them.

'He wouldn't go to one, anyway,' George Mudie said when Simon told him. 'Not if he's been used to somewhere grander. The Western isn't luxurious, but . . .'

Still a big step above a common lodging house; Simon understood that. Fox wanted to believe he was still somebody. He couldn't stoop that low; it would be an admission of defeat.

Then where was he?

Someone came blundering through the undergrowth. As soon as she heard the noise, Jane was ready, standing with a knife in her hand. For the first time in a while, she felt her missing finger.

Sally stood, pulling out her blade, eyes wary. Wilfred followed, the fear showing on his face.

It was a boy, nine or ten years old. Lean as a whip, skin weathered and raw from months of living outside. He came to a sudden, terrified halt as he saw the weapons and held up his hands, looking from one face to the other. Sally's blade slid out of sight. Jane was the last to put hers away.

'Have you found something, Danny?' Sally asked, smiling at the boy to put him at ease.

Still scared, the words came hesitantly. 'That man. The one you want. Anna saw him.'

Jane opened her mouth, but Sally gestured with her hand. Let her take care of it.

'Where was this?'

'By St Mary's Church.'

It stood at the bottom end of Mabgate, close to where it joined with Quarry Hill, not too far from where the Foxes had lived on Middle Fold. Back where they'd originally found him, and the last place anyone would look now.

'Why did Anna think it was him?' Sally asked. She kept her voice low and gentle, coaxing the words out of the boy.

'She said he looked like the man you told us about.'

'Where was he going? Did she see?'

'She said he started to walk up Mabgate. Then she ran off. She knew we needed to tell you.'

Jane took out a silver sixpence and handed it to him.

'You've done well, Danny,' Sally assured him and took out another coin. 'Give that to Anna.'

He crashed away, beaming wide.

'We have to tell Simon,' Jane said.

'She might have been wrong. Remember last time?'

She did. The chances were that it wasn't Fox; even the best description would seem vague to a child. But it *felt* right. Her heart was thumping at the idea, a tingling in her fingers. This was it. Nothing she could explain, but somehow she was certain that this was it.

'What about Barton?'

Time to decide. 'He won't come out again today.'

Even if Fox appeared, he wouldn't get into the house. It was safe to leave.

'It's possible,' Simon agreed. They'd found him close to the courthouse, on his way to see Porter. He was rubbing the sweat from his forehead with a handkerchief; the afternoon heat had turned thick and oppressive. 'He could be up there.'

It would be clever. Mabgate was by Middle Fold. Nobody would expect him to return there. But the man was taking a chance.

Still, this was the best they had for now. It wasn't much. Nothing more than a guess built up from a child's belief. He wouldn't wager everything on it. But . . .

'Go up and watch. It might not be the same house. Maybe not the same street. Ask people if they recognise his description.'

Or it might be nothing at all. But they knew that as well as he did.

Her head was filled with anticipation as she marched through town. Looking straight ahead, aware of Sally to one side, Wilfred to the other. She twisted the lucky gold ring that Mrs Shields had given her.

As they passed Seaton's old mill at Millgarth, Jane remembered the screaming girl who'd been carried from there was where all this began. The one who still visited her dreams. Maybe she'd managed to stay alive and find some sort of peace.

Over Sheepscar Beck at Lady Bridge and into the chaos of workshops and small factories that had grown up along Mabgate. The houses that she recalled along here had gone. It was all industry now. Making money.

She stood at the top of Middle Fold, staring down the street.

'What can we do?' Sally asked. Possibilities shone in her eyes. She wasn't drained; her eyes were shining, thrilled by the chase. Jane turned her head and glanced at Wilfred. Scared, looking very young, but not backing down.

'Ask people we see.' She nodded towards a woman walking towards them. 'If we don't find anything, we'll have a look further along.' They'd just passed New Church Place and the corner of Ward's Fold stood a dozen more yards along Mabgate. 'Porter will be coming with his men. They'll need information.'

Jane was never comfortable talking to strangers. She noticed how they moved away and eyed her with suspicion. It was no surprise; in her work clothes, she might have been a beggar asking for money. People shook their heads as she asked about Fox.

An hour of patience and persistence with the background music of machines and hammers from the big Hope Foundry. Suddenly she picked out the sound of someone running, reaching for her knife as she turned. Wilfred, dashing over the dirt road and waving his arms.

'The houses down the other end.'

'Has someone seen him?'

The boy nodded as he caught his breath.

Sally was out of sight, deep in the shade of an old tree. Her face was drawn with exhaustion as she watched a group of four houses that trailed down towards St Mary's Place. Farther along Middle Fold than the house the Foxes had taken before.

'Which one?'

'The man I asked didn't know, but he seemed sure it was Fox.'

'The last time was nothing, Westow,' the constable said. 'I'd thought you'd have learned not to trust a gaggle of children. All they're after is your money.'

'If they help us find him, they're welcome to some of it.'

Porter's men had still been asking about Fox around Eye Bright Place.

'If.' Porter snorted. 'Chances are he's nowhere near here, and you know it.'

'Do we have anything else?'

The constable was right; it would probably turn out to be nothing, but for some reason he felt a small surge of hope. He'd sent a note to Rosie, asking her to go and keep watch over Barton's house. The constable had left his inspector in charge and brought one man with him, a veteran of the watch named Tom. With Simon and the others, it ought to be enough.

If Fox was there.

Jane was waiting by the graveyard in front of St Mary's Church. Simon watched Porter's face as she explained what they'd discovered.

'Let's say for a moment that he really is like a dog returning to its own vomit and he's back in Middle Fold.' Porter considered the possibilities. 'It's easy enough for him to run from there.' He pointed. 'That open ground to the north, it goes right through Sheepscar, up to the turnpike and the barracks. Over to the east, Burmantofts Hall. We have to be able to stop any escape that way.'

He was right. If Fox came out, the man would be running hard. With his bad leg and stick, Simon knew he had no chance of moving quickly. Had Sally recovered enough to run and fight? Maybe if she was with the new boy who'd been following Jane like a puppy . . .

'Why don't you two take that stretch of ground up there?' he said, pointing north. 'You know what to do if you see him.'

Sally nodded. He could see it in her eyes. She was ready for this.

'What about me?' Jane asked.

'Down towards Burmantofts Hall,' he told her. 'In case he tries to get out that way.'

He watched them leave and turned to Porter.

'How are we going to do this?'

'We go from house to house.' A row of four of them together. 'I'd bet good money we're wasting our time. But since we're here, we're going to look thoroughly.'

'If he's there?'

'I'd prefer him alive.' A snort. 'Don't take any chances.' The constable turned to the night watchman standing beside him. He had a jutting chin and an expression that looked eager for violence. 'You understand, Tom?'

'Yes.' The word came reluctantly.

Porter stood in front of the first door, Tom at his shoulder, hand on his knife. Simon stayed a yard behind them, ready in case he was needed. But Fox was wanted for murder; this was the constable's business.

The rap of knuckles on wood and the door was pulled open. Before they could breathe, Fox was standing there, no panic on his face, a pistol in each hand.

# THIRTY-ONE

He fired. No hatred, no emotion on his face as he pulled the trigger and the watchman fell with a scream, clutching his belly. Porter had begun to turn his head to stare at him as the second shot exploded in his face.

He crashed backwards, already dead as he toppled against Simon, landing heavily on top of him. His skull was shattered, blood and gore running over his flesh.

Simon was pinned, the weight heavy on his chest. He struggled to move, to push himself from under the body. He squirmed, yelling out, tearing and pulling at the ground to try and squeeze his way out. All the while he wondered if Fox was waiting, reloading, ready to kill him, too.

The air was heavy with the smells of blood and death. Tom was moaning, screaming in agony and crying, but Simon couldn't help him.

Then someone was there, hands dragging Porter away, putting his stick in his hand and helping him rise to his feet. A pain like fire shot through his leg as soon as he tried to put weight on it. He staggered, but held.

He saw Jane gazing at him in horror, looked down and realised he was covered in blood.

'It's not mine.' The words were a croak, hard to believe. He was too stunned to be scared. As Simon stared at what remained of Porter's face, none of it seemed real. Only the watchman's screams had any substance. Porter couldn't be dead. It wasn't possible. It . . . dear God, he didn't know. How had he survived?

He didn't want to speak the name, but he had to know. 'Fox?'

Jane shook her head. 'Gone.'

'We need . . .' He turned at the sound of people running.

'We heard shots . . .' Sally began, then stopped when she saw what Fox had done. She was out of breath, panting hard.

The boy with her was on his knees beside Tom, holding his hand as he talked gently to him, trying to soothe him.

The thoughts arrived clear and calm. Things that had to be done. Some order.

'The inspector's down near Eye Bright Place,' Simon said. 'Tell him what's happened, that we need someone to take charge. A surgeon too, someone to take him to the infirmary.'

Without another word, Sally nodded, gathered the boy and left. Simon looked around. He couldn't take it in. He'd never be able to accept, to understand. He tried to walk. A couple of stumbling, painful steps; he must have twisted his knee when Porter landed on him.

'Go to Barton's house,' he told Jane. 'Rosie's there.'

'You think Fox is on his way?'

'He has to be.' The man had run out of time and choices now. He needed to finish his business in Leeds, then try to run. It was the only course.

'What about . . .' Jane asked. 'Will you be all right?'

He took a breath and kept the truth hidden inside. Rosie could hear it later. 'I'll be fine. I'll stay here and tell them.' Simon tapped his leg and tried to smile. 'I can't help you chase, anyway.' Another glance at Porter. 'He has pistols.'

Jane ran, not caring if anyone turned and stared. The scene kept playing in her mind. Dead, wounded, Simon trapped under a corpse. So much blood that she'd believed he was dying, too, her heart desperate.

Fox had a good start on her. She forced herself to move faster, twisting the gold ring on her finger again for luck.

She ducked between carts and behind horses, feeling the rushed breath of a coach a few inches away.

Finally she reached Barton's house. She felt as if it had taken her an age to arrive.

Moving quietly through the bushes until Rosie was standing in front of her, tall and dangerous with her knife ready to cut.

Her expression changed as she listened, shifting from disbelief to shock to anxiety.

'Simon?' she asked as soon as Jane finished. 'Is he hurt?'

'No.'

'Fox hasn't come yet.'
'He will. We need to be ready for him.'
He'd be here; she knew it.

Simon began to shake again, the third time since Fox pulled the trigger. He couldn't stop it. The shuddering took over for a minute before gradually subsiding again.

Inspector Fry had arrived, bringing more men. He glared, filled with rage, then stared at the body on the ground. Simon knew there was nothing he could have done to stop things. No one could have guessed what Fox would do. There hadn't even been time to try and push the constable out of the way. It had been over before he could blink.

A neighbour had brought out a piece of sacking to cover Porter, but blood had soaked through the material and a crowd of flies had gathered to feast on it.

At least Tom the watchman had been taken to the infirmary. He looked bad. But he was still alive. More than the constable.

'Where's the bastard gone?' Fry yelled, pacing up and down the street, smashing one fist into the other.

'Barton,' Simon told him as soon as the shaking passed.

'You saw him.' A glance down at the ground. Pure fury in his voice. 'Murder.'

'Yes.' Fox would go to the gallows for this, and everything else he'd done. No reprieve this time. But he'd never live long enough to climb on to the scaffold.

'I'm going up there. Jameson, Ford,' he called. 'You're with me. Turner, stay and look after the body. They'll come and collect it soon.'

The sun was still bright and the air thick with dust. It didn't seem like a day for death. The door to Fox's house still hung open. Simon took a step, then two, testing his leg. Painful, but he could still walk.

A little cooler inside. All the shutters were closed; it took a while for his eyes to adjust to the dimness.

Simon poured water into a bowl and tried to wash his hands and face. It took the worst of the stink off him, but the water quickly turned the colour of rust. His clothes were ruined, only good for burning.

He still felt as if he was moving through a dream. That he'd wake with Porter and the watchman standing and talking. Then the shots would echo in his ears again.

He searched the rooms. Habit. But there was little to find. A pipe and a twist of tobacco. A half-read newspaper. No spare clothes: Fox was wearing everything he owned.

Simon came out again, blinking under the sharp sunlight, and began to hobble away. He needed to be at Barton's house. Thank God for the stick.

Jane stood out of sight against the tree, hidden by its shade. Rosie was on the other side of the drive. They'd be able to take Fox as he entered.

She closed her eyes for a second and saw the dead and destroyed on Middle Fold; she had to shake her head to force it away.

He should have arrived by now.

A faint sound and she was alert. Fingers tight around the hilt of her knife. She sensed something and turned. Sally, sliding in behind her.

'I sent Wilfred away. He's not made for this.'

A nod. No need for words.

Jane turned her head. The scuff of a shoe on the ground. She pressed herself against the tree and pulled the shawl tight over her hair before she looked.

Fox. Crouching, moving cautiously, trying to keep out of sight.

She let him pass, then crept from the undergrowth. From the corner of her eye, she saw Rosie emerge, silent, dangerous.

Sally would be moving between the bushes. Ready when the time came.

When he was five yards from the door, Rosie called out: 'Stop.'

The man turned. No pistols in his hands. Not even a knife. His face showed nothing at all. No anger, no fear. Empty.

'This isn't your business.'

Jane took two paces to the side. A better angle to attack him. She saw Sally ease into view behind Fox, carrying a small, stout branch along with her knife.

'You've murdered,' Rosie told him. 'You're going to stand trial.'

'I've come to finish things.'

'Finish them, then.' A man's voice.

Jane hadn't seen the front door open. Barton stood there. The withered husk she'd followed to the churchyard and back had vanished. The man she saw now wasn't stooped and old. He had a fire about him, the hope of finally discovering the truth. Finding some redemption.

'Let him be,' Barton said.

Jane didn't move. Rosie, Sally, all three of them stood firm.

'You killed my son.' Not an accusation. A judgement.

'Do you know what he did? He betrayed you.' Fox's voice rose. 'He wanted us to fleece you dry. He hated you.'

Barton stood, eyes fixed on the other man. 'Perhaps he did. But he failed.'

'Do you know why he killed himself?' Fox asked.

'Why is that?'

'Guilt. It had been growing in him for months. It must have become too much for him to carry.'

Barton stepped forward. A knife appeared in his hand.

Fox was ready, suddenly holding his own weapon and sneering. 'What are you going to do? See if you can kill me?'

'Andrew was fine until you appeared.'

'My wife,' Fox continued as if the other man hadn't spoken. 'She was the one who spotted your son. That hatred of you was already there inside him. She brought it out, that's all, and it was easy enough to do. She seduced him. But she grew a little too close. Do you know what she said? She was going to leave me to be with him. The last time I saw your son, I told him he was the reason I had to kill her.'

His wife leaving would have been a humiliation, Jane thought. Fox wouldn't have been able to stomach that. Now he'd turned it into a weapon.

'Why have you come here?' Barton asked.

'To finish the story.'

'You had plenty of chances before.'

'I wasn't ready. I wanted you terrified, always looking over your shoulder. Never knowing when I'd come for you. Now . . .' He shrugged. 'There's nothing else.'

Enough, Jane thought. The time had come to end all this. They'd been employed to keep Barton safe.

She glanced towards Rosie; her eyes were fixed on Fox. Sally saw her look and nodded.

'Fox,' Jane said.

He turned his head to look at her. She waited, aware of the minute hesitation before Sally darted in and brought the branch down on his arm and made him drop the knife. Before he could move, Jane and Rosie were close.

She stared into his face. Still empty, as if the emotion had been wiped away. 'It's over.'

'No.' Barton spoke. The light caught his eyes and for a second they seemed to glow. He lunged forward.

She saw the knife plunge into Fox's belly, as deep as he could force it, then it slid slowly back out.

'He killed my son.'

Jane and Rosie both moved forward to hold Fox as his knees buckled. They lowered him to the ground as the thin trickle of blood from the wound grew into a dark, sodden stain that covered his trousers.

No doctor could save him now. Barton stared with a gleam of satisfaction. Jane recalled how he'd looked when he saw Andrew drowned in the beck. This would bring him an hour's joy, but it would fade into more pain to weigh down his heart.

Then the inspector pushed her aside. She'd been caught in the moment, never heard him arrive. He had his men beside him. The toe of his boot prodded Fox.

'Nobody to reprieve you now.' He spat; the phlegm landed beside the man's hand. 'You attacked Mr Barton and he defended himself. I saw it happen with my own eyes.' He let the words hang in the air. Nobody would challenge him.

Fox moved his hand to cover the wound, as if he could stop the blood leaving his body.

'Why did you kill Shackleton?' Rosie asked quietly.

The man breathed in and gasped with pain. 'Gave him money to kill him . . .' He nodded towards Barton. 'Got here and he refused. Gave him food and lodging. Tried to persuade him three times.' Another gasp. 'He had to pay.'

Jane cradled his head. Pale pink foam was starting to come out of his mouth. Death had its hand on his shoulder.

Sally's question took her by surprise. 'How did you get your pardon?'

His lips turned up as he tried to smile. It turned into a laugh. A clot of blood flew from his mouth. 'Luck,' he said. 'Pure luck. I prayed for it and it happened.'

The blood became a torrent and his eyes closed. Jane waited a moment then placed her hand against his neck. Nothing.

She lowered his head and stood.

All of them standing, staring down at a dead man. Whoever he'd been, however bad, that was done.

Barton was the first to leave. He turned, went into his house and closed the door on the scene.

With a final kick at the body, the inspector left, his men falling in behind as Simon hurried in, face contorted and bathed in sweat.

He knew how he must look. Dangerous, like a madman with the blood and gore spattered all over. People on the streets had moved away in horror. One man had shouted something; he'd paid it no mind, intent on getting here.

Too late. Fox's blood had soaked into the dirt, his life gone. Jane, Sally and Rosie were standing by the body.

'Who?' he asked them.

Rosie replied, 'Barton.'

That shook him. 'Is he . . .'

'He's fine.'

He'd seen too much death and pain today. He could smell it each time he breathed in. Taste it on his tongue. It was going to live with him for years.

'We can't do anything more,' he said. 'Nobody can.'

He needed to wash off the stink and the blood. To destroy the clothes. To try to feel clean again.

There were days, weeks ahead to discover what had happened.

# THIRTY-TWO

The town clattered and thrummed as they walked, but neither of them seemed to notice it. Jane heard a few faint notes from Davy Cassidy's fiddle, but for once she knew it couldn't soothe her. This was a time for silence.

Sally stayed by her side. The girl's face was pinched tight from all the effort and strain of the day. She'd pushed herself too far. Time and rest would cure that. Her body had recovered well; she was almost back to the way it had been. Her mind, though . . . Jane had seen the small hesitation before she acted against Fox. Another time that could be fatal.

Maybe they needed to spar; a little practice with her knife could help. But that was an idea that could wait for another day, when the air wasn't so full of blood and dying.

At the house behind Green Dragon Yard, they sat outside on the bench. Mrs Shields looked at them both with knowing eyes and vanished to the kitchen. She brought out two mugs holding a drink whose smell Jane didn't recognise.

'Drink it,' the old woman told them.

It tasted of . . . she wasn't sure. Nothing unpleasant. Something that reminded her of fields and forests. She drained the cup and rested it in her lap as she thought about Barton.

He'd had a hollow joy in his eyes as he used the knife on Fox. The grief for his son had been building in him since that afternoon by the tiny church out at Lead. This wouldn't rid him of his devils. After this, they'd ride him harder than ever.

Now he'd carry the guilt of murder on top of everything else.

Jane turned her head. Sally was staring without seeing. Her eyes glistened as if she was on the edge of tears.

'Can we start reading again tomorrow?' she asked.

'Yes. Of course.'

The girl nodded. She was silent for a while.

'Do you know why I want to learn?'

'No.' She'd wondered about it, but hadn't managed to find a reason.

'When I was ill, I realised what I want to do. Not yet,' she added quickly. 'Once I'm a few years older.'

'What is it?' It was hard to imagine Sally making plans like that.

She began slowly. 'My parents had a farm. Animals, growing things.'

The silence returned. Jane waited.

'I'm not happy in town. I'm never going to be, not really. I've tried.' She turned her head. 'Does that make sense?'

'Yes.' She'd seen it on the girl's face, the way she seemed to come alive when their walks took them out of Leeds, among the fields and the woods. 'What are you going to do?'

'I'm going to find a little piece of land and buy it. Mine, where nobody can make me leave. Ever. A farm. The children can live there and help me. You know working for Simon pays. I can save my money.'

A dream, a wish, Jane thought. But the resolution was set on Sally's face.

'What does that have to do with reading?'

'If I know how to read and write, no one can cheat me.'

So simple, so straightforward. She had it all clearly laid out in her head. It would never be that easy, but Jane stayed quiet. She'd teach and be glad to see her pupil blossom.

Sally stood, suddenly looking flustered, as if she'd said more than she intended.

'Don't tell anyone. Especially Simon.'

'Our secret,' Jane promised. She had plenty of those, more than she could count, all tucked away in her mind. 'Do you want me to walk with you?'

A quick shake of the head. 'No need.' The knife flashed in her hand. 'I'll be safe now.'

The clouds threatened, dark and dreary. But no rain. Simon stood by the coffee cart on Briggate, listening to people talk about Fox's killing. Plenty wanted to know his version, but he could honestly tell them he hadn't been there for it.

Rosie had recounted it all to him as he scrubbed his skin

bright pink and rinsed pieces of brain and bone from his hair. His mind was still numb, not wanting to believe any of it. But under that, he knew the truth far too well. He'd heard the shots in Middle Fold, he'd seen the body outside Barton's house. However much he wanted to deny it, it was all real.

Rosie was filled with regrets that she hadn't been able to stop Fox's death, but what could she have done?

The man was a murderer. There was never a chance he'd stay alive long enough to stand trial. If Barton hadn't killed him, the inspector would have done it.

The luck that had pardoned him had ended.

'You beat me.'

Simon turned. Alexander Brady was facing him.

'Was it a race?'

'You know damned well it was.' The man glared. 'There was money to be made from him. We could have shared it.'

'There was justice to be done.' He glanced at the battered valise by Brady's feet. 'I wish you a comfortable journey home.'

He placed the tin cup on the trestle and began to walk away, knee throbbing. Easier than yesterday but twisted and aching from the fall. Sally appeared at his side. She still had the fading remains of bruises from her black eyes, and the scar would never go, but she seemed to be almost recovered.

'What do we have to do today?' she asked.

'Nothing,' he told her. 'Nothing at all.' Nobody needing their services, and for once he was glad. His mind, his body, they both needed rest. He had to see Barton, but that would wait for a little while.

She nodded and hurried away. Alone, he turned, moving slowly through the people who crowded Briggate, over the Head Row to Mudie's shop.

At the circulating library, Jane picked the book from the shelf and opened it to the title page. *The Betrothed*, she read, *by The Author of Waverley*. A favourite writer; this was the one to read next. She bought two pies from Kate and took them home to share with Mrs Shields.

A return to the comfort of familiar routines and faces.

Wilfred hadn't returned that morning. She had nothing for

him to do, anyway. Maybe he'd decided this life wasn't for him.

Throughout the afternoon she sat outside, caught in the strange, tangled plot and the world of men in the wilds and castles of the Welsh Marches. She was startled when Mrs Shields tapped her on the shoulder.

'I called you to eat, child. You must have been miles away.'

'I was.' Glad of it, too; the words on the page banished thoughts from her mind.

Last night she'd expected Fox or Porter with his vanished face to come to her dreams. Instead, it was the girl again, her screams cutting through sleep, bringing her awake and gasping. She sat up in bed, staring down the darkness while her heartbeat slowed again and the dread that filled her mind receded.

There was the first hint of an autumnal chill in the early evening air outside the cottage. She gathered the shawl around her shoulders, and was about to move indoors when Sally arrived, eager to read and learn. An hour with her, then they walked down to Swinegate as the twilight grew around them.

Friday night and the alehouses were doing good business, roaring and racketing. Jane didn't feel any fear of the drunken men. She kept a hand in her pocket, fingers loose around the hilt of her knife, and stayed aware of everything around her.

She returned up Briggate, pools of light from the windows illuminating the street. Stopping for a word with Dodson, the old soldier with the wooden leg, as he folded his blanket ready to return to his room for the night.

Up by the market cross, Davy Cassidy was playing a sprightly tune that ended as she drew close. He gazed around with his sightless eyes and a girl appeared, whispering a word into his ear. He lifted his bow and began to play again. Low, mournful. Then the girl stepped forward and began to sing.

Jane knew her face. She'd lived with it for months. She'd seen it contorted with pain as the girl was carried from the mill, her leg in shreds, then when it returned night after night in her dreams. Now she was here, one-legged, supported by a crutch, her voice as unearthly sweet as a visitation as she sang about a girl who moved through the fair.

She stood, transfixed as her disbelief fragmented and

disappeared. The pain she'd heard in the girl that day in February had become beauty. The small crowd was silent, caught in the words, the singing, while the world receded around them.

The last note ended. A stunned silence, then applause and people pushing forward to put coins into the hat on the ground. Jane added her money, then looked up. She couldn't see the girl. It was almost as if she hadn't been real.

The memory of it lifted her home and into bed. No need for a book tonight. She had the song in her head.

Inspector Fry came to see him during the morning. Fury still burned in his eyes, but his voice was sober. Until a new man was appointed, he was the constable, responsible for the law in Leeds.

'I need to know how it happened, Westow. What happened when Fox opened that door?'

As he told it, Simon understood yet again that there was nothing they could have done. No reason to believe Fox had his pair of pistols, that he'd shoot.

Once he'd finished, Fry looked up at him. 'One more question.'

'Ask it,' he said, although he knew what it would be.

'Why is he dead and you're still alive? You don't have a mark on you.' He stood, nodded, and let himself out.

Simon had kept wondering the same thing. Fate. Luck. But the man was wrong. No mark on the outside, but plenty in his head and his heart.

'He thinks he should have been able to stop it,' Rosie said. 'Then he came too late to take his revenge against Fox.'

No screams to rip open her sleep. Not even the memories of Porter and Fox. Jane woke to daylight seeping through the shutters. She stretched, feeling the rare joy of a deep, unbroken rest.

Last night's chill remained and she was glad of the shawl around her shoulders as she strolled down to Central Market to buy food, a basket over her arm. Carts and coaches filled Briggate, women stopped on the pavement to stare into shop windows.

The market came as a relief. Crowded and familiar, men shouting their wares, women searching for a bargain. She bought what she needed, then wandered down Kirkgate, past Grey's Court, down beyond the parish church and East Bar to the butcher she liked on Timble Bridge.

On the way home, Kate the pie-seller took her pennies as she handed over the food.

'You look different, pet.'

'Do I?' How? she wondered.

'I'm not sure. Content, perhaps?' The woman smiled. 'Whatever it is, I'm pleased to see it. I've known you all these years and I can count on one hand the times I've seen you happy.'

Maybe she was. Jane thought about it, then let her mind drift. No plans beyond reading and spending time with Mrs Shields, learning one or two more of the old woman's secrets with herbs and remedies.

She was reading, deep in the evening and caught up in the book, when she heard the footsteps and the pounding on the door. She opened it to see Sally.

The girl was pale, drained, panting after running.

'What is it? What's happened?' Jane felt the panic rise.

'Simon's heard a rumour that the men are going after the children again. He said a couple of people were talking.'

Jane glanced over her shoulder at Mrs Shields. The woman stared at her, then gave a reluctant nod.

'Where are they?' she asked as they marched side by side.

'That empty land the far side of Great Waterloo Street.'

The other side of the river. A large open space, some houses rising out of the ground.

'Are you sure you're ready?' Jane asked.

The girl looked exhausted, but her eyes were fixed straight ahead. 'Yes,' she answered after a moment. Then, more firmly: 'I have to be.'

Fifty yards away, where they were building, the walls of a house offered protection. A pile of bricks and wood provided ammunition to defend themselves. Better than being caught in the open.

No need to douse the fire in the middle of the open ground.

'We'll let it burn,' Sally decided. 'The men will go there and then we can take them by surprise.'

Now they had to wait.

As soon as he overheard the men speak about the attack, Simon had hurried home to warn Sally of the danger. Now he was back out, fading into the heart of a Saturday night. The end of the work week, men out drinking their wages, seeking pleasure and a fight.

The whores of Briggate were enjoying a crisp trade. By the Turk's Head, the drinkers had spilled out into the yard. A voice close by called out, 'Billy, you're back in Leeds,' and he turned.

That was the man. Billy Harding. As soon as he saw him, he remembered the eyes. One of the pair who'd attacked him. Simon eased away, finding a spot in the gloom outside the door to wait for the man to leave.

Almost an hour passed before Harding emerged, walking alone, wearing his high crown hat at an angle, the tails of his coat pushed back as he walked with hands thrust in his pockets. Not a care in the world, completely unaware of the man following him.

Town was busy, but by the time they reached North Street, people had melted away. One faint echo of footsteps that faded to silence. They were alone.

'Mr Harding,' he said quietly, and Billy turned, surprised.

'Who . . .' he began, but Simon was already on him, holding the flat of his knife against the man's face. 'You can have my money. My watch—'

'Don't you remember me?'

He smelled the man's terror, seeing his eyes move, searching for any chance of escape.

'You seemed to know who I was when you and Mr Collins met me. Or have you forgotten so quickly?' He tapped the stick on the ground. 'How's his knee now? It was still bad when I talked to him the other day.'

'What . . .' He tried to swallow. 'What do you want?'

'Just a word, Billy. Nothing more. What did you think? That you'd never have to face me? That I'd forget?' He shook his head. 'Life doesn't work like that.'

'I . . .' he began, and hung his head. 'We'd been drinking. Charles goaded us on.'

'I'm not here for him.'

'I'm sorry.' He looked into Simon's face and the repentance was there. 'I truly am.'

Suddenly Simon tired of the game. The idea of revenge withered. He wasn't going to kill the man or cut him. What would be the point? Harding would remember tonight for years. That was enough.

'I'll trust you mean that.'

'I do.'

'Then I'll wish you a good night.'

He stood and watched the man walk off, constantly glancing over his shoulder. It was done. Let him think whatever he wished.

# THIRTY-THREE

The children were growing restless. The young ones were fretful, a few crying and scared. The older ones tried to show nothing, but fear crackled through the air.

Waiting for battle.

Sally moved around the groups, with plenty of reassurance and smiles. Hannah stayed with her, looking relieved to have her to look after them all.

Jane caught a glimpse of Wilfred in the deep shadows at the edge of the group.

'What do you think about being a thief-taker after all that happened?' she asked. He hadn't come to see her since Fox's death. 'Did you decide it's not for you?'

The boy blinked and looked down at the ground. It was an answer. 'I'm sorry, miss.'

'It doesn't matter. You made yourself try.'

'I . . . I don't have the courage for it. I'm sorry, miss,' he said again. 'I'm going to look at the factories, miss.'

'They might have a job for you.' Twelve hours or more a day, six days a week for starvation wages was all children could expect. That took a different kind of courage. 'That might suit you more,' she told him. 'If I can . . .' Jane stopped and raised her head. They were coming.

She stood with Sally, watching as they appeared from the far side of the empty ground. Four of them. No, five; one was lurking behind. They were carrying sticks and knives. In the curl of firelight she recognised one face: Henry Harrison. One of Andrew Barton's friends, part of the group that attacked Sally.

The girl spoke before Jane could open her mouth. Her eyes never moved from the men. 'I've seen him.' Her voice was barely more than a hiss. 'There's another one, too, with the fair hair. He was with them. They're mine.'

They stood still and silent as the men charged the fire. Drunk and stumbling, not realising nobody was there, and confused when they found no opponent.

'Now,' Sally called out, and the children screamed as they threw their bricks and stones.

The men moved back in blind disarray. One ran off into the night. Jane glanced; Sally had slipped away.

Everything was quiet for a minute, only the crackle of the flames and sparks rising into the night. Then a cry, and she saw one of the men bent over, clutching at his face as if it was on fire. Sally had begun her revenge.

Jane sensed the children behind her. Wary, ready. But the attack was wavering before it could really begin. Only two left. And the other one behind, urging them on. She knew his voice. She'd last heard it when she cornered him in Rockley Hall Yard and sliced his cheek. Charles Ibbotson.

A clash of knives, metal on metal and she dashed forward. Sally was squaring off with Harrison. The other man stood, unsure if he had the courage to join in. As soon as he saw Jane, he fled.

Sally was carried by fury, forcing Harrison back step by step. He made the mistake of turning his head towards Jane. That was all the girl needed. She darted in with a single, lightning cut, then away again, out of reach. The man's eyes filled with horror as his fingers moved to his cheek and came away bloody. He dropped the knife, whimpering like a child as he scurried off into the night.

'It's over,' Jane said. So fast, so easy. No battle, not even a scrap, just young men full of drink and bravado that wilted at the first challenge. But Sally shook her head.

'No, it's not. There's still one more.'

'I cut him. I told you.'

'But I haven't.' Her voice was iron. She began to move. 'Are you coming?'

Ibbotson had waited too long. Now he was running, trying to keep himself safe.

Sally was already moving, forcing her legs to push hard. Jane began to run; she couldn't let the girl go alone.

He looked over his shoulder. They were gaining on him. Thirty yards between them by the time they reached Leeds

Bridge. Jane heard the lapping of water and the deep wooden creak of barges against the wharves.

Suddenly they couldn't see him, as if he'd somehow vanished into the night.

At the corner, they stopped. Briggate ran on ahead of them, Swinegate trailing away to the left, the Calls going the other way.

Sally cocked her head, raising a finger: wait.

A few seconds, then, silently, she turned right. Four yards and right again. Down Pitfall.

Hardly wider than a ginnel, leading to the river. As she stood, Jane could hear a rasping breath. A few more seconds as her eyes adjusted, then she made out the shape cowering against the wall of building, as if its shadow would hide him.

He was trapped. The only way out was past them.

Sally took a pace forward. Jane followed.

Sally moved again.

Ibbotson began to shuffle back, moving down Pitfall towards the water.

A step. Then one more.

The girl didn't speak. She clutched her knife and stared at his face. The livid scar on his cheek that matched her own.

The echo of her boots came back off the walls as she moved forward again. Ibbotson held up his arms, as if he could push her away. Panic flared in his eyes.

Sally stopped. 'Well?' she asked. 'What do you have to say now?'

He shook his head. The words stumbled out: 'I'm sorry.'

'Are you?'

'Yes,' he said.

Jane saw his legs tense, ready to spring, the knife coming up in his hand.

'He—'

Before she could say any more, someone rushed past them. A boy, dressed in drab clothes – Wilfred. He crashed hard against Ibbotson. The man's blade arced loose through the air as the impact carried them both backwards. Tumbling over the bank, landing heavily in the water.

They saw a small hand rise and fall, stabbing wildly with a

knife. As the splashing finished, the ripples slowly spread to nothing remained on the oily surface of the river. Wilfred had discovered his courage.

Jane stared until she felt the chill seeping under her skin.

'Now it's all done,' Sally said. She sounded empty. Drained.

'Yes.' Jane's voice was dull. 'I . . .' she began, then realised she didn't know what to say. She had no words for the storm in her head.

No screaming girl to haunt her rest tonight. Instead, it was a boy running.

Jane was standing by the coffee cart outside the Bull and Mouth before Simon arrived the next morning. As he paid for his cup, he gave her a curious look. At least he knew better than to ask questions. Sally was there, too, keeping watch on the other side of Briggate.

Jane had been listening closely to the gossip. No whisper of any bodies in the river.

She listed the names in her head. Wilfred, Ibbotson, Porter, Fox, Andrew Barton.

So many dead, she thought, and the only legacy was pain.

# THIRTY-FOUR

Wilfred's body was brought ashore downstream at Knostrop. Two days to travel a mile. It was news for five minutes.

Sally asked Simon to arrange everything with the parish church; they'd listen to a man, never to her. All the homeless children stood quietly as a curate read the burial service by the grave. Hannah tossed the first clod of earth down on to the coffin, Sally the second, then Jane.

'Poor boy,' Rosie said as they walked away. 'Does anyone know what happened?'

'No,' Simon told her. 'Nothing more than guesses.'

Someone had told him about two young men with their cheeks sliced open in a knife fight. Another mentioned that Charles Ibbotson had disappeared. Rumours swirled but the truth stayed hidden. If anyone knew, they were staying silent.

Time passed. Once or twice, he wondered about Barton. Someone said that he and his wife had gone away; nobody seemed to know where. But what would Leeds hold for them now, anyway?

Jane returned to her tidy routines. Shopping each day, living through the books she read. Simon hadn't asked for her help. That was fine. She had money; Barton had paid them well. She was happy with her small circle: Mrs Shields, Kate the pie-seller, Dodson the beggar, Davy Cassidy and the girl who sang with him.

Sally arrived three times a week for her lessons, her reading improving steadily as she grew more confident in her ability.

Rest had helped her. She moved easily now, she'd regained a little weight, she was smiling, carefree again. Still covering her hair with the shawl when she walked, but no longer covering the scar on her cheek; she seemed to have decided to wear it with pride.

'That one has a purpose about her now, doesn't she?' Mrs Shields remarked one day after the girl left.

Jane thought of the future Sally had told her about. Maybe she'd make it happen. 'Yes. She does.'

# Acknowledgements

As always, my thanks go to the excellent team at Severn House, who help make these words in my head into what you read. They all do outstanding work, but I have to single out my editor, Sara Porter, whose stunning eye for detail had been a saving grace several times, and Piers Tilbury, whose cover designs always take my breath away.

My huge thanks, too, to Lynne Patrick, a longtime friend and editor whom I've trusted completely for a long time now. Her work improves my writing.

I'm also grateful to all who review these books, and to those who buy them – please don't stop! But it always comes down to you, the readers. I value you more than you can ever know.